THE GUARDIANS' GIFTS

THE RISE OF THE THREE

A Novel by

M.J. BELL

Books by M.J. Bell

Chronicles of the Secret Prince Fantasy Trilogy:

Book 1: **Before the Full Moon Rises**

Book 2: **Once Upon a Darker Time**

Book 3: **How Dark the Light Shines**

Next Time I See You

A time travel suspense thriller

The Rise of the Three

Book 1: **The Guardians' Light**

Book 2: **The Guardians' Gifts**

THE GUARDIANS' GIFTS

THE RISE OF THE THREE

THE GUARDIANS' GIFTS, The Rise of the Three Book II

Published by MTB Publishing Inc. LLC

First paperback printing, January 2024

ISBN 978-1-7365003-2-3

MTB Publishing Inc. LLC

Centennial, CO 80122

Printed in the United State of America

Book cover design by Steven Novak

For my family and friends, whose love and support helped bring this story to light.

And for my readers, who are the reason I write.

ONE

How could I not have known? Sofia Kaye asked herself for the gazillionth time in the last four days. Though had it really only been four days? It seemed more like four years.

Four days ago, she'd gotten the money she needed for her first year at the Massachusetts Institute of Technology. Four days ago, she also found out she was an alien, and not one from a different country.

Oh sure, Sofia knew she was different. Always had been. Her special abilities, for lack of a better word—seeing in the dark as good as in the light, seeing UV light, feeling other people's body vibrations, and tears dripping from her nose instead of her eyes to name a few—were not normal. And no matter how hard she had tried to hide those abilities, they'd set her apart from everyone else.

But never, not even in her wildest dreams, had she considered herself anything other than human.

A wave of lightheadedness swept over her. She placed one hand on the floor-to-ceiling, multilayered glass wall in the room she called the Observatory. In the other hand, she held the stone pendant, the only object she owned from her real parents, and closed her eyes.

This has got to be a dream. When I open my eyes, I'll wake up and be back in Iowa.

Sofia swallowed hard and opened her eyes a crack, then squeezed them tightly shut again. She was still in the Observatory on some kind of abandoned space vessel. And Earth, the planet she had called home her whole life, was a luminescent blue marble floating serenely in an endless black sky outside the window.

She pressed her forehead against the cool glass, a hundred "what ifs" churning in her brain. Her gut had told her not to do the reality TV show her friends had talked her into doing. But she'd been desperate for money to pay her first-year college tuition and the show had been the only way to get it in the short time she had.

She should have listened to her gut, or at least to her synesthesia, which filled her mouth with the taste of rotten eggs every time she heard the name Main Daher, who was the multi-billionaire producer of the show.

At that time, though, she hadn't known Daher was the leader of the Anunnaki, an alien race from the planet Nibiru. Or that the Anunnaki hated the Pleiadians, who were *her* people. She was one of the three Pleiadian *Guardians* to be exact, Zach and Liv, two other contestants of the bogus reality show, being the other two. She hadn't known that back then, either.

And she certainly hadn't known the reality show was a trap to capture the three of them.

It was only through pure luck that they and Nick, an innocent human contestant of the reality show, were able to escape Daher in the Great Pyramid by jumping through a portal. Although she couldn't help but wonder now if being stuck in space was really a better outcome.

A feeling of helplessness welled within her like a geyser ready to erupt. It wasn't just helplessness, though. It was frustration at being kept in the dark and knowing that someone else had control of her life, like when she was in foster care. Though the situation now was even worse and was literally a matter of life or death.

If they couldn't find some food and water in this place soon, it would be death.

Sofia blew out a long sigh, making a foggy patch on the window. Zach was convinced that Will, their supposed Pleiadian benefactor and protector, was working with Daher. She hadn't wanted to believe it, but it was becoming harder to deny after four days of being trapped on this vessel with no contact from him or anyone else.

And though she tried not to think dark thoughts, sending them into space would be an ingenious way to get rid of them if that was truly Will's intent. Who would ever find their cold, dead bodies up here?

Sofia shook that thought out of her head and defiantly sniffed back a drip from her nose.

No, this isn't how it's going to end! No rich, evil, narcissistic alien like Daher is going to take my dreams and life away from me. I'm gonna find a way out of this place and then no one is ever going to have control over me again!

TWO

Four days earlier

Sofia twisted around on the cold, hard floor. Her head was swimming as if she'd just gotten off the Monster rollercoaster at Adventureland. She held her breath and stared at the iridescent whirlpool of light of the portal she, Zach, Liv, and Nick had just jumped through to escape Daher and his men. The light suddenly flared as bright as the sun, then blinked out. And just like that, the link to the subterranean chamber in the great pyramid of Khufu was gone, along with Will, Daher, and the threat the Anunnaki posed to them.

The four of them hadn't a clue where the portal would take them when they stepped into it, or more accurately, were propelled through it by a force that struck them from behind. Thank goodness she had an invisible shield to protect her and the others from that strike. Though her shield was another thing she had no clue about. She only knew that it always seemed to be there when she needed it. And she was pretty certain without it, they might have all been killed or at the very least badly injured.

She was also certain that if they hadn't used the portal, they would have either been crushed under the ceiling of the subterranean chamber when it collapsed or been captured and forced to help destroy Earth.

"Where the fuck are we?" Liv said under her breath.

Sofia scanned the small, empty metal cube they'd been dumped in, her heart pounding in her ears as if she'd run a four-hundred-meter sprint. The square room was illuminated by a soft blue light radiating from floor-to-ceiling metal panels on two of the walls. The other two walls had no distinguishable markings at all. There was no door, either. And she felt no other body vibrations except for the three in the room with her.

"What was that back there?" Liv asked. "Who were those guys?"

Before anyone could answer, a mechanical voice came out of the air, speaking in a language that sounded somewhat familiar to Sofia, though she didn't understand a word of it. And by the questioning looks on Zach and Liv's faces, they didn't understand it either.

Sofia scrambled to her feet and almost fell back down as a bout of dizziness hit her. She put her hand on the wall, closed her eyes, and took deep breaths until her head stopped spinning, then cautiously opened her eyes. A few feet from her, a tray, holding four pairs of goggles, was sticking out of a rectangular-shaped slot in the wall.

Liv looked up from the floor. "What's that?"

The mechanical voice spoke again in the same unintelligible language.

"This is bullshit," Zach muttered as he got to his feet, then called out, "We don't understand what you're saying."

Without missing a beat, the mechanical voice switched to English and sounded just like Scarlett Johansson with an unusual accent. "Please put on the goggles and prepare for decontamination."

Liv jumped to her feet and grabbed onto Zach's arm to steady herself as Scarlett began to count down from ten.

"What's the decontamination for?" Zach asked, looking at Sofia.

She shook her head and shrugged in answer.

When Scarlett reached five, the three of them each grabbed a pair of goggles from the tray and slipped them on.

"Get up!" Liv hissed at Nick, who was still sitting on the floor.

He made no effort to move.

With a disgusted snort, Liv took hold of his arm and tugged him up to his feet. He swayed and stared blankly at the wall, his arms limp at his side.

"Damnit, Nick, snap out of it. Do you wanna go blind?" Liv grabbed the last pair of goggles from the tray and pulled them over his head just as Scarlett reached zero.

A second later, the goggles automatically adjusted to Sofia's head, becoming as tight as a second skin. The lenses then went black, and her senses went on high alert.

She tried hard not to panic, but she could feel the tension rolling off Zach and Liv like an avalanche rolling down a mountainside, and her pulse accelerated at the same rate of speed.

As the pressure in the room increased and the air grew denser, Nick's already labored breathing turned into a wheeze that echoed through the silence.

A warm sensation spread over Sofia's feet and ankles. Then slowly moved up her body to the top of her head and back down again.

Her hands grew clammy, and an itch, like spiders crawling under her skin, ran up her bare arms and legs. Her chest grew tight as if a python had slipped in and wrapped itself around it and all she could take were quick, shallow breaths.

But just as a dark abyss began to move in from the edges of her vision, a hand closed around her fist. Her heart came to a dead stop, and she jerked back with a gasp before she realized it was Zach.

He gave her hand a squeeze and instantly his calming energy restarted her heart and drained away her tension as if he'd opened a spigot. She covered his hand with her other and hung on as if he was the only thing keeping her from falling into the darkness.

The decontamination seemed to go on forever before the pressure in the room began to decrease and Scarlett informed them they could remove their goggles. Her statement was followed by the hiss of a hermetic seal being released, and a peculiar but not unpleasant scent of ozone and something else that smelled like welding fumes drifted into the room.

Sofia ripped off the eye protection and turned her head in the direction of the sound. One of the bare walls now had a door in it and the door was open.

Zach and Liv, their goggles dangling from their hands, also turned to face the opening. The uncertainty on their faces matching what Sofia felt.

When no one appeared after several seconds, Liv whispered, "What're we supposed to do now?"

Zach licked his lips. "I, um—" His voice cracked. "I guess I could go see if I can find out where we are."

He didn't move.

There was a long, awkward pause before he cleared his throat and added, "Hey, Nick, you wanna ..." He looked around and did a double take. "Jesus, Nick! Are you okay?"

Nick made a gurgling sound and collapsed against the wall, then slowly slid to the floor.

"Ohmigod, Nick!" Liv dropped to her knees beside him.

Nick's face was a pasty white and the right side of his t-shirt was completely stained red.

Liv gently peeled up the hem of his shirt and gasped at the marble-sized hole right below his ribcage that was oozing a steady stream of blood. She put two fingers on his throat to check his pulse.

His eyelids fluttered open, then closed again.

"Hey, Nick," Liv said, her voice a pitch higher than usual, which accentuated her Texan accent. "You're going to be okay, buddy." She bunched up his t-shirt and pressed it against the wound. With her other hand she smoothed his hair back from his forehead. "We're going to find someone to fix you up, so, hang in there for me, okay?"

"Guys, this looks real bad," Liv said telepathically to both Zach and Sofia. *"He's burning up. You've got to go find someone to help him and fast."*

"I'll go," Zach replied out loud. Before anyone could say anything else, he turned and dashed out the door.

Sofia felt like a hollow cavern had opened in her chest and her stomach turned queasy, but not from the sight of the blood. She was used to that. She had always been the first one her younger foster brothers and sisters sought out when they needed their numerous scrapes patched up. But this was far worse than a skinned knee or elbow, and it was all her fault. Her invisible shield had protected her, Zach, and Liv, but for some reason hadn't extended to Nick.

She looked around helplessly for something to do. "Um … maybe I should go out and look for someone, too."

When Liv didn't respond, Sofia added, "Okay then. Will you be all right here alone?"

Liv gave a slight nod of her head without taking her eyes off Nick.

Sofia shifted her weight from one foot to the other, wanting to say more but the words stuck in her throat.

She had never been able to cry real tears from her eyes like everyone else. Her tears, if you wanted to call them that, ran from her nose. And she could feel them building.

She sniffed them back and raced out the door into a corridor that looked like a long metal tunnel with thick arched girders spaced every ten feet or so. The girders all radiated the same soft blue light as the panels in the room, but only to the left of the door, which she guessed was the way Zach had gone.

Without thinking twice, Sofia took off to the left after him. But after a short distance, she stopped and looked back at the dark, empty hallway behind her.

Would they find someone faster if she went that way, instead? Or should she and Zach stick together?

Ughh! She never used to doubt her every move. But the last twenty-four hours had shown her she wasn't as smart as she'd thought she was. Heck, she hadn't even seen what was right there in front of her her whole life. That she was an alien. A Pleiadian. And there were so many obvious signs—like the invisible shield and her eyes not being able to produce tears—how could she have missed it?

Sofia closed her eyes. *Come onnn. There isn't time for this. Nick's gonna bleed to death if we don't find someone to help him.*

She shook her head to rid it of the doubts and squared her shoulders.

"I gotta do this for Nick," she whispered to the air and retraced her steps.

The second she placed a foot in the dark section blue lights clicked on. She jumped, then groaned again, and quickly looked behind her to see if anyone had witnessed her being a big wuss. The hall was still empty.

She rolled her eyes, balled her hands into fists, and started again.

Her feet barely touched the ground as if she was jogging inside a bouncy castle. Or like the gravity was different here.

Sofia's brow wrinkled. How could that be? Where did Will send us to?

An uneasy feeling settled in her stomach the farther down the never-ending curving tunnel she went. And the question of why there were no doors or windows nagged at her like a pebble in her shoe.

Also, where were all the people? She hadn't felt another person's body vibrations other than Zach, Liv, and Nick since they'd gotten here. That was super weird. She'd always been able to feel other people when they were around.

It felt like Sofia had been jogging for miles when finally a lone figure appeared up ahead.

Thank God, some help! A bubble of hope rose within her, but as Zach's familiar vibration swept over her, that bubbled popped.

What was this tunnel? One big circle?

Zach looked over his shoulder as if he had felt her too.

"You see anyone?" he asked as she ran up to him.

She shook her head.

Zach raked his fingers through his hair. "I didn't either. There wasn't even another room or a window to look outside. What kinda place—"

The golden ring around his pupils sparked and he cocked his head and stared into space for a few seconds. When he looked back at Sofia, the tic in his jaw was pulsing.

"Liv just contacted me. She said Nick is getting worse. She can't get him to wake up. We gotta hurry and get him some medical help."

A wave of guilt swept over Sofia. She lowered her gaze as questions swirled in her mind. Why hadn't her shield protected Nick like it did the rest of them? Was it because he was human?

"I think—" she glanced up through her eyelashes, then jerked her head up. Zach was gone, racing down another long corridor that branched off the tunnel she was standing in. He was going so fast, he was just a blur.

What the ... How can he ...

The answer came to her like a punch in the gut. He was a Pleiadian, and Pleiadians can do things normal humans can't, like run as fast as a cheetah apparently.

And he'd left without her.

Frustration, along with a hint of hurt, pushed her guilt asid, and without a second thought, she took off after him, praying that speed was a trait *all* Pleiadians had.

Again Sofia's feet barely touched the ground, and the air whipping past her face made her feel like she was flying not running. In no time at all, she slid to a stop beside Zach, flushed and feeling a little giddy. But as soon as she realized they had reached another T-junction to a third corridor, her spirits dropped.

Oh, God, what is it with this place? Is it another maze or something?

Sofia had never been in such a strange place before. One that felt so sterile, and ... well, kind of alien. She blew out a disgusted sigh. Of course it was alien. They had come through a dang portal to get here.

She followed Zach's gaze to the wall across from them where three large beams were arranged in a triangular shape. The beams were at least twelve feet high at the peak and ten feet wide at the base and looked to be made of the same metal as the support girders in the tunnel, except they were thicker and didn't glow. Intricate designs of strange-looking animals and winged creatures that were definitely not found on Earth were etched into the beam's surface. Intermixed with the designs were lines of unfamiliar shapes and symbols that appeared to be some kind of written language.

This is a door! Sofia flinched at that thought, not knowing where it had come from. For it looked nothing like a door and the wall in the middle of the beams looked pretty solid. There were no hinges or door handles either. Yet she had a strong feeling she was right. It *was* a door.

As she studied it, cocking her head one way, then the other, a new revelation came to her—there were no body vibrations coming from the other side.

Zach took a step toward the beams.

"Wait!" Sofia caught hold of his arm. A small jolt of electricity shot through her hand and up her arm, but she ignored it. "There's something you should know about me. I can, um ..." She looked at the floor. "I can feel other peoples' body vibrations when they're around." Heat creeped up her neck to her cheeks. "I don't feel anyone here in this place except you, Liv, and Nick."

Zach's muscles flexed. "I can feel people, too. So can Liv."

Sofia's head came up and her mouth formed an O. "Do you think that's something all Pleiadians can do?"

He stared at her for a moment, a range of emotions from disbelief to anger crossing his face. He then shook his head and heaved a sigh. "I think this might be a door. I'm gonna check it out and see if I can get it open."

He took a step forward, but Sofia kept a tight hold on his arm.

"Zach, you're the same guy you've always been. Putting a different name on it and learning you can do more than you thought doesn't change that."

He yanked his arm free. "I don't want to talk about it. We need to get Nick help."

Sofia bit her tongue to keep from saying more. This wasn't the right time to talk about being an alien. Though to be honest, she wasn't sure if there would ever be a "right time" for Zach.

THREE

Pyramid Khufu, Egypt

Makin Daher blinked into the darkness that felt as deep and dense as a black hole. The stale smell of decay, bat guano, and urine told him he was still in the subterranean chamber of the pyramid Khufu. But where were his men and the Guardians?

His mind was a little groggy, but he did remember being hit by a powerful energy blast from the Guardians. He had no idea what had happened after that, but the silence surrounding him wasn't a good sign.

Daher strained to lift his arms, but something heavy had his whole upper body pinned down. He opened his mouth to call out, but the air was so thick with dust he lapsed into a coughing fit. But in between his coughs echoing off the walls, he heard the sound of rubble being thrown about.

When he was finally able to speak again, he croaked, "Help! I'm over here."

The only response he got was a grunt, and with the disorienting darkness, he couldn't tell where it had come from.

Something beneath Daher suddenly moved, and the weight on top of him shifted onto his upper shoulders. He grimaced, but not with pain. The Nibiruian body armor he and all Anunnaki Elite wore could withstand an armored truck sitting on top of it. But now he couldn't even raise his head an inch off the floor.

Someone groaned to the right of him.

"Who's there?" Daher called out.

There was no answer.

Several more silent minutes passed before the sound of debris being thrown about started up again.

"I'm here!" Daher yelled, turning his head as far as he could. "Over here."

A strong scent of swamp gas suddenly permeated the air and the hulking thermal signature of a Dracuzian enforcer came into view. The behemoth wheezed short, ragged breaths, as he clumsily felt around in the darkness with one hand. As he shifted positions, his foot brushed the side of Daher's head.

"Watch where you're stepping, you son of a *zugik*!" Daher bellowed. "I'm right here."

The Dracuzian bent over the Anunnaki. A makeshift tourniquet had been wrapped around the stub of his left arm, which was severed just below the elbow. Still, a drip of his foul-smelling blood splashed onto Daher's cheek.

Daher turned his head and snarled a continuous stream of insults as the enforcer fumbled around to find the edge of the slab. Finally getting a grip on it, the Dracuzian grunted and heaved one-handed, lifting it up enough for Daher to pull his arms free.

Daher turned his palm outward, projecting a light on the rubble. The dust and darkness swallowed up the light within a few feet of the beam, but it was enough for him to get a good look at the slab of bedrock lying on his chest.

"*Ezafak*!" he cursed. "Get this thing off me."

The Dracuzian again strained to lift the thick chunk of rock as Daher pushed. Little by little, the two of them got the slab moved to the side enough that Daher could sit up and survey the area.

Most of the cavern was obscured by the thick dust, but the Anunnakis all had the ability to see thermal signatures, and he spotted two of them about fifteen feet away. By their size, as well as the darkish blue color with a hint of orange in the abdomen area of their thermal signature, he knew they were both Dracuzians.

"The Guardians?" Daher snapped at the enforcer who was now struggling to free his legs. "Where are the Guardians?"

The answer came from the other side of the room. "They made it through a gateway before the ceiling collapsed."

Recognizing Ukani's voice, Daher twisted around and scanned the area until he located the enforcer. "You! I told you what would happen if you failed me again!"

"I didn't fail you. I delivered you the Guardians. My mission was complete."

Daher gnashed his teeth together. "Do you see any Guardians around here? No! Because you let them get away."

A rumble from above brought another cascade of dust and pebbles raining down.

"Get me out of here!" Daher roared. "And one of you secure Ukani. He's going to pay for the trouble he's cost me this time!"

Guttural grunts rang through the chamber as two thermal signatures came together and slung each other about. In less than a minute, one of the two went down and did not get back up.

"Did you get him?" Daher called out to the standing thermal signature.

The figure didn't answer but turned and bolted through the hole in the wall that led out of the chamber.

"Ukani!" Daher yelled after him. "You've forfeited your final chance! You cannot hide from me forever. I *will* have your head if it's the last thing I ever do!"

FOUR

Zach's stomach twisted into a knot as he stared at the rectangular panel on the wall beside the triangle frame. The top half of the panel was shiny black like a biometrics scanner. And if it was, they could be screwed.

Below the black section were two lines of a strange text he'd never seen before. Beneath the writing was a tiny red light speeding around a circle within a circle within a circle.

He knew that symbol well. It had been on the letterhead of the letter he'd gotten from the fake reality show that had started this whole mess. It was also what had guided him through the maze—the supposed first challenge of the show that was really a trap to capture them.

So, what was that symbol doing here? This was a Daher-free zone. Or that's what he had assumed since Will, the Pleiadian who was supposed to be keeping them safe, had sent them here.

A fresh spark of anger ignited within him. Had they been set up?

Zach never had fully trusted Will. And this symbol showing up here was additional proof he was right not to. Will might have been working with Daher all along, which would explain a lot. Like how Will had known where to find them in the maze. It would also explain why Will had drugged him and Sofia and taken them to Egypt, then fed them a ridiculous, made-up story about them all being Pleiadians.

Zach's tic started to pulse in his jaw. How gullible did Will think they were? Sure, Zach had some unusual abilities, but that hardly made him an alien. Will on the other hand, was obviously one, and the portal he created had brought them to one of Daher's secret compounds.

He whipped his head around at that thought, half-expecting to see a line of Daher's goons in the hallway. The corridor was empty, except for Sofia, who was gaping at the symbol on the panel.

"Have you seen that symbol before?" he asked.

"The lollipop one … yeah," Sofia muttered. "It was on the letter I got from Conway and Vik, you know, the lawyers from the reality show. I saw it in the maze, too. In fact, that's how I got to the cavern under the tower. And …" She pulled the neck of her t-shirt down and turned sideways so he could see the tattoo on her back left shoulder.

Zach's throat tightened. *What the fuck?* Sofia's tattoo was almost an exact match to the one he had on his right bicep. He locked eyes with her and raised the sleeve of his t-shirt. "This came to me in a dream."

Sofia looked from his tattoo to his eyes and back. "I saw mine in a dream too, but …" She shook her head. "I don't understand. How could Daher possibly know about it?"

"That's the million-dollar question, isn't it?" Zach fought the urge to punch the panel. "I think Will's been playing us from the minute he showed up. And we've just been blindly following him while the whole time he's been working with Daher."

She shook her head vehemently. "No, that can't be true. I won't believe it. He's done everything he can to keep us away from Daher."

"Has he? He sent us here, didn't he? And that right there," he pointed to the red light racing around the circles, "is the symbol Daher used to trick us. How do you explain that?"

Sofia frowned and stared at the symbol. He could almost see the wheels spinning in her head.

"You don't know that symbol is Daher's. Will could have been the one who planted it in the maze," she said, though she didn't sound all that convinced herself.

Zach gaped at her, but as he opened his mouth to reply, Liv's voice came into his head.

"Zach, where are you? Have you found anyone yet?"

His words stuck in the back of his throat. He dropped his chin to his chest. How did this all go so wrong? That stupid reality show was supposed to get his life back on track, not blow it up.

"I never should have let you and Liv talk me into jumping through that portal," he mumbled and raised his head, the fire in his belly flaring anew. "Now here we are, stuck in God knows where, and Nick's probably gonna die, and you're still defending Will?"

A wave of hurt washed over Sofia's face, the kind of hurt that cut straight to Zach's heart. Then, just as quickly, her blue eyes turned to steel, and she shifted her stance, planting her hands on her hips.

"Are you serious?" she asked, her voice as hard as her eyes. "No one talked you into anything. We would've died if we'd stayed there, and you know it! So, don't be—"

Zach held up his index finger and cut off her words as Liv's voice once again came into his head.

"Zach, are you there? Why aren't you answering me?"

He turned his back on Sofia. *"I'm here and just fixin' to check out what I think is a door. I'll let you know what I find."*

He closed his eyes, took in a deep breath, then slowly emptied his lungs, releasing the tension in his muscles from the top of his head down to his toes as his basketball coach had taught him. It was pointless to stand there arguing with Sofia. They had enough problems as it was.

He cracked his neck left, then right, and turned back to face Sofia.

"Look, I don't want to argue with you. Nick's life is depending on us, so let's just focus on finding help. Okay?"

To Zach's relief, Sofia's face softened at the mention of Nick. She dropped her hands to her sides.

Zach turned to the triangle, squared his shoulders, and extended his arm. "Get behind me. I'm going to see if this really is a door and what's on the other side."

Sofia gave a loud huff and shoved his arm aside. “I don’t need you to protect me. I’ve been taking care of myself my whole life.”

Before he could stop her, she stomped up to the door and placed her palm over the circle symbol. Nothing happened. She rubbed her palm on the leg of her shorts and tried again, lining her hand up so it completely covered the symbol. Still nothing happened.

Her shoulders drooped and she stepped back. “I thought the lollipop thing would open the door like it did in the maze.”

Zach stepped up and pressed his right palm against the symbol. When nothing happened, he pressed his left hand. Then, with his head cocked to the side, he squinted and placed one fingertip at a time on the biometric scanner.

He could feel Sofia’s glare on his back like a dozen frozen ice pick plunging into his spine, and he knew he deserved it. He’d been acting like a complete jerk and had said all the wrong things. And he didn’t even know why. Something about her just completely scrambled his mind.

He clenched his teeth and scowled at the door. Then, without warning, he let out a roar and lunged forward, ramming his shoulder into it. Though all that did was make him look like a fool and made his left arm hurt like hell.

He walked away cursing to himself and rubbing his upper arm.

“Wow. Really smart,” Sofia said, the corners of her mouth twitching.

He whirled around, walked back, and gave the door a kick. “Open, dammit!”

Sofia jumped, but the door remained closed.

Zach pressed his forehead against the door’s cool surface. A small shock shot through him. Then a searing pain stabbed the nape of his neck. He reared back and grabbed the neck of his head. But as a long-forgotten memory flashed behind his eyelids the pain was forgotten.

He was young, maybe three-years-old, and sitting in wood chips under a slide on a playground, his forehead on his knees that were drawn into his chest. A girl his same age sat beside him. She had auburn pigtails and the bluest eyes that seemed to take up most of her face.

She held his hand in both of hers and said in her squeaky little girl voice, "It's okay, Z. I'll always be here for you. I swear. I won't never ever leave you."

He grimaced and twisted around to face Sofia. She was staring at him with big, round eyes … just like the little girl's.

"We knew each other when we were kids." There was no question in the statement. "I saw it in a flashback. Or I think it was a flashback."

Sofia's eyes rounded, but she didn't say a word.

Will had told them they would start getting their memories back.

Zach stared into her eyes, trying to remember more, but the feeling of hot knives stabbing the back of his head returned. He closed his eyes and another memory immediately started to play.

He was still about three and standing in the doorway of a room with Liv, watching Sofia follow some strange woman down a hall. Sofia was wearing a backpack, and when she twisted her head to look back, he saw her nose was bright red and her chin was quivering.

At the top of a staircase that led down to the first floor, Sofia yanked her hand free of the woman's and started toward him and Liv.

The woman reached out, caught Sofia around the waist before she could take a second step, and picked her up.

Sofia didn't make a sound as the woman hurriedly carried her down the stairs. She just raised her arms and reached toward Zach, who had rushed to the railing to watch.

He stretched his arms out as well, but it was too late. The woman and Sofia went out the front door and were gone.

Zach's insides turned to stone. *I let them take her. How could I have let them take her away?* He looked back at Sofia and searched her eyes for the answer, but all he could see was sorrow and the pain of loneliness and alienation.

Sofia shifted uncomfortably and looked away.

"Oh, look!" she exclaimed, pointing down the hall. "Down there. It looks like there's a door frame."

She took off in that direction, as if anxious to get away from him.

Zach wiped his hand over his face, still shaken by the memory. It had happened a long time ago and he had been too young to be able to do anything to stop it, but the sting and the ache in his heart of that moment was as strong as if it happened yesterday.

A solid brick of guilt settled on his chest over his sternum, and it gave him a little stab with every heartbeat.

Sofia had stopped in front of a typical square door frame. But there was nothing typical about the door, if it was a door. It looked like a plain wall inside the frame, and there was no door handle. It did, though, have a rectangular panel with the same strange writing and circle symbol as the one next to the triangle beams. But instead of a red light racing around the circles, the light was blue.

Zach slipped up beside her, keeping a good foot of space between them.

She shot him a questioning sidelong glance when he didn't make a move toward the door. Then, clicked her tongue and stepped forward.

The door vanished on its own as she reached her hand toward the panel.

They both jumped back.

"Did you see that?" Sofia inched closer to Zach. "It just disappeared like magic!"

Zach sidestepped away from her and squinted into the bright white light coming from the other side of the door. "Who cares? It's open and that's all that matters."

When she flinched and pulled back, he realized he'd said the wrong thing again.

"I didn't mean that the way it came out. I'm just anxious to find someone and find out where the hell we are."

Sofia didn't respond and he couldn't blame her.

"Come on, let's check this out," he said and together they tentatively stepped over the threshold, stopping just inside.

The stark white room before them was sparsely furnished with only a large oblong capsule on an accordion-style base on the left side of the room and an egg-shaped capsule with what looked like a dentist chair inside it on the right side. Both end walls were lined with cabinets and a countertop with drawers and more cabinets below.

"Weird," Zach mumbled to himself as he took in the sterile-looking room.

He pointed to the cabinets on the right. "Check out those cupboards. Please," he added, so it wouldn't sound like he was issuing her a command. "I'll check out the ones on this side."

I'm such a moron, he thought as he walked toward the cabinets, slowing when he came to the long capsule.

The top half of the pod was transparent except for two feet at one end. Above it, a large metal box with robotic arms folded up against each side hung from two metal tracks on the ceiling.

Is this a … MedPod? Zach mentally scoffed at the thought. MedPods were the figments of imagination pulled out of the brains of Sci-Fi authors and Hollywood set designers, not real things. Still …

He took a step closer and peeked inside. An interior blue light flicked on. He jumped back, then shot a glance over his shoulder to see if Sofia had seen him. Thank God her back was to him.

Maybe this *was* a MedPod, though. He'd always thought portals were a Hollywood thing, but he'd just jumped through one to get here.

"All I've got over here is medical supplies," Sofia called, pulling him out of his thoughts.

"Hmmm," he mused out loud, looking back at the capsule. "So, if this is a medical office, then that might actually be a MedPod."

Sofia turned to the capsule and looked at it as if seeing it through new eyes.

"This might help Nick." Zach's voice carried a note of excitement. "I'll go get him. Stay here. I don't want you wandering about by yourself until we know more."

Sofia's hands went to her hips.

Uh oh.

Figuring another argument was coming and he would end up making things worse, he bolted out the door.

As he raced back the way he'd come, the strangeness of the lengthy corridors with no doors or windows struck him again. Neither of them had seen a single person either. A bad feeling twisted in his stomach.

Then another unnerving thought hit him like a gut punch, and he almost stumbled over his own feet.

If no one else was there, and there were no exits, how were they going to get out to go home?

FIVE

Sofia watched Zach race out the door.

Who the hell does he think he is, telling me what to do?

She stormed into the corridor, but Zach was already out of sight.

She glared down the empty hall, remembering his earlier suspicions of Will. She had no explanation for why the lollipop symbol kept showing up everywhere, but she couldn't bring herself to believe this was a setup. And the thought of Will working with Daher was just ridiculous. She'd seen the look on Daher's face when Will showed himself in the pyramid. No one could fake that kind of hatred.

She seethed through her clenched teeth and began to pace. If only Will had come with them. He had the answers they desperately needed, but he was back in the pyramid and there was no way to reach him … *Wait.*

Sofia came to an abrupt stop. *What an idiot I am! We can talk telepathically.*

She crossed her fingers, closed her eyes, and pictured Will's face.

"Will, are you there? It's me, Sofia. Nick's been hurt bad. We think he might even be dying. What are we supposed to do?"

She waited with bated breath, but her own thoughts were the only thing that came into her head. And as the seconds ticked off, those thoughts got worse and worse.

Sofia bit down on her bottom lip and turned her head to stare at the blue light racing around the symbol on the wall panel. Nick was going to die if they couldn't find someone to help him.

She squinted down the empty hall in the direction Zach had gone, then turned her head and looked the other way. If the tables were turned, would he sit here and wait for her to get back? She clicked her tongue. Of course he wouldn't.

So, why was she standing there?

"Sorry, Zach. I can't let Nick die," she whispered to the air and headed into the unknown.

Unlike the other two corridors, this one was more open and felt less like a tunnel. Though the floor was just as bouncy, and it was just as deserted.

When she came to another door, a seed of hope sprung to life, then wilted just as fast when she saw the room was nothing more than an empty lounge. Farther on, another door led to a closet filled with bulky padded suits that looked like super-charged hazmat suits. She also discovered two additional corridors, but both had a wall blocking them off a short distance down. And the doors in those two walls were locked.

With each new discovery that led nowhere, her steps dragged a little more, but she kept going all the way around until she found herself back at the triangle beams.

This can't be right. There has to be more to this place than empty lounges, closets, and an ER.

She slowly turned in a complete circle and surveyed the entire area. Everything was the same as it had been when she and Zach first found it: the triangle beams, the panel with the red light on the wall, the other corridor that they had initially come down straight across from beams, and the ER down the hall.

Aghhh, what is this hell? Why would Will send us here?

She dropped to the floor and buried her face in her hands. She could only imagine what Zach was going to say when he found out there was nothing here and no one else here. But she was sure he was going to be mad.

"Sofia!"

She could already hear his angry voice in her head.

"What are you doing?" Zach demanded, sliding to a stop beside her.

She looked up in surprise. She'd thought she was imaging his call.

"I told you to stay in the room," he said, his eyes glistening with concern. Or was it anger?

Sofia bristled at his haughty tone and jumped to her feet. "Yeah, you did, but you're not the boss of me."

The second those words came out of her mouth, she realized how juvenile they sounded, and her exasperation fled as quickly as it had come. She turned her back on him to hide the heat moving up her neck.

"There's no reason to worry anyway. No one else is here." She half turned toward him. "What about you? Did you have any trouble getting Nick to the ER?"

Zach looked like he wanted to yell, but instead, he let out a weary sigh. "No, no trouble. Liv's cleaning his wound, so we can see how bad it is."

"Oh … good." Sofia didn't know what else to say.

The air between them remained thick with tension.

"Maybe I should go see if she needs help," she added and hustled toward the ER like she was trying out for the Olympian speed walking team.

Zach caught up to her within a couple steps. "I wasn't insinuating you couldn't take care of yourself, you know."

Sofia picked up her speed, hoping to avoid another fight.

"Look, I know you don't want to believe it, but we can't rule out that this isn't another of Daher's traps. And until we know for sure, we should all stick together. You know … strength in numbers. Because if anything would've happened …" He glanced at her and then straight ahead again. "I just don't want anyone else to get hurt."

Sofia felt her ears grow hot. If her brain wasn't so scrambled with everything that had happened, she would have thought of that herself. Or maybe not. She'd always had to fend for herself and never had to worry about her actions affecting others.

She gave him a sidelong glance. "You're right. It makes sense for us to stick together, but I haven't seen anything here that suggests Daher's involved."

"Yeah, but we haven't checked out the whole place yet. I passed some doors on my way here, but I didn't stop to look in, 'cause—"

"I checked them," she cut in. "One was a lounge with some cushy chairs and sleep cubicles. Another was a closet full of hazmat suits. And the two doors in the blocked off corridors were locked."

Zach's tic began pulsing in his jaw.

When they reached the ER, Sofia stopped in front of the door. It immediately vanished as it had done before. She started forward, then did a double take. The inside of the room was almost a direct replica of the lounge she'd explored earlier.

"What happened to the ER?" she asked.

Zach's eyes turned hard as steel. "They're playing with us. This place is really a prison."

"No," Sofia shot back. "I mean, yes, this place is strange, but it doesn't feel like a prison."

"Yeah?" His hands balled into white-knuckled fists. "Well, what do you call a place with no exits or windows?"

"I don't know," she said and turned to look back the way they had come. "But there must be two of those triangle things, which means we haven't checked out that corridor there yet." She pointed to the one across from the beams. "Maybe we'll find something down it."

Zach didn't look convinced.

"Come on. We've at least gotta check it out." Sofia took his arm, pulling him with her toward the new passageway.

They walked in silence, each lost in their own thoughts, until the corridor ended at another T-junction and a tunnel like the first one they had explored. They gave each other identical exasperated looks.

"Why do I have a feeling there's an identical room to the one we arrived in around on the other side of this tunnel?" She didn't let

Zach respond but pointed to the left. "I'll go this way, you go that way, and we'll meet at the room."

Zach headed off without comment, though she could feel the frustration rolling off of him. And she was right there with him.

She raced around the long, curved hallway straight to the room that was exactly where she'd expected it to be.

Zach was already there waiting for her and gestured toward the panel on the wall. "Be my guest."

Sofia lifted her hand and pressed her trembling palm over the lollipop symbol. The door vanished, but no light came on inside the room.

She slipped her hand into Zach's and together they walked into a small dark cube the size of an elevator car. The door closed behind them, and dim lights snapped on along the base of the walls.

A strange feeling suddenly swept over her—a feeling like she was being pressed into the floor. Zach must have felt it too because he tensed and put his arm around her shoulders. Then spun around taking her with him.

"Let's get out of here." He put his hand over the symbol on the wall. The door didn't open.

Sofia moved in closer and slipped an arm around his waist. "What's going on?" she whispered.

"I don't know."

As Zach raised his fist and started to pound on the door, the floor gave a slight jolt and a bright light from behind lit up the cube. They swiveled around in unison and froze.

"What the fuck?" Zach whispered, expressing Sofia's exact thought.

The back wall of the cube was gone, revealing a room beyond. The room was dark except for a thin slit of brilliant light shining at floor level. The slit was getting wider by the second as if the wall was rising toward the ceiling. But when the slit had grown to about a foot wide, Sofia realized it wasn't a wall that was moving. It was a shield over a wall of glass.

Inch by inch the windows were uncovered, and the bottom of a glowing blue ball came into view.

Zach's fingers dug into Sofia's shoulder, but she was so mesmerized by the object outside the glass she hardly noticed.

By the time the ball had become a half sphere, her pulse was racing so fast she thought for sure her heart would explode.

This can't be possible.

"That's Earth!" Zach exclaimed, turning to her with a mixture of awe and confusion in his eyes.

Sofia hesitantly took a couple steps into the room.

The room was domed shape, and except for the floor, was solid glass. The dark shell still covered the back side of the room, but the glass ceiling was exposed, and through it she could see a billion stars shining in pure blackness.

This has got to be a trick. A hologram like in the maze.

She truly wanted to believe it was a hologram, but a sinking feeling in her gut told her it was real. She looked over at Zach, who was gawking at something beyond her.

"Jesus, what the hell is that?" he said.

Sofia's heart jumped into her throat. She flipped around and her mouth dropped open.

Beyond the glass was a long metal arm branching off a wide, thick ring. At the end of the arm was a structure that looked like a flying saucer. The saucer had a band of blinking lights circling its middle and an open bay door on its side. A rocket-shaped vessel that had three oblong tanks stacked one on top of another attached to both sides was slowly approaching the bay door. Off in the distance, another metal arm with an identical flying saucer structure at the end came off the same wide ring. She couldn't see past the second arm as the dark shell covering was in the way.

Ohmigod, are we really in outer space?

She swallowed hard and looked back at Earth. "Did Will send us into space?"

All at once, an even worse thought popped into her head. She gripped Zach's arms with both hands and looked into his stunned face, her panic reflecting back to her in his wide eyes.

"How are we going to get home from space?"

SIX

Rivulets of sweat ran down the side of Tabari's face as he stood in the foyer of Daher's Katameya Heights villa, even though the temperature in the forty-five thousand square foot mansion was kept at a cool sixty-six degrees. He'd gotten a call that Daher was on his way back from the pyramid. The night had not gone as planned and the entire staff was on edge, knowing that no one was safe when the leader of the Anunnaki was upset.

At the sound of a car door slamming, Tabari snapped to attention. A second later, the front door burst open and made a loud boom as it slammed into the wall. Daher stormed in like a hurricane, his face the color of a lobster just pulled from a boiling pot, and brushed past Tabari as if he were an insignificant piece of furniture.

Tabari had to hustle to keep up with his boss, but he knew better than to say anything until spoken to.

The Anunnaki stomped into his office like a bull on a rampage, waking the doctor who had been dragged out of bed to attend to the billionaire's injuries. The man reared to his feet, but Daher didn't give him so much as a glance.

Daher rounded his desk, yanked his chair back, and with a resounding, "*Ezafak*," swiped his arm across the desktop. A fist sized gold nugget from his gold mine, a desk lamp, and a cup of Egyptian karkade tea Tabari had prepared for him went crashing to the floor.

Then, with both hands splayed on the polished wood, he stood and seethed, his chest heaving with each breath.

The doctor glanced at Tabari with raised eyebrows. Tabari shook his head no and ran his tongue around his mouth to bring back some moisture.

The seconds ticked off like a bass drum in Tabari's head, but he didn't dare move.

Finally, Daher grabbed his chair, sat down, and fixed Tabari with a murderous glare. "Where's my information?"

Tabari's muscles seized, and his tablet slipped from his hands.

"S-sir," he stuttered as he bent and retrieved the tablet from the floor. "I have it right here, sir."

As Tabari's fingers flew over the keyboard on the tablet screen, the doctor crossed the room. He set his medical bag on the corner of the desk and pushed Daher's hair away from the cut on his forehead.

"That's quite a gash. How did you get it?" the doctor asked in his best bedside manner, seemingly oblivious to the danger stewing about him.

Daher knocked the doctor's arm away. "Not now."

"But, this looks like it might need stitches. You might also have a concussion."

"I *said* not now," Daher hissed through his teeth. "Get out!"

The doctor looked as if he was going to protest, but when Daher turned his penetrating glower on him, he raised both hands in the air and backed away. He then snatched up his bag and strode from the room, mumbling about irrational billionaires wasting his time.

Tabari's hand was trembling so hard he kept tapping the wrong keys. At last he found what he needed. He pulled a small crystal pyramid from his pocket and placed it on the desk in front of Daher. A 3D image of the Guardians' applications immediately appeared in the air above the crystal.

The crease between Daher's eyebrows deepened as he studied the display. "Interesting," he mumbled to himself. "Is this right? Zachary and Olivia were adopted out as twins to one family?"

"Yes, sir. It appears the Pleiadians made up fake birth certificates and listed the two as twins so they would be harder to track. The adoptive parents have no idea the children aren't biologically related."

"And it says here Sofia was adopted but ended up in the foster system. How did that happen?"

"From what I could gather, the adoptive mother died when Sofia was five. The father didn't want to raise a child on his own and turned her over to the welfare system. She remained in Child Protective care until she aged out at eighteen."

Daher swiped through the pages of the report. "Who's this Madeleine Lewis listed as an emergency contact on Sofia's application?"

Tabari checked his tablet. "She was a student at Urbandale High School. Sofia has been staying with her since leaving foster care."

Daher drummed his fingers on the desktop, his face growing darker by the second. Then, with a growl of frustration, he swept the crystal from the desk. It landed on the floor at Tabari's feet.

"The Guardians think they have outsmarted me, but they don't understand the power I wield. Kill the parents, and that Madeleine girl, too."

"I'm not sure that's wise, sir," Tabari replied.

In the next instant, the air in the room became heavy as if a storm cloud had moved in, and Tabari's heart skipped a beat as he realized he'd spoken those words out loud.

Daher's yellow eyes glowed like warning lights beneath his brow. "Not wise?" He said, lifting his hand and curling his fingers in like a claw.

Tabari let out a gasp and gripped his throat, which suddenly felt as if a garrote had been wrapped around it. "Murder … three people … bad for show." He could barely push the words out through the pressure that was strangling him.

"The show?" Daher's voice grew louder and more ominous with each word. "What do I care about the show? It was nothing but a ruse to expose the Guardians."

Tabari cowered, but he knew the only way to save himself was to make Daher understand their entire operation would be jeopardized—or worse—if he killed the humans.

He tugged on the collar of his shirt, which did nothing to ease the pressure.

"You the sponsor … under intense scrutiny … if t-t-three murders … are tied to contestants. A-Americans m-might freeze your assets … and hurt s-s-search for the Guardians. … The Elite w-would not like … the attention."

Getting those words out took the last of the air from his lungs. A grey fog began to move over his vision. But right before the abyss claimed him, the pressure around his throat eased.

Tabari grabbed the back of a chair and coughed. After several deep, painful breaths, the fog began to lift, and his voice came back.

"May I continue, sir?"

A long, uncomfortable silence followed, but Tabari held his ground, his knees shaking only slightly. At last, Daher gave a barely perceptible nod.

Tabari cleared his throat and winced. "In order to take Earth back, you're going to need the energy grid turned off, which only the Guardians can do." His voice was raspy. "I believe a way you could manipulate them into cooperating is by making them think their parents and friend are in danger."

Daher tapped his index finger on the desk and stared straight through Tabari.

Tabari fidgeted, wanting badly to rub his throat, but afraid to make a move.

"We'll use the humans as bait," Daher bluntly stated as if he'd come up with the idea on his own. "Force the Guardians to come out of hiding to save their loved ones."

Tabari sagged in relief but went rigid again when Daher slapped his hand on the desk.

"Send the enforcers out immediately to pick up the three humans. And advise them not to harm the humans yet."

"Yes, sir. I'll get right on it, sir."

As Tabari turned to leave, Daher added, "If any Sons of Ea get in the way, the enforcers can deal with them in any way they want. But I do not want the humans witnessing any of it. They can *not* know what is actually going on."

Tabari nodded his understanding and hustled to the door. Just as he reached the threshold, Daher spoke again in a tone as cold and sharp as an ice pick.

"If you enjoy your life and want to continue living, never question my orders again."

Tabari's shoulders jerked as if he'd been stabbed in the back. He stumbled over his own feet, caught himself, and hurriedly turned toward his office with full knowledge that he was lucky to have made it out of there alive.

How much long would his luck hold, though?

SEVEN

Liv chewed on her bottom lip as she stood beside the capsule, holding Nick's hand. A small pile of bloody gauze lay at her feet, but the wound was still bleeding.

The events of the last twenty-four hours were running in circles in her mind, but the more she tried to understand them, the more questions she had. It was like she was caught in a nightmare that kept going and going and none of it made a lick of sense.

She had literally been on the verge of winning the competition and being named Daher's heir. It hadn't been officially announced yet, but she knew without a doubt she had nailed it, especially after hearing Nick and Hannah had cheated to get through the maze. But then everything fell apart, and the next thing she knew, men were trying to kill her. And she still couldn't fathom why.

A familiar butterfly fluttered in her chest. She looked over her shoulder at the door in expectation. A few seconds later, it opened, and Zach and Sofia walked in. Her heart gave a small lurch.

"So?" Liv asked telepathically, praying he had good news.

When Zach shook his head, it felt as if the floor had been ripped right out from beneath her feet. She clutched the side of the MedPod, dropped her chin to her chest, and willed the room to stop spinning.

This can't be happening.

She lifted her head and softly closed the MedPod's lid to keep Nick from hearing the bad news, though he seemed to be out cold. She hurried to the doorway where Zach was standing with Sofia.

"You found no one at all?" she whispered, not wanting to believe it was true.

"No one." Zach didn't meet her eyes. "And we went over every inch of this place. Or what we could get into, anyway."

Liv stared at Zach, but it was Nick's pale face she saw in the back of her eyes. "I don't know how much longer he's gonna make it. He's—"

A loud beep interrupted her words. All three of them spun around to face the capsule. At its head a red light was blinking in time with the beeping.

Liv rushed over.

The pad Nick was lying on had lowered at least six inches and laser-like beams, coming from small holes along the exposed sides, were crisscrossing over his body. Projected on the transparent lid was a full anatomical diagram of Nick's body with circles drawn around certain body parts. At the bottom of the diagram were lines of the weird alien writing and a bunch of numbers, which appeared to be his vitals. Two of the numbers were pulsing red. A red shaded square over the wound on his right side was also pulsing.

"Oh God, is he dying?" Liv wailed.

Her burst of emotion caused the image on the lid to waver and blink off for a second.

She reached for the handle of the lid and tried to lift it, but it wouldn't budge. "Help me," she said, tugging to get it open.

Zach and Sofia didn't make a move. They were staring at the foot of the pod where a thin, rectangular piece of clear glass had risen out of the side of the capsule. The glass displayed Nick's heartbeat in a wavy line, as well as several other graphs and more of the alien writing. In the bottom corner was a small green circle, blinking on and off.

"Where did that come from?" Liv asked.

"I don't know. It just popped up." Zach touched the green circle on the display.

From the ceiling, the whirl of a motor started up.

Zach threw his hands up as if to surrender and hurriedly stepped back.

A row of small light bulbs on the metal box overhead had lit up and the entire box was starting to inch forward on its rails. Then, with a hiss, as if air was being released, the top half of the lid slid backward toward the foot, and the box on the ceiling came to a stop directly over Nick.

"What'd you do?" Liv cried.

"Nothing," Zach replied in defense. "I just pushed the green button to see if it would give us more information."

With a whine that sounded like a dentist drill, the robotic arms began to lower.

Scarlett Johansson's voice came out of the air, "Please stand back."

The three flinched at the same time and obediently took a step back as told.

A drawer slid out of the bottom of the pod and rose level with the side. One of the robotic arms took some kind of medical instrument from the drawer and dipped inside the capsule.

"What's it doing?" Liv squeaked and started forward.

Zach grabbed her arm and held her back. "Let it be. If it's what I think it is, it can help Nick."

Liv felt like she'd swallowed a boulder. *Please let him be okay.*

Scarlett spoke again, "Attach the blood supply now."

Liv and Sofia both looked over at Zach as if expecting him to know what to do. He shrugged and shook his head, as clueless as they were.

"Where are we going to get blood from?" Liv asked in a quaking voice.

Sofia's heartbeat pounded in her ears, supplying a rhythm to the words "your fault" as they echoed in her head.

"He can have mine," she blurted and rushed to the MedPod's side.

Nick's shirt had been cut down the middle, exposing his full upper torso. Small bubbles of blood dotted a line that ran from his navel to a blackened area on his side where the robot fingers had spread the tissue apart. The coppery scent of blood and rubbing alcohol burned Sofia's nose and her stomach clenched.

"Attach the blood supply now," Scarlett repeated.

Sofia forced her gaze away from Nick, held her breath to avoid the smell, and rummaged through the drawer for a syringe and IV tubing, which, according to what she'd seen in the movies, you needed for a person-to-person blood transfer.

"How do you know your blood's compatible?" Liv asked, coming up beside her. "You could kill him if it's the wrong type."

Sofia's hands stalled. She hadn't thought of that. Could a human body even accept alien blood?

Nick's cheeks were blotchy, and his eyelids were tinged blue. So were his lips that were visible through a clear oxygen mask the robot arms must have put over his nose and mouth.

Sofia squeezed her eyes shut. He needed blood, and she, Zach, and Liv were the only sources available.

She brusquely swiped a drip from her nose with a trembling hand. "What choice do we have?" She aggressively shoved around the supplies in the drawer beside the MedPod. "He'll die for sure if he doesn't get blood. I have to …" her voice cracked.

"Wait." Zach laid his hand over hers. An electric shock ran up her arm.

"No … you don't understand—" Sofia's throat closed up.

"I know you want to do whatever you can to save him, but Liv's right. Giving him the wrong blood won't help."

Sofia dropped her chin on her chest. *I can't let him die. I just can't!*

Liv made a small, surprised squeak.

Sofia looked up and did a double take as a robot streaked past her, making a beeline for the wall behind the capsule. The back of its head was an opaque plastic shell stamped with different size circle-shaped impressions that made it look like it had curls. Its hands, sticking out of a long-sleeved white jacket, looked human, complete with skin that could have passed for the real deal. But its lower half was a wide shaft with a wheel on each side of a short platform at the bottom, similar to a Segway.

As the robot approached the wall, a large rectangular section opened, revealing a hidden cabinet. The bot spent a minute at the cabinet, then rolled back to the MedPod carrying several small pouches, two filled with a clear liquid and another with what looked like red powder.

Like its hands, the robot's face had porcelain flesh as well as perfectly shaped eyebrows, eyelashes, lips, and brilliant blue, human-looking eyes. It paid no attention to the three of them standing there staring but went right to work on Nick.

"What's it doing?" Liv whispered.

No one responded.

Long, torturous minutes passed until the Segway robot dropped its arms to its side and moved back, where it stood at attention and stared into space.

A thin metal pole, holding a small pouch of red liquid and two pouches of clear liquid had been attached to the head of the MedPod, and two IV drip lines were running from the bags into Nick's arm. And the robotic arms from the ceiling box continued to work on Nick's wound.

Liv swiveled around to face the Segway robot, her eyes spitting fire. "What'd you do? Whose blood is that?"

The bot remained silent, its eyes blank and staring straight ahead.

Liv huffed and stomped up to it. "I demand to know where you got that blood," she repeated, poking the robot in the chest with her finger to emphasize her words.

It made a jerky movement backward, blinked its eyes, then resumed its "at attention" stance.

"Liv, don't—" Zach started.

She turned on him with the same fury she'd shown the robot. "You can't possibly be okay with this! How do we know these things know what they're doing? They're not even human."

"It looks to me like they know what they're doing," Sofia stated.

"You stay out of this!" Liv screeched, rounding on Sofia. "If it weren't for you, we wouldn't be in this mess. And Nick wouldn't have gotten hurt!"

Sofia physically flinched as if she'd been punched. Her guilt over Nick's injury flared for a second, then a wave of anger roared through her like an avalanche. She balled her hands into fists and looked down at Nick.

His face was still blotchy, but his lips were more pink than blue.

She straightened her back. "Let me remind you that you were the one back in the pyramid who said we should jump into the portal, so there's plenty of blame to go around." Her tone was as sharp as a scalpel. "And it doesn't take a doctor to see that Nick looks a whole lot better than he did a few minutes ago, so I'm going to say that these things, as you called them, know a whole lot more than any of us. So stay out of their way and stop pretending you're concerned about him. Because we all know you're not."

Zach hastily stepped between them. "All right, all right. We're all running on adrenaline here, but going at each other isn't going to help anything."

He grabbed Liv's hand, which was clenched into a fist. She tried to yank it back, but he wouldn't let go.

"Look, it's obvious these robots were designed for medical use. Let's give them a chance to do their thing and see what happens ... okay?"

As if Zach's words were a command, the Segway bot came to life and returned to the pod. But again they couldn't see what it was doing.

Zach put his arm around Liv's shoulder and pulled her into his side. "We're all in this together. If we don't work as a team, we're never going to get back home."

Liv glared at Sofia another second, then turned and melted into Zach's shoulder. "I didn't know Nick was hurt when I said we should jump. I never would have—"

"I know." Zach wrapped both arms around her and shot Sofia a warning glance over Liv's head. "No one's blaming you. We all knew that jumping was our only option. It would've been nice to know in advance we were gonna end up on a spaceship, though."

Liv stiffened, then pulled back. "What? We're on ..." She flipped around to Sofia. Her face was almost as white as Nick's. "Is that for real? Are we on a spaceship?"

Seeing the haunted look in Liv's eyes, Sofia's indignation waned.

"I wish I could say no," Zach answered. "But I can't. And it gets worse ... I think we're up here all alone."

Liv recoiled and closed her eyes, then slowly sank to the floor, putting her head in her hands.

Sofia stepped forward, but Zach waved her back and sat down next to Liv.

"It's gonna be all right," he said, rubbing small circles on her back. "We just have to figure it out. But we'll be home before you know it, and all you'll have to worry about is how to cram all your crap into your dorm closet."

Sofia lowered her eyes and picked at her cuticles. Zach's tender reassurance was nice, but she knew it was just lip service. No way could their lives ever go back to the way they were before this all happened.

Still, she'd give anything to have him care enough about her to lie like that.

Or for anyone to care that much about her for that matter.

EIGHT

The three spent the night curled up on the floor of the ER, though for Sofia, sleep only came in short spurts. After waking for the fourth time, her brain refused to shut down and instead regurgitated the few facts she and Zach had discovered over and over, even though there weren't all that many.

If the others hadn't been asleep nearby, she would have let out a scream of frustration. They had so little information to work with, she didn't see how they'd ever find a way out of this mess.

They'd explored every inch of the place except for four corridors that were blocked off, one of which she felt certain led to the flying saucer looking structure she'd seen from the Observatory. Whoever was on the spaceship she'd seen arrive never appeared, though. Which gave her another mystery to solve and made her wonder if they were being kept apart on purpose because someone didn't want them to find out what this place was really used for.

Sofia let out a weary sigh and gingerly got to her feet so she wouldn't disturb Zach or Liv. She tiptoed to the display at the foot of the pod where Nick's heartbeat made a steady line of peaks and valleys across the glass.

After watching it for a bit, her gaze drifted to a line of icons at the bottom of the screen. She hadn't paid much attention to them before, but as she studied the unfamiliar icons, a question popped into her head.

What if this system hooked into the facility's mainframe?

If it did, and if she could hack into it, she might be able to finally find something that would help them.

She raised her hand to select an icon, then paused as second thoughts squirmed their way into her brain. What if one of the icons stopped the robots from working on Nick?

Sofia turned her head to look at the Segway robot attending to Nick after having taken over from the overhead robotic arms. Sitting on a tray beside the bot was a metal bowl holding a bloody blob that she didn't even want to try to guess what it was.

Another wave of guilt swept through her.

Crap! She let her hand drop and looked back at the icons.

She had no idea what any of them were, but the last one in the row, a blue circle with vague green shapes on it, kind of looked like an abstract version of Earth, which made a certain amount of sense. The Pleiadians on Earth would want to have a channel of communication with this spaceship if it was theirs.

That thought perked her up. Maybe it would even help her get in touch with Will.

A bubble of anticipation formed inside her as she reached out and hovered her finger over the icon.

Please don't let anything bad happen.

She held her breath and tapped the glass.

In the blink of an eye, a full image of Earth filled the screen.

She sagged in relief.

The globe slowly rotated until North America was front and center. Then the image zoomed in on Texas and continued to close in on a town, then a street, then a nice-looking brick home.

Her eyebrows together as she stared at the house. Why had the app gone directly to it? Was it the Pleiadians' headquarters or something? She scrunched up her nose. Texas seemed like an odd choice for an alien headquarters. Though, what did she know?

She lifted her finger to the search bar at the side of the glass to see if the app would let her zoom in on Maddie's house in Urbandale. But just then a black SUV pulled up in front of the house and her hand stalled in midair. Two large, hulking men that looked similar to Daher's guards in the pyramid got out of the car and walk up to the stoop. The door of the house opened a second later and the two men disappeared inside.

As she watched and waited for the men to come back out, she noticed the word, "Live," in the bottom corner of the screen. An uneasy shiver ran up her spine.

"Um, guys ..." she called to Zach and Liv. "I think you should come see this."

Zach roused, rubbed his fists in his eyes, then perked up when he saw Sofia standing in front of the glass screen. "Is something wrong?"

He jumped to his feet, then pulled Liv to hers.

Liv let out a sharp gasp when she saw the screen and elbowed Sofia out of the way. She gripped the glass with both hands and stared as if she was looking at a tragic accident.

"That's our house! Why is our house on the screen?"

NINE

Martina Schultze stood cross-armed in the doorway of Liv's bedroom, contemplating the antique desk she had painstakingly refinished and installed in the corner.

"Standing here isn't going to bring her back any sooner, you know," her husband, Scott, said from behind.

She made a small sound in her throat without taking her eyes off the desk. "I know. It's just been bugging me. I think maybe I should have painted it instead. White is all the rage right now."

Scott's arms snaked around her waist. "It's perfect just the way it is. Liv's gonna love it. Don't you worry."

Martina sagged against him. "I hope so."

"You do know that one of these days she's gonna move out no matter how nice you make her room look."

"I know, I just—"

Both of their watches buzzed at the same time. The doorbell then chimed.

"Were you expecting someone?" Scott asked, pulling his phone out of his pocket.

"No."

The doorbell app showed two men standing on the stoop.

"How many times do I have to tell these guys I'm not interested in new windows!" he muttered as he headed down the stairs.

A moment later, Martina heard Scott say, "May I help you?" She couldn't hear what the men said back, but a few seconds later, he called up the stairs, "Sweetheart, can you come here, please?"

The desk was still on her mind as she descended the steps.

Three-quarters of the way down, Scott said, "These men are from *Road to Riches.*"

Her heart skipped a beat, and she rushed down the remaining steps. "Is something wrong? Are the kids okay?"

"Zachary and Olivia are fine." The voice came from a tablet held out by one of the men.

She looked down at the dark, intimidating face on the screen. The man's smile looked forced and did not reach his piercing eyes that were as cold as a shark's.

She involuntarily shuddered.

"Actually, they're better than fine," the man on the tablet added. "And I must ask that you do not repeat what I'm about to tell you, but I'm happy to say your children are in the running for the grand prize."

Martina's hand flew to her chest. "Oh my! That's …" She was at a loss for words.

"Yes, it's amazing, but I'm sure not a surprise."

She put a hand on Scott's arm to steady herself. She never had any doubts the twins would stand out in the competitions, but win it all? And why would this man … she inhaled sharply as recognition suddenly set in.

Oh. My. God. That's Makin Daher!

"You're—" her mouth had gone dry and she couldn't spit out the rest of the words.

He nodded and gave another smile that looked as fake and cold as his eyes. "I'm Makim Daher, executive producer of *Road to Riches.*

"I've been extremely pleased with the aptitude your children have demonstrated," Daher continued. "They really are quite exceptional, but I'm sure you've heard that before." He winked.

"Keep in mind nothing is official yet because the final challenge isn't finished, but let me just say, I've seen no other contestant come close to exhibiting the kind of abilities I've witnessed in your children. And it's a safe assumption for me to say they'll finish as the rightful victors."

Martina was speechless.

Scott grinning like a Cheshire cat put his arm around her and gave her a one-arm hug.

"You've done an incredible job raising the two of them for which I applaud you," Daher went on. "And that brings me around to why I'm calling you today. Since you two have obviously played a big part in Zachary and Olivia's success, I feel it's only fitting that you also be a part of the finale. So, I'm inviting you to come and be there to watch them cross the finish line."

"Come there?" Scott asked, his eyes going wide with disbelief. "To France?"

"Actually, the final episode is taking place in Cairo, Egypt."

"Oh Lord." Martina's chest swelled with pride. "Egypt," she looked dreamily at Scott. "We've always talked about going to Egypt."

"Excellent!" Daher interjected before Scott could answer. "My private jet is sitting at the airport, ready to depart as soon as you can get there. I've already set you up with accommodations at one of my guest houses at Katayama Heights."

"Wait just a second … you aren't expecting us to leave right now, are you?" Scott sounded even more incredulous.

"Yes, I am," Daher replied, a hint of annoyance coming through in his tone. "We don't know when the twins will finish the challenge, and the whole point of you coming is to be there for the finale."

"But our j-jobs … " Scott stuttered.

"My assistant, Tabari, has already spoken to both of your employers and explained the situation. Your time off has already been cleared and taken care of."

Martina started and frowned at the tablet. She'd always heard Hollywood types could be pushy but going to their bosses before checking with them first was flat out arrogant.

"I don't know—" she began but was cut off.

"You better than anyone can understand how much it would mean to Zachary and Olivia to have you there with them in their finest hour." He sadly shook his head. "Think how disappointed they would be to learn you turned down this opportunity to support them. It could ruin the entire victory for them, not to mention break their hearts. Would you really want to do that to them?"

"No, of course, we d-don't want that," Martina stammered.

"Good! Then, it's all settled. These two gentlemen, Mr. Jacobson and Mr. Adler, will wait while you gather a few things, and will then take you to the airport. Your suite will be fully stocked with essentials and toiletries, so you do not have to worry about packing those items. You'll also have access to the hotel's exquisite designer boutique, compliments of the show, of course, so you don't have to bring much in the way of clothing either."

The hairs on the back of Martina's arms stood on end. This was overly excessive and starting to sound more and more like a scam every second. How did she even know this guy was the real Makim Daher? He could be an impostor.

She smiled at the tablet, the kind of smile she'd give an overly aggressive salesman. "Your offer is very generous, but it's a lot to take in. If you could give us some time to talk it over—"

One of the men reached out and put his hand on her arm. The other man put a hand on Scott's shoulder.

Martina's thoughts instantly became fuzzy, then disappeared altogether. She blinked rapidly and tried to remember what she was going to say. She was sure it was something important, but for the life of her she couldn't think of what it was now.

Scott's face relaxed and a wide grin replaced his frown. "Guess we're going to Egypt. Livy and Zach are going to be so surprised when they see us."

Daher's mouth turned up into a genuine smile. "Very good. I look forward to meeting you both."

With that said, the screen of the tablet went black.

Scott turned to Martina, looking as awestruck as she felt. "An all-expenses paid trip to Cairo! Can you believe it?"

Martina let out a girlish giggle. "No, I can't! It's like winning the Lotto." A twinge of doubt sparked in her mind, but it was fleeting.

"I've never been prouder of the kids. How did we get to be such lucky parents?" Scott said, giving her a hug.

One of the men cleared his throat.

Martina screwed up her face and whispered, "It looks like our driver is getting impatient."

She took Scott's hand and pulled him toward the stairs. "The first one packed gets the window seat!" She let out another giggle and raced up the steps.

TEN

Sofia flinched as Liv rounded on her. "Why'd you bring our house up on this screen?"

"I didn't…" She looked to Zach for help, but his attention was on the display. "I was looking for information to help us and clicked on an icon that I thought looked like Earth. That's all I did. It zoomed in on your house on its own right before that black SUV drove up." She pointed to the vehicle sitting in front of the house. "Some men got out of it and went inside."

"What men?" Zach asked, leaning in for a better look.

"There were two of them. They looked like the guys Daher had with him in the pyramid."

Liv let out a small squeak and clutched Zach's arm.

"I couldn't get a good look at their faces, though," Sofia quickly added. "So I may be wrong about that."

Liv turned to Zach. "We have to get home. Right now!"

Zach kept his eyes locked on the screen. "And how do you suggest we do that? It's not like we can jump on a plane and fly to Texas. Even if we could, we wouldn't get there in time."

Liv frantically looked around. "Well, we can't just sit here and do nothing." She started for the door, then stopped and turned back. "What about that other guy in the pyramid … the one you called

Will. He's the one that spoke in my head, right? Maybe he can do something … send someone to the house. And tell us how to get out of here, too."

The tic in Zach's jaw pulsed as he clenched and unclenched his hands. After a long pause, he turned to Sofia. "I'm not sure it's wise to trust Will, but he's the only one I know who can tell us how to get home. I think you should be the one to reach out to him, though. He's more likely to answer you."

Sofia could see a mixture of worry and rage burning in Zach's eyes. She could feel it radiating off of him, too. She shifted her weight and looked down at her hands. She'd never told him she'd tried to contact Will earlier and that she had no success. She knew it would just make him more suspicious. And she didn't want to make matters any worse.

She squeezed her eyelids closed and said a quick prayer that this time would be different.

"Will, are you there? We really, really need your help. Please answer me."

She waited, the silence growing heavier as the seconds ticked off.

"Where are you? Why won't you talk to me?" she asked desperately, ignoring the suspicions trying to wiggle their way into her mind.

Was she not doing it right? Or was it that he couldn't answer? The last time he spoke to her telepathically was right before the ceiling collapsed in the pyramid. Her stomach dropped.

Ohmigod, what if he didn't make it out and was crushed under all those rocks?

Sofia looked up through her eyelashes. Both Zach and Liv were staring at her.

"Did you get a hold of him?" Liv asked, her voice squeaky with desperation.

Sofia shook her head. "He didn't answer." Seeing Zach's nostrils flare, she hurriedly added, "But we don't know if he made it out of the pyramid. The ceiling collapsed right after we jumped. He might have gotten ..." She couldn't finish the sentence.

"What are you saying?" Liv asked. "The only person who knows we're here is dead?" She turned back to Zach, her eyes wide with fear. "I don't understand why this is happening. Why did Mr. Daher try to kill us and those men back there in the pyramid?"

Sofia eyed Zach, but his mouth was set in the stubborn scowl she was becoming to know all too well.

"Zach," she said telepathically. ***"Liv deserves to know the truth. You've got to tell her."***

He tensed and turned his head away.

Sofia blew a huff through her nose and pressed her lips together. Her and Liv's relationship had started out on shaky ground and hadn't gotten any better, so she was sure Liv would have a much easier time accepting the truth if it came from Zach instead of her.

But one way or the other, Liv needed to be told.

Sofia shot Zach a sidelong glare. *God, why do you have to be so dang stubborn?*

"Okay, fine. If you won't tell her, I will," she said telepathically and waited another second to see if he would do the right thing. When he remained silent, she let out a heavy sigh and cleared her throat.

"Daher's an Anunnaki. They're an alien race from another planet."

Zach visibly flinched, but Liv's face remained blank.

"Think of it this way," Sofia said. "The Anunnaki are the equivalent of the Galactic Empire in Star Wars—the bad guys who go around conquering planets to enslave the inhabitants and strip the planet clean of its natural resources. The Pleiadians are the good guys like the Rebel Alliance. They're the ones who are keeping the Anunnaki from coming in and destroying Earth."

Liv gave a snort, similar to the one Zach gave when Will first tried to explain this to him. "I don't need a lecture on Star Wars. I've seen all the movies. Just tell me why those men tried to kill us and why they're at our house!"

It took all of Sofia's willpower to not grab Liv by the shoulders, shake her, and tell her to shut up.

"I was trying to make it easier for you to understand," she replied through clenched teeth.

Liv narrowed her eyes and lifted her chin in defiance. "Whatevs, just get to the point."

Sofia swallowed back the "go to hell" that came to the tip of her tongue.

"Okay, you want the point… here it is. The Anunnaki hate the Pleiadians and want to kill every one of us so they can rule Earth. Is that better?"

Liv tsked. "I still don't see what any of this has to do with us."

"Well, if you'd just shut up and let me tell you the whole story, you'd see."

Liv crossed her arms over her chest, stuck out her hip, and glared at Sofia.

Sofia rolled her eyes, then shot another glance at Zach's back, hoping he'd help out, but his body language made it clear he wanted no part of it.

"Just let me finish. Okay?" Sofia tried to keep the edge out of her voice, but she wasn't a miracle worker. "I'll try to make it as short as I can."

Liv glared back but held her tongue.

Lord, give me strength, Sofia prayed and started in, summing up the story of the Anunnaki getting kicked off Earth, the Pleiadians building the energy grid to keep them from coming back, and how Daher got a few of his ships in when the grid went down.

"So Daher needs the grid turned off to bring in the rest of his troops," Sofia continued. "But there are only three Pleiadians who can actually turn the grid off. The Guardians."

She paused, expecting Liv to react to the name *Guardians*, but for once Liv had nothing to say.

She glanced over at Zach's back. "Do you want to finish this?"

His head swiveled around to glare at her over his shoulder, but his lips were pressed tightly together. She let out a sigh, shook her head, and looked back at Liv.

"Daher has been desperate to find the Guardians, but no Pleiadian would give them up. So he came up with the idea of the reality show and rigged the maze so that only a true Pleiadian could make it to the center. When you, Nick, and that other girl got to the tower, he thought he'd found us. But what he didn't know is that Will had helped Nick and the girl cheat, so he only actually had one of the real Guardians ... that was you. Me and Zach are the other two."

Sofia had never called herself a Guardian before and it felt like an invisible hand had a hold of her heart and was squeezing it.

Liv's eyes grew rounder, and her lips parted, but she looked lost for words.

"Daher killed our biological parents when we were toddlers and would have probably killed us too if Will hadn't placed us with human families and had us raised as ordinary humans." A wave of emotion clogged Sofia's throat at the sacrifice her parents and so many others had made for their sake.

She swallowed hard and cleared her throat, but her voice still came out raspy with emotion. "But then we went and messed everything up by stupidly walking into Daher's hands on our own. And now, here we are ... stuck in space."

Liv stared straight ahead, her expression deadpan. The only sound in the room was the whirl of the robotic arms. But after a long awkward moment, her golden aura, as well as the gold ring around her pupils, lit up like a solar flare. And, without warning, she spun around and punched Zach hard in the arm.

He staggered backwards. "What the fuck, Livy. That hurt!"

"How long have you known?" Liv's nostrils flared, and her glare shot daggers. "Why didn't you tell me I'm an alien? Didn't you think that was something I should know?"

Zach rubbed his bicep and glowered back. "Because I don't know that I believe it! Will is a stranger who showed up in the maze and started feeding us this insane bullshit about aliens taking over Earth. It sounded so far-fetched and ridiculous, you would have reacted the same way. And how do we know he's who he says he is? I mean, we all thought Daher was a good guy, and look how that's turned out."

Liv gave a disgusted snort. "Really? That's what you're going with?

You expect me to believe Will made it all up, then picked us out of billions of people? Why would he do that? Why pick us?"

Zach scowled but didn't answer.

Liv threw her hands in the air with a frustrated groan and walked away.

The doors of the wall cabinets all slammed open at once.

After a few steps, she whirled around and stomped right up into Zach's space. "You've never admitted to anyone, not even to me, that we're different. But we both know we are and always have been. I can move things with my mind. You can jump like two stories high. Those aren't things within normal human capabilities. And what about what happened at the pyramid? How do you explain that?"

Zach visibly flinched. "How do you know I can jump that high?"

Liv's face lost some of its hardness. "There's very little I don't know about you."

She closed her eyes for a moment, her lips firmly pressed into a thing line as if trying to get control of her emotions. Then she opened her eyes and took both of his hands in hers.

"I had a vision of this … well, not this exactly," she gestured with her head to indicate the room, "but close enough. We were in some place that looked like an arsenal, and we were learning how to use our special powers and these super weird looking weapons and stuff. It was a scene straight out of a sci-fi movie, so I thought it had to be a dream. But …" she spread her arms wide, "here we are."

Zach's face went pale.

"Look, we've both been through hell trying to be someone we're not," Liv said in a softer voice. "And though you may think this guy, Will, made up the story, I think it's the answer we've been looking for. And to be truthful, it's a relief to finally know who we really are."

She took his hands again and squeezed. "We're not freaks, Z. We're Pleiadians, the good guys."

He stepped back and tried to pull his hands free, but Liv wouldn't let go.

"You can't run from it," she added. "We are who we are, and I'm tired of pretending to be someone else. Aren't you?"

Liv's words echoed in Sofia's head.

She turned away and stared at the house on the monitor. All this time she had pegged Liv as a manipulative prima donna, but maybe Liv was just as confused and scared of being herself as she was.

A movement on the screen caught Sofia's attention. She narrowed her eyes and watched as a smiling man and woman exited the house arm in arm and started down the walk.

"Guys, quick. Come see this."

Liv and Zach nearly tripped over each other in their hurry to get back to the screen.

"Mom, Dad!" Liv squeaked, and stared in horror as her dad opened the back door of the SUV, helped her mom in, then got in himself.

Daher's men stowed the Schultze's suitcases in the trunk, then settled into the front seat.

"No, no, no," Liv whispered as the SUV drove away.

Zach wrapped his arms around her and pulled her into his chest. "Shhh, it may not be what you think. They looked happy. They were smiling, and it didn't look like they were being forced to go with those men."

Sofia could see by the look on his face he didn't believe his own words.

Her insides twisted into knots and a blanket of guilt threatened to suffocate her.

She wrapped her arms around her middle.

Deep down inside, she knew none of this was her fault. But that didn't stop the feeling she had somehow let Zach down. Even worse, she had no idea how to fix it or make it better. Or how to fight an alien who had enough money to buy loyalty as well as any weapon he wanted.

ELEVEN

Maddie Lewis flipped a lock of hair out of her eyes and grimaced as she hefted a tray loaded with glasses of water, iced tea, and sodas. Her back gave a twinge of protest, reminding her that this was the twenty-first tray she'd carried since clocking in. And it wasn't just today. For three shifts in a row, she'd been lugging the trays for both her and Meredith's tables, and she was not just feeling it in her back, but in her arms and legs, too.

"Bitch," she whispered through clenched teeth as Meredith brushed by her wearing a pleased smirk and waggling her ace-bandage wrapped wrist.

Everyone knew that Meredith's claim of a sprain was just another lie to get out of work and to make Maddie suffer for being Sofia's BFF. Because, for whatever unhinged reason, it seemed Meredith still harbored an intense dislike for Sofia even though they were no longer roommates at the foster home.

In all honesty, though, Maddie knew that was partly her fault. She had taken great pleasure in telling Meredith that Sofia had been picked to be on the new reality show, *Road to Riches*. And though she knew she wasn't supposed to and knew it would put a target on her back, the look on Meredith's face had been totally worth it.

She was paying for it now, though. But, thank God, she only had a couple more months before she left Meredith and her nastiness behind for college, albeit they could very well be the longest couple months of her life.

"Order up," Sam the cook yelled.

Maddie checked the clock on the wall and internally groaned. *Ughh, two more hours to go!*

With a weary sigh, she grabbed another tray and began to stack the plates. Before she finished, a second order was pushed through the pass-through window.

"I'll be right back to get those, Sam," she called and swiveled to take table two their dinner, not knowing Meredith was standing right behind her.

Meredith didn't move out of the way, and accidentally, or not, caused the tray to tip. For the next couple seconds, Maddie looked like a circus act trying to balance the tray to keep the plates of fried chicken, meatloaf, mashed potatoes with gravy, and coleslaw from sliding off as Meredith stood there and watched. Luckily, another waiter happened to walk up in time to grab the tray and prevent a complete catastrophe. The only loss was a plate of meatloaf smothered in brown gravy, which was now running down the front of Maddie's uniform.

"What the hell, Meredith!" Maddie yelled, feeling the heat of anger and embarrassment move up her neck. "You totally did that on purpose!"

"I did not. Don't blame me for your clumsiness," Meredith fired back, not even trying to hide the laughter in her voice.

"That's enough, girls," the manager said, coming up behind the two. "Sam, we need another meatloaf," he barked to the cook. Then, to Maddie, "You, go clean yourself up. Get a new shirt from the office." He turned to Meredith. "And you get that order out."

"But my wrist?" Meredith whined.

The manager's jaw squared as if he really wanted to say something but knew he couldn't.

"Ella, help Meredith get this order out," he said to one of the waitresses who had gathered around. "The rest of you, get back to work. We need those tables turned over."

To a pimply-faced boy, he added, "Get this mess cleaned up."

Maddie took off her name badge, slammed it down on the order station, and turned toward the restroom, fighting the urge to slap the victorious grin off Meredith's face. But she knew if she did, she'd probably get fired and Meredith would score a double win. Still, it was tempting.

"Aghh, the end of summer can't get here soon enough," she seethed through her teeth.

A hulking man with wide shoulders and bulging biceps that stretched the sleeves of his polo shirt to the max approached Meredith as she stood at the order station, entering an order she'd just taken into the system.

"I'm looking for a Madeline Lewis," the man said in a heavy, unrecognizable accent.

Meredith gave a disgusted snort. "Do I —" Her words abruptly cut off as she glanced up through her eyelashes and caught sight of the *Road to Riches* logo on his shirt.

She straightened her shoulders, which pushed out her chest, and asked in a low, sultry voice, "May I ask what this is about?"

"Mr. Makim Daher is wanting to speak to her," the man said.

The clatter of dishes and voices of the hundred or so people in the restaurant faded as Meredith's brain whirled with thoughts of how to take advantage of this once-in-a-lifetime opportunity.

She darted a glance around to make sure no one else had heard what the man had said and made a motion to the door. "Would you mind if we talked outside?"

The man gave a curt nod, turned, and walked out.

Ohmigod. Meredith wrung her hands and stared at Maddie's name badge lying next to the computer. As nonchalantly as she could, she moved her hand over the badge.

"Hey, I'm gonna take my break," she called out to Ella, who was standing at the cook's pass-through window. "Table three's order is in and five needs drink refills," she added and sprinted for the door before Ella could reply.

Outside, a mob of people had congregated around the entrance, waiting for the hostess to call their names, but the man was easy to spot. He stood a head taller than everyone else.

"Let's go over here." Meredith pointed to the corner of the building. She let him lead the way and quickly pinned Maddie's badge on her chest, then gave her armpit a quick sniff.

"What's this all about?" she asked.

Instead of answering, the man handed her a tablet.

"Ms. Lewis?" a dark, brooding face said from the screen.

Recognizing the billionaire, Meredith's hand flew to her chest and her mouth dropped open, but she was too flustered to speak.

"What I'm about to tell you must be held in the strictest confidence. I need to have your assurance you won't disclose any part of this conversation to another person. Especially not to the press."

Meredith nodded emphatically.

"Very good. If I could get your signature on the non-disclosure agreement Mr. Smith has there in his hands, I can continue."

The burly man handed her a clipboard with a sheet of paper clipped to it.

Meredith felt as if all the blood in her body had drained to her feet. She looked at the paper, then back at the tablet. "I—"

"It's just a technicality. Lawyer stuff, but nothing to worry about." Daher's smile was that of a wolf eyeing its prey.

Mr. Smith pushed a pen in Meredith's hand. She swallowed hard and made an illegible scribble on the designated line that was neither Maddie's signature nor hers.

"Very good. I can now happily report to you that your friend, Sofia Kaye, is in the running for the grand prize on our show, *Road to Riches*."

A green claw of jealousy twisted inside of Meredith. She bit down on the inside of her cheek to keep from growling.

"Sofia's such a remarkable young lady and deserves to have someone close to her cheering her on at the finale. And since she has no family, I was hoping that person might be you."

"Me?" Meredith croaked, forgetting for a moment that he thought he was speaking to Maddie.

"Yes, Madeline Lewis, you. I would like you to come to Nice to represent her family as she celebrates her victory. Although, I must stress that the competition is not yet finalized, and her victory is not one hundred percent assured. But from what I've seen, and the fact she is so far ahead of the pack, I don't believe this would be a waste of your time."

"Nice … as in the city in France?" Meredith's mouth was so dry she could hardly speak the words.

"Yes, my dear, Nice, France." Daher's chuckle sounded fake, but Meredith didn't care. "What do you say? Are you willing to support your friend and come to France?"

Oh, my fucking God … France! Meredith's mind was spinning with excitement. Could she really get away with pretending to be Maddie and going in her place?

"I'm afraid time is of the essence at this point," Daher added. "As I mentioned, the competition is in its final leg and could end at any time. So, with that in mind, and because I know you are a good friend and wouldn't want to let Sofia down, I've sent my personal jet to bring you across the pond. It's scheduled to leave the minute you get to the airport."

Meredith flinched. "You're talking like right now? But I … I don't even have a passport."

Daher waved his hand in the air. "No need to worry. There are advantages to being the richest man in the world. It will be taken care of once you get here. You also don't need to worry about packing. The show will provide you with a healthy line of credit at the hotel to take care of whatever you need in the way of clothing, toiletries, and such."

Meredith opened her mouth, then closed it, and looked down at her feet.

What would happen if they found out I lied about being Maddie?

Her mind churned with options.

Well, I never actually said I was Maddie, so they can't say I lied. And I do know Sofia, so there's that.

She chewed on her bottom lip.

And once I'm in France what are they going to do?

"I would hate for Sofia to have no one here to witness her finest moment," Daher added. "But, if you don't think you can do this for her, maybe there's another friend who would?"

Meredith's head jerked up and she shouted "No!" louder than she meant to. Heat rushed up her neck. "I mean … of course, I'd be happy to be there for Sofia. Me and her were practically sisters."

"Perfect! I had a feeling you wouldn't let her down. Mr. Smith and Mr. Green will escort you to the airport."

"What? Right now?" Meredith was giddy with the thought of going to the French Riviera and wasn't sure she'd heard right.

"Yes, now. As I've already mentioned, the last leg of the competition has begun, and the whole point is for you to be there to see Sofia cross the finish line. Is this a problem?"

"No … no. Absolutely no problem."

"Great, it's settled. And let me remind you, the NDA you signed means you're legally bound and cannot mention this trip or that you've even talked to me to anyone else."

"Oh, sure. I totally get it," she said, nodding as if she understood the legalities of what she'd signed.

"Enjoy your flight then, Ms. Lewis."

Meredith blinked as the screen went black and tried to grasp onto what had just happened.

"This way, Madame," Mr. Smith said, swinging his arm toward a black Porsche sitting at the curb in the No Parking zone.

Meredith swallowed hard. "Um … sure. Just let me get my purse out of my locker. I'll be right back."

She was screaming with excitement on the inside, but somehow, she managed to keep a straight face as she ran through the restaurant to the employee locker room. She quickly scribbled a note saying she quit and placed it on the manager's desk.

"What's up?" Ella asked as Meredith came out of the office.

Meredith glanced around to make sure Maddie wasn't in the vicinity before she whispered, "I just got my ticket out of this hillbilly town." She pushed past her and headed for the door. "I'm going to be living the high life on the other side of the pond and I won't ever have to deal with you losers again."

Grinning like the Joker, she ran to the car, climbed into the back, and leaned her head back against the soft leather seat.

Sofia's gonna totally lose it when she sees me. She giggled to herself. *But she won't be able to do anything about it because I'll already be there ... in France!*

She held back the squeal bubbling up her throat.

God really does work in mysterious ways sometimes.

TWELVE

Four days without food or water had begun to take its toll on Sofia. Bouts of weakness would hit her out of the blue and her reflection in the window showed sunken eyes with blacker than usual circles, giving her the look of a raccoon.

She, Zach, and Liv had each taken a turn in the MedPod chair and received a bag of intravenous fluid. They only did that once, though, because they had no idea how much solution there was on hand, and they all agreed Nick needed it more than they did. Although, if they didn't find water or a way out of this place soon, they might have to rethink that.

Sofia sank to the floor of the Observatory and stared out at Earth. It was so bright and so amazingly beautiful it almost didn't look real. And looking at it from space like this, it was hard to imagine there were seven plus billion people roaming around on it.

She blew out a wistful sigh. Not one of those seven billion people cared or would probably even notice if she never returned. Except maybe Maddie, her BFF who had signed her up for the reality show in the first place. But even Maddie would eventually forget her.

No one here cares about me, either. That unbidden thought hit her hard. She grimaced and closed her eyes.

She'd been a fool to think she and Zach had a connection. Someone like him would never be interested in someone like her. She was totally unlovable. The long list of rejections she had accumulated over the years was proof of that. And even though Zach did seem different than the others, she should have known better than to get her hopes up.

Sofia brought her knees into her chest and rested her forehead on them. A stream of salty tears ran from her nose onto her shorts, and an ache of loneliness slithered out of the hollow of her bones and wrapped its icy tendrils around her heart.

She sat that way for exactly sixty seconds. Then, as if an alarm clock had gone off in her head, she swiped her hand under her nose to wipe away the drips, pushed the self-deprecating words out of her mind, and looked up. Her subconscious had never allowed her to wallow in self-pity for longer than sixty seconds at a time. It obviously knew that if she did, she'd fall into a black hole and never come out.

It doesn't matter, anyway. I'm better off on my own. She knew that was a lie, but she had no problem lying to herself. She just couldn't lie to others.

Sofia stared past Earth and whispered to the unseen entity she'd always felt was controlling her future, "Why can't you ever, just once, give me a break?"

She clenched her teeth as a wave of lightheadedness swept over her.

Ughhh, I just wanna forget about Daher and Zach and everything that's happened and get on with my life! There's got to be a way to get back to Earth. Think harder and figure it out!

Sofia closed her eyes and took a deep breath to clear the fog that had taken up permanent residency in her brain in the last day. She'd already gone over the events that took place in the pyramid a dozen times, sure that the answer was there somewhere. But there were so many things she didn't understand, it was hard to know what to even look for.

Like the beam of light that had shot up when the three of them joined hands. What was that about?

At first she'd thought the beam was what had opened the portal.

But the three of them had tried duplicating it several different times over the course of the last few days, and though the light shot up, no portal appeared.

Another thing she didn't understand was how she and Zach had produced the energy to throw Daher and his men across the cavern. They'd tried to replicate it to open one of the locked doors as well, but all she felt was the usual tingle that ran through her whenever Zach touched her. And that was nowhere near the power she'd felt in the pyramid. That energy had been so intense she was sure it would have split her apart if she hadn't released it.

Ahhh, I'm missing something. But what?

Sofia massaged her temples and tried to ignore the thought that Will had actually been the one who opened the portal. But even if it had been him, the three of them should be able to open one, too. After all, they were Pleiadians the same as him.

The thought of being a Pleiadian still felt weird—like more of a dream than reality. A dream she couldn't wake up from.

She pulled her pendant out of her t-shirt and curled her fingers around it. The stone's energy had become much stronger since arriving in this place and she could feel its buzz all the way up her arm to her shoulder. She squeezed it and raised her eyes to the dome. Rachmaninoff's, *Rhapsody on a Theme by Paganini*, began playing in her head the way it always did when she looked up at the stars. But neither the song nor the swirls of colors her synesthesia created brought her the sense of calm it usually did. Instead, her insides felt as hollow as a chocolate Easter bunny.

All of a sudden, she felt a small flutter in her chest, which was a warning that Zach was nearby. She sat up straighter.

"Is it alright if I join you?" Zach asked from the door of the lift.

Not sure she could trust her voice, Sofia nodded but continued to look up through the dome.

Zach plopped down on the floor a foot away from her. Then after a long awkward pause, he said, "I figured you'd be here."

She fixed her gaze on a single star and concentrated on taking slow even breaths, but it wasn't easy to do with Zach so close.

"I know you've been avoiding me and don't want anything to do with me," he added.

Sofia's jaw dropped. He thought *she* was avoiding *him*?

"I can't say I blame ya," he went on. "I've been a real jerk. But …" he sighed. "It's just that you don't understand what I've gone through. I worked my ass off to be a regular guy and to keep Liv from exposing us to the world. You might think these fu … weird powers or whatever are cool, but for me they've been a living nightmare. I've tried everything to hide what I can do, but it was like people could sense I was different. I saw it in their eyes and in the way they acted around me."

He turned his head, presenting her his profile. "Only one time in my whole life have they helped me out. That was my basketball scholarship. But then those same stupid-ass powers took it away. And now, Mom and Dad are in danger because I'm …"

Zach's misery and vulnerability swirled around him like a black cloud of smoke.

Sofia scooted around to face him, wishing she could tell him everything was going to be all right, but she wasn't sure it would be, and she couldn't lie even if she wanted to.

He picked at his fingernails that were already chewed down to the quick. "I can't say I was surprised when Will showed up with the story that we were aliens. I think I always knew in the back of my mind that I wasn't exactly human. But it's one thing to deal with a couple weird powers, and a whole other ball game to be told you're an alien, which means on top of everything else, I now have to worry about being hunted down, caged, and having experiments performed on me."

Sofia involuntarily shuddered. She hadn't thought about that aspect of being an alien.

"I'd like to say that'll never happen," she said, putting a hand on his leg.

An electric shock rushed through her awakening a swarm of butterflies in her stomach.

"But in reality, who knows what people would do if word got out there were real, honest-to-God aliens among them?" She moved a little closer. "But if you think about it for a second, Will said Pleiadians have been here for thousands of centuries, and in all that time, nobody's found out. We've been around for eighteen years, too, and no one's managed to discover who we are. Not even Daher. So, why would it be different now?"

Sofia couldn't tell if her words had gotten through to Zach, but his golden aura still looked washed out and a sense of anxiety and hopelessness circled him like a satellite.

She reached out and enclosed both his hands in hers, just like she had done back then.

"You're not alone in this, you know. I'm here for you and I'll help you get your parents back. I swear."

Zach raised his head and looked her in the eye. "I remember you swearing you'd always be there for me once. But you left anyway."

His words reached into her chest and ripped out her heart, but he was right. She'd made him a vow back then and hadn't kept it. It hadn't been her choice, of course. And she would have given anything to have stayed with him and Liv, but she had been too young at the time and had no say in her own future. Still, a lead balloon of guilt settled in her abdomen.

Sofia lowered her gaze to keep from having to look at the betrayal shining in his eyes.

Zach pulled one of his hands free, took a loose strand of her hair, and tucked it behind her ear, then brushed his knuckles down her cheek.

She went stiff as a rush of heat sparked in her lower regions and swept through her faster than a comet, vaporizing every thought in her head except for one: what would his lips feel like against hers?

Stop it! You're going to make a fool of yourself, just like you did in Cairo.

She had almost kissed him then because she thought she was dreaming. This time she was fully awake and she knew it, but her body didn't seem to care. It was fully attuned to her desires and everything else, even common sense, got pushed aside.

Sofia's chest heaved up and down to fill her lungs, but there didn't seem to be enough air in the room. In the back of her mind, a small voice screamed that she was playing a dangerous game, but her head spun from his heady, musky scent and she couldn't help herself.

She reached up and trailed a fingertip along his jawline to his mouth. His lips were dry and cracked from dehydration, but as tempting as ever. And they were slightly parted, begging to be kissed.

She ran the tip of her tongue over her bottom lip, wondering what he would do if she pressed her lips to his for real this time.

As if Zach had read her thoughts, he leaned in until his mouth was a hair width away from hers. "What have you done to me?" he whispered into her mouth, then teasingly brushed his lips over hers.

A desire like nothing Sofia had ever experienced welled up inside, driving away what little logic was left. She whimpered in complaint as he drew back, and one corner of his mouth lifted in a provocative smile.

She stared back, her eyes saying what her mouth couldn't: I want you.

Then, almost like in a trance, she slipped her hand behind his neck and pulled his mouth to hers.

He let out a low groan, and for a heartbeat didn't respond. Then, with the same abandonment she'd shown, he cinched her to his chest, parted his mouth, and kissed her back with a fervor as if she was the last person left in the galaxy.

"Guardians!"

They both recoiled at the voice coming out of the air and scooted away from each other as if they'd been negatively charged.

"Guardians, can you hear me?"

"Will?" Sofia said, blushing to the tips of her toes as she scrambled to her feet.

Zach leapt to his feet as well and yelled, "Yes, we can hear you!" at the same time Sofia said, "Is that you?"

"Thank Ea you're safe. Forgive me for not contacting you sooner.

I was …" He made a small, strangled sound, the kind a person makes when they're in pain. "My current circumstances are of no concern to you. The important thing is you're safe and out of danger. I can rest easier now that I know everything's all right."

"All right? No, everything's not all right!" Sofia shouted.

"Where did you send us?" Zach roared over the top of her.

"Please … I can't understand any of you when you all talk at once. I know I have a lot of explaining to do, but this isn't a secure line. I'll contact you again once I get back to our base. Until then, may Ea watch over you. Asenja."

"Wait, don't go! We need help," Sofia cried out, but he was gone.

"What the fuck?" Zach murmured to himself, his pulse racing as if he was trying out for pole position in an F1 race.

How could I be so stupid? She's gonna think I was taking advantage of her and the situation. Shit! Things were already messed up enough. How's she supposed to trust me now?

Sofia cleared her throat. "We should get back to the ER and let Liv know that Will called."

Zach closed his eyes and silently groaned, *Ah, shit … Liv! If she finds out about this, I'm so fucked.*

Sofia touched his arm. "Zach?"

Her touch sent a jolt through him as if he'd stuck his finger in an electrical outlet. He reared back and glanced at her through his eyelashes. Her lips were red and a little puffy, and her eyes shone with the same question and uncertainty that was in her voice. His chest constricted, and it took every ounce of his strength to keep from taking her into his arms again. But she deserved so much more than a freakshow like him.

Zach raised his head. "What makes you so sure Will's on our side?"

He'd hoped the question would get Sofia riled up enough to forget about what had happened. But the trace of hurt that crossed her face before she could mask it made him feel even worse.

She shook her head in an I-can't-believe-we're-doing-this-again kind of way. "You know why," she sighed. "He saved us from Daher in the maze and in the pyramid."

"Did he?" His emotional state made his voice come out harsher than he intended. "If Will knew Daher was so dangerous and that joining the show could possibly get us killed, why didn't he stop us at the airport? Or before we even got on the plane? It's obvious he knew where we were the whole time."

Sofia visibly cringed.

He turned away and rubbed the back of his neck.

"Z, where are you?" Liv said in his head. *"I just heard from Will. He's going to call again, so you need to get back here and get ready to go home."*

"I know, I heard him, too," he replied. *"On my way back now."*

He raked his fingers through his hair, pushing it back off his forehead. "Liv wants us back at the ER."

To keep his urges from betraying him again, he cut a wide path around Sofia on his way to the elevator. He stepped inside and turned around. She was still standing where she was, her head bent and her shoulders slumped. His throat thickened and his resolve nearly broke.

He knew the right thing to do was to say he was sorry, but instead, he croaked, "You comin'?"

Sofia heaved a big sigh, swiped her hand under her nose, and turned. She didn't look at him as she walked into the back corner of the elevator, as far away from him as she could get.

The silence that rode down to the main floor with them was torture, but Zach didn't know what to say. And it was probably for the best to have Sofia disgusted with him. That way he could focus on what he needed to do—get them home and find his parents.

But no matter what else happened, the taste and feel of her lips was now embedded in his head and in his heart forever.

THIRTEEN

Liv was waiting right inside the door of the ER when it opened. Her stomach flipped when she saw Zach, then turned hard as stone when Sofia walked in behind him. The guilty looks on their faces and the palpable tension between them set off a warning bell inside her head, and it felt like an elephant had suddenly sat down on her chest.

"What happened? Where were you guys?"

Zach shrugged. "I ran into Sofia in the Observatory."

He was trying to act nonchalant, but Liv knew him too well.

"So, you heard Will, too?" he added in an obvious attempt to change the subject.

Liv narrowed her eyes. "Something's go—"

Zach stepped forward and pulled her into a hug. The rest of her words dissolved on her tongue.

"We're gonna get out of this place, find Mom and Dad, and put it all behind us," he whispered, squeezing her tight. "And we aren't going to let Will put us off the next time he calls. It's obvious he wants something from us, but he's not going to get it 'til he tells us how to get back to Earth."

Her ear was pressed against his chest, so she could hear his heart beating way too fast. But it wasn't loud enough to drown out the nagging voice in her head telling her something had happened between him and Sofia.

She pulled back and looked into his eyes. They were dilated and his nose was red, but the lost little boy look on his face that she hadn't seen since they were kids melted her heart.

She reached up and placed her hand on his cheek. "You're right. You and me are going to find Mom and Dad before we do anything else when we get back to Earth."

"Well, actually, first we'll need to get Nick to a hospital," Sofia said, breaking into Liv's moment.

Heat raced up Liv's neck. *Or maybe we just send you back to Iowa first!*

Ignoring Sofia, Liv replied to Zach, "Maybe Will can open a portal right into a hospital and make it quick and easy for us to drop Nick off."

Sofia clicked her tongue. "I don't think that's the way portals work."

Liv clenched her teeth and rolled her eyes. "As if you would know."

She wrapped her arms around Zach's waist and laid her head on his shoulder. "It'll be so nice to get home where it's just you and me," she whispered to Zach loud enough for Sofia to hear.

Zach looked past her head at Sofia. "Yeah, but who knows when Will will get back to us. It took him four days to contact us this time." He untangled himself from Liv's arms and stepped back, looking very uncomfortable. "I'll go grab a couple chairs from the lounge and bring them in here, so we'll at least be comfortable while we wait. It could be another long one."

He scurried out the door like he couldn't wait to escape.

Sofia started after him, but Liv jumped in front of her, cutting her off.

"Where do you think you're going?"

"To help Zach get some chairs."

"No, you're not. I'll go."

Sofia blew a disgusted snort through her nose, and opened her mouth to fire back, then froze as Zach's voice came into her head.

"Livy, Sofia, lock the door if you can and don't open it for anyone."

Hearing the alarm in his voice, Sofia ran out the door. He was standing in the middle of the hall a few feet away. Liv was right next to him.

What the heck? Sofia threw a glance over her shoulder into the empty ER, then looked back at Liv. *How'd she get up there so fast?*

That question was pushed to the back by a bigger one: where did the tall woman standing in front of the triangle beams come from?

The woman, who stood perfectly still with her eyes closed and her hands pressed together in a prayer pose, had short, black, spiky hair. She was dressed in a long, pale blue, sleeveless robe with a shimmering, gauzy scarf that draped over her shoulders and the tops of her arms, crisscrossed over her bodice, then circled her waist. But the most intriguing thing about her was, she had no body vibrations, no aura, and her skin was sort of radiating.

Sofia ran up to Zach's side.

He shot her a disapproving glance then looked back at the woman.

"Excuse me … ma'am?" he called out.

The woman calmly lifted her head and turned their way, appearing not at all surprised to see them. Her eyes were a unique lime green-color and seemed to twinkle.

But her eyes weren't what Sofia focused on. It was the woman's stone pendant that was identical to the one Sofia wore around her neck. The pendant was the only thing she had from her real parents and was her most prized possession.

The woman put both hands over her heart, one on top of the other, and gracefully bowed her head. "I and Atlantis II welcomes you home, Garaile, Alesandese, and Mirari." Her voice had the same odd accent as Scarlett's.

Atlantis II? The name filled Sofia's mouth with the taste of chocolate covered strawberries.

The woman raised her head. "I am Elleci, your mentor. I have been instructed to see to your comfort. If you would come with me, your quarters are prepared and waiting." She swung her arm toward the triangle beams.

"Who instructed you?" Zach asked.

"Gilamu did."

"That's Will," Sofia whispered out of the side of her mouth.

"I know," he hissed back. To Elleci he added, "Is Atlantis II what you call this spaceship?"

"Atlantis II is a Pleiadian space station located one point five million kilometers from Earth and four hundred forty-two light years from our home planet, Pleiades."

A space station? The imaginary python that had been wrapped around Sofia's torso since the moment she'd arrived tightened, squeezing her heart into her throat.

Over the past three days, she'd been trying to convince herself that this whole space thing was an elaborate prank like the reality show. But if what this woman said was true, it was one more thing Sofia had gotten wrong.

"Now, if you will, please follow me to your quarters," Elleci said, gesturing again toward the beams.

Zach straightened his back and squared his shoulders. "Sorry, ma'am, we can't do that. Will told us to stay where we are."

"Of course." The woman's calm demeanor didn't waver. "But I am not suggesting you leave Atlantis II. Only that you come in from the outer ring to where it is more comfortable. You are in obvious need of food and water, both of which are available inside."

All three of them perked up.

Sofia was the first to find her voice. "You have water?" The dryness in her throat made her words raspy.

"Atlantis II has everything needed to satisfy your body and mind."

"But ma'am, what about Nick?" Liv stammered.

Elleci cocked her head. "The boy in the CDT unit?"

"If the CDT unit is what you call the capsule thingy back in that room there," she pointed behind her, "then, yes, that's Nick. He was hurt in the pyramid and is in bad shape. We need to get him back to Earth and to a hospital right away."

"Atlantis II's medical facility is far more advanced than what you would find on Earth. I will have him transferred inside and see that he is well cared for."

Sofia and Liv both looked at Zach. He tilted his head to the side, signaling them to follow as he walked away several feet.

"Where has this woman been this whole time?" he said in a loud whisper. "Sofia and I checked every room. She wasn't in any of them."

"Yeah, but we couldn't get into a couple of the doors, remember?" Sofia replied, sneaking a glance back at Elleci and wondering if the woman had been on the spaceship she'd seen through the windows of the Observatory.

"Okay, let's say she was," Zach replied. "Why wait four days and let us nearly die of thirst before showing up?"

"Does it really matter?" Liv sounded like she was holding back a scream. "I for one am thirsty as hell. If she has water, I'm all for going with her. Besides, she's only one person," she glanced over her shoulder as if making sure no one had joined Elleci, "... and she doesn't look all that strong. The three of us should be able to take her if she tries to pull something."

Sofia spoke up before Zach could respond to that. "I agree with Liv. We're not going to last much longer without water. I don't see we really have much choice here."

"You two thought it would be a good idea to jump through the portal, too," Zach responded.

Sofia winced, then pressed her lips together and lifted her chin. "No one's twisting your arm. If you want to stay here, that's up to you. I'll try to bring you out some water if I can."

With that said, she turned and walked toward Elleci.

Liv signaled Elleci to wait a moment and faced Zach. Though she couldn't read his mind, she could read his vibrations. She also knew from past experiences that he was overly analytical, and it would take a good deal of coaxing to get him to go along with something he'd already set his mind against.

Sidling up to Zach, she put her hand on his chest, pursed her lips, and gave him the I'm-just a helpless-girl-and-you're-my-hero look even though she knew it seldom worked on him. But it was the only tool she had to use at the moment.

"I know this is hard for you. You like to be in control."

"You don't know anything," Zach pushed her hand off his chest.

"Yes, I do!" she snapped before she could stop herself. She paused a second, reapplied her innocent look, and lowered her voice. "You're not the only one who found out they're an alien, you know. Me and Sofia are facing the same thing. And we don't know how to deal with it any better than you, but we're not being asshats about it."

A flicker of comprehension crossed his face, and just like that, he deflated like a balloon losing air. He dropped his head and rubbed the back of his neck.

Liv moved in and rested her forehead on his. "I'm sorry I sent in that application to the show. And I'm sorry we're stuck here," she whispered. "If I'd known what would happen, I never would've done it. But we're here, and as far as I know, Pleiadians can't time travel and change the past. So, cowboy up and let's work with this Will and Elleci to get home."

When Zach didn't respond, Liv stepped back and slapped him hard on his chest. "Stop sulking. I wanna go home and find Mom and Dad!"

Zach's head jerked up, but his startled look lasted a mere moment before his eyes sparked with anger. "I'm not sulking!"

Liv's mouth twitched, but she held back her grin. "Then let's go and see what information we can get out of this woman."

She picked up his hand and squeezed it between both of hers. "Come on. The three of us need to stick together." She tugged him to where Elleci and Sofia were standing.

To Elleci Liv said, "What are we waiting for?"

The woman smiled and turned to the triangle beams. "Right this way, my Guardians."

"Our names are Zach, Olivia, and Sofia," Zach stated.

Elleci paused, looked over her shoulder, then gave a slight nod.

The corners of Liv's perfectly shaped mouth turned up in a smug smile as she made a show of looping her arm through Zach's for Sofia's benefit. She didn't say a word, but she didn't need to, the message was clear: Zach was all hers and Sofia needed to keep her hands off.

FOURTEEN

Daher stormed out of the room, wiping dark, leafy-green blood off his hands with a towel. The swamp gas stench couldn't be wiped away, though, and it followed him through the warehouse.

Four days had passed since the incident in the pyramid and the Guardians had yet to be apprehended. The human bait wasn't even working.

He gnashed his teeth and swore under his breath. How was it possible the Guardians could elude the best Dracuzians trackers in the galaxy? They were just kids, untrained, and from all reports, ignorant of their Pleiadian capabilities.

The Dracuzian enforcers were insisting the Pleiadians must have a base off Earth, but Daher refused to buy that theory.

It was true the Pleiadians were a technically advanced race, but he had not heard of them having the capability of cloaking an entire space station. It was easier for him to believe the enforcers had learned they would be shipped back to Nibiru as soon as their work here was finished, and they made a conscious decision to slack off to delay their departure so they wouldn't have to give up the leisurely lifestyle this planet had to offer.

Daher, too, had gotten used to this luxurious lifestyle and didn't want to give it up any more than the Dracuzian's did. But the Anunnaki Elite were getting tired of waiting and were threatening to replace him if he didn't start making some progress in taking Earth back.

So, if he had to take a few Dracuzian heads to get them motivated, he would, because better their heads than his.

The driver waiting to take Daher back to his mansion snapped to attention and said nothing about the foul smell of Dracuzian blood that followed Daher into the armored SUV.

Daher slumped in the back seat and steepled his fingers, tapping his two index fingers together. His original plan had been to have the Dracuzians take care of the Pleiadians while he worked on replacing the world leaders with Nukiri. The new leaders had been tasked with starting wars that would wipe out a good portion of the human race, which had grown to uncontrollable proportions. That would leave the planet open for him to step in, declare Earth an Anunnaki colony, then take up his rightful position as Supreme Leader of this section of the galaxy.

Unfortunately, his plan hadn't gone as intended.

The replacement leaders had caused massive chaos and deaths as they were supposed to, but humans were much more resilient than he thought.

On top of that, he got word that the Elite were sending a full fleet of Anunnaki ships, and he was expected to have the energy grid turned off by the time it arrived. If not, he would lose his commission and be exiled and disgraced.

Daher's upper lip curled into a snarl and his thoughts turned to Ukani, who had found the Guardians not once but twice. For a brief moment, he considered contacting the traitor, but his ego wouldn't let him. The Dracuzians under his command were enough. And now that they knew their lives depended on them finding the Guardians, they should bring him some results. *Should* being the operative word here.

"*Ezafak*!" he shouted, pounding the armrest of his seat with his fist. "Why am I surrounded by imbeciles?"

Tabari, tablet in hand, waited at the entrance of Daher's estate, the front of which sported a fake façade that mirrored the front of the Katameya Heights golf clubhouse.

He braced himself at the sight of the tightness around Daher's mouth and the fury in the Anunnaki's eyes as Daher exited the SUV. Tabari's abdomen then clenched even tighter when he noticed a green smudge on Daher's forehead.

Daher brushed past Tabari as if he wasn't there and hurried into the foyer, which had also been transformed into a smaller version of the clubhouse's lobby, complete with a boutique, a golf pro shop, a lounge, billiards and bridge room, and a bar.

Tabari hustled after Daher, stretching out his hand holding the tablet for Daher to see. "The news—"

Daher's forearm flipped up, signaling silence.

At that moment, Martina Schultze rushed out of the boutique.

"Mr. Daher!" she called, hurrying toward the small group. "Mr. Daher, may I have a word, please?"

A low rumble came from Daher's throat, and he shot Tabari a murderous glare, then turned to Martina before Tabari could say anything in his defense.

"Mrs. Schultze, how nice it is to see you. I trust you've been supplied with everything you need, and your accommodations are good?" He stretched his mouth into a semblance of a smile that was as cold as the dry ice under the shrimp platter on the buffet table.

"Everything is very nice, thank you," Martina said, although her flustered expression said otherwise. "I don't mean to bother you, but I was wondering if you've heard from the kids. If you know when they'll be back?"

Daher's forced smile slipped. "I believe I mentioned to you when we talked on the phone that they'll be back when the task is finished."

There was no mistaking the edge of annoyance in his voice.

"Yes, but we've been here three days, or has it been four?" She looked confused. "And—"

"I'm not a psychic, madam, and I have no way of knowing how

long they will take." Daher edged around her. "Now, if you'll excuse me, I have important matters to attend to."

He gave Tabari a stern take-care-of-this-look, turned, and rapidly walked away.

Martina lifted her chin and called after him just as sharply, "These are my children and y'all can't keep information from me. I demand you let me talk to them."

Daher kept walking without so much as a faltering step.

Tabari put on what he hoped was a sympathetic smile and took Martina's elbow to turn her around. "We completely understand your concern, madam. You're anxious to see your son and daughter, but you must understand the show cannot legally divulge the status of the challenges or the challengers."

"But I'm their mother."

"True, but they are eighteen and considered adults, and they, along with everyone else involved with the show, including Mr. Daher, are legally bound by a non-disclosure clause. We've already overstepped the line by bringing you and Mr. Schultze here. If our lawyers knew, they would be incredibly upset with us."

"I don't care if the lawyers get upset."

Tabari struggled to keep his smile in place. "It should make you very proud to know Mr. Daher holds Zachary and Olivia in such high regard he is putting their needs above the legalities."

Martina straightened her shoulders. "I only want to talk to the kids for a minute. I just … I have a bad feeling."

"There's no need to worry," Tabari reassured her. "Trust me. They have high security surrounding them at all times. If there were any problems, you'd be the first to know.

"You know we're all anxious for this to be wrapped up, but unfortunately, reality TV doesn't abide by a standard timeline. So, I must ask for your indulgence and patience a little while longer."

Martina's brow crinkled as she silently glared down the hall Daher had gone.

"In the meantime, might I suggest a guided tour of the Dahshur pyramids?" Tabari said in an effort to distract her. "They're not as popular as the Giza pyramids, so it's much more peaceful and you're not as rushed. I would be happy to arrange a special tour of the interior of the Bent Pyramid of Sneferu if that would appeal to you and your husband."

When Martina didn't reply, Tabari waved a hand at the Dracuzian standing by the front door, signaling to him that her mind control needed to be refreshed.

The hulk of a man blinked in acknowledgement.

"Tell you what," Tabari put his hand on her back and guided her toward the door. "Uroil here will escort you back to the guesthouse and I'll send over our best masseuse to give you a relaxing massage. I could even add a manicure to go along with it if you'd like. How does that sound?"

He handed Martina over to the Dracuzian, who took her arm.

The worry lines around her eyes instantly relaxed and she gave Tabari a glowing smile as he walked her to the car.

Tabari kept his wide grin in place, as he waved at the car as it drove off toward the opposite end of the compound. Long after the car disappeared into the shadows of the palm trees, he stood at the curb rehearsing in his mind what he would say to Daher.

He was well aware of each minute that ticked by and when he knew he could no longer delay the inevitable, he wiped the sweat from his brow with the back of his hand and turned with a grimace to make his way to Daher's quarters.

Without looking up from the triple monitors on the desk in his office off the master suite, Daher growled, "You were supposed to be handling the humans."

"Yes, sir. I am, sir. Mr. and Mrs. Schultze were scheduled for a round of golf today. She should have been out on the course."

"So, the mind control's not working?" Daher glowered over the top of the screen.

Tabari shook his head in denial. "It may have weakened a bit, sir, but I had Uroil apply a stronger suggestion. She was fine when she left for the guesthouse."

"If they become more of a problem, I'll have the Dracuzians take care of them as what should have been done in the first place."

"I'll make sure they don't bother you again, sir."

Daher drilled his assistant with a long glare that chilled Tabari to the bone. He then returned to the monitor without saying anything more, but the air remained thick with tension.

Tabari stood for another intense moment, then slowly began to back out of the office, praying he could slip away before Daher noticed.

Since the pyramid incident, Daher's mood had been increasingly volatile and his temper closer to the surface. Tabari was still able to talk Daher down on most of the Anunnaki's outlandish schemes, but he also knew when to not press his luck.

He had just about reached the threshold when Daher smacked his hand on the desk with a loud crack and yelled, "*Ezafak*!"

Tabari froze in his tracks.

"I am an Anunnaki Elite. I do not cater to humans or kowtow to Pleiadians. And it's high time I show them all who has the upper hand here. I want Sofia's friend brought to Cairo."

Cold dread washed over Tabari. "Is that—" he started, but a brusque wave of Daher's hand cut off the rest of his words.

"The holiday is over for these humans. They're my prisoners and will be treated as such. I need to show the Guardians I'm not playing around and that their humans are in danger of being tortured and killed if they don't present themselves."

Tabari's stomach dropped.

"Once the girl arrives, take her and the Schultzes to the desert camp. Then, release a video of the hostages bound and gagged on social media."

Tabari knew this was not the time to challenge Daher, so he muttered a meek "Yes, sir" and hurried down the hall, cursing the Anunnaki leader under his breath.

Years ago, Tabari had come to the realization that it was just a matter of time before he fell into disfavor with Daher and would end up at the bottom of a volcano. That's when he made a decision to start embezzling money and buy himself a private island where he could disappear and live out his life in the luxury he'd grown accustomed to on this lavish planet.

His offshore account was getting close to having enough to buy the island he'd picked out, and, once he was on the beach sipping frosty drinks with those cute little paper umbrellas, he could care less if Daher blew up his entire empire. In fact, he was looking forward to the day that very thing happened, so he wouldn't have to worry about Daher anymore.

But first he had to make sure the Anunnaki fleet never landed on Earth, which meant he had to see that the Guardians never turned the grid off. Luckily, the Dracuzians hated Daher as much as he did. If he could keep them on his side, Daher would be doomed for sure.

Tabari closed his eyes, picturing that day. Maybe I could even talk the Elite into letting me run this planet.

A smile spread across his face as his thoughts mulled over the possibility of Emperor Tabari.

Fifteen

Elleci held her pendant up to the rectangular panel on the wall. At once, the red light turned blue and the section between the beams vanished, exposing a cube-shaped room similar to the one they'd arrived in, only smaller. She gestured to a row of chairs along the wall.

"Please take a seat."

Sofia settled into one of the high-back seats and laid her arms flat on the arm rests, expecting another round of decontamination.

"Are we going to need goggles?" she asked.

"No, goggles are not needed," Elleci replied. "However, for your protection, you must wear a seat harness."

A metal band snapped around Sofia's waist.

Liv let out a startled squeak as her band also snapped into place.

Sofia gripped the armrest, the thump-thump of her heartbeat drumming in her ears.

"It is possible you will become a bit drowsy. That is normal, especially your first time," Elleci added and took a seat in the last chair.

Without warning, a strong force pressed Sofia down into the seat, and the skin on her cheeks felt like it was being stretched to the floor. Her eyelids grew heavy. She fought to keep them open, but soon lost the battle and drifted into a sea of blackness.

Someone shrieking, "Holy shit!" brought Sofia back to the present. Her eyes shot open wide.

"Wake up, Z," Liv said, shaking Zach's arm. "I think we're back on Earth!"

Sofia blinked to focus and looked around. The strap holding her in the seat was gone. So was the wall across from where they'd entered. On the other side of the opening were trees and lush green foliage.

She rubbed her fists in her eyes, sure she was imagining things. But the greenery was still there when she looked again.

What the heck?

She gulped in a big breath of air that had an earthy smell and was thick with humidity. She looked over to where Elleci had been sitting, but she, too, was gone.

Okay, this has got to be a dream. Or else the dehydration is affecting my mind.

She slowly pushed herself to her feet and walked to the opening where Zach and Liv were standing.

Liv mumbled something under her breath and cautiously walked out of the opening a few feet. A look of wonder covered her face as she picked up a long, narrow leaf on a tree and snapped it off from a branch.

"It's real!" she exclaimed, then giggled. "So, this has to be Earth. No space station would have real trees like this in it."

"I don't know," Zach replied, frowning as he looked up at a thick, grayish cloud of fog that obscured the sky and the tops of the taller trees. "It doesn't feel like Earth. The gravity's all wrong."

Sofia agreed. It didn't feel like Earth.

She walked to another tree and ran her hand over the bumpy skin of a maroon football-shaped pod hanging from the thin trunk. *These are cacao trees!* She knew that from a school trip to the botanical gardens. She also knew cacao trees only grew in rainforests. So what were they doing *here*?

Mixed in with the cacao trees were several different varieties of palm trees, all of which had signs of berries, seed pods, or fruit.

A four-legged dog-like robot was picking cacao pods not far from where Sofia stood. The robot's neck looked like a vacuum hose, but instead of a head there was a triangular-shaped tool that opened like the mouth of a snake, gripped the pod, and snapped it off.

Sofia closed her eyes and sucked her bottom lip in through her teeth, feeling very much like Alice inside the rabbit hole with everything getting curiouser and curiouser by the minute.

"We're going to go find Elleci or someone who can tell us where we are," Zach called, jolting Sofia out of her thoughts.

She twirled around.

The two of them were already heading down a path that cut through the trees. "Wait!" she called after them. "Do you really think it's a good idea to go off on your own not knowing what else is out there?"

"Yes," Liv answered without looking back.

Sofia let out a disgusted sigh and mumbled to herself, "So much for sticking together."

It was eerily quiet except for a faint rustling of leaves and an occasional soft mechanical whine when the robot moved.

"Hello," she called out.

No one answered.

Crap! She didn't know if leaving the transport was a good idea or not, but staying there alone wasn't any more appealing. With one more look around, she took off in a run to catch up with the others, hoping she wasn't making a mistake.

Her gaze darted from side to side, looking for something that would give her a clue as to where they were. And with her attention focused on that she didn't notice Liv had stopped in the middle of the path and ran right into her.

"Oh, I'm—" Sofia started to apologize.

Liv shushed her. "Do you hear that?"

Sofia froze. A faint buzz flew by her ear. She flinched and swatted at it, but it flew off before she could see what it was.

"Is that water?" Zach asked.

Sofia turned in the direction he was staring and held her breath to listen. Nothing but trees surrounded them. But off in the distance, there was a soft trickling sound.

Water? The mere thought of water brought on an intense sensation of thirst.

Without saying a word, Liv took off in that direction.

Sofia didn't think twice and followed on Liv's heels.

"Wait!" Zach yelled to no avail, and ran after them.

The grove gave way to a wide stretch of hard-packed dirt that gently sloped down to a wide aqueduct filled with water trickling in from several pipes placed at intervals along its banks.

Behind the aqueduct, rocky cliffs rose high into the air. Up to the right about twenty yards away, a stone bridge arched over the water leading to a façade of a neoclassical building that was carved right out of the side of the cliff. The façade looked like an ancient temple more likely to be found in Greece or Petra than in a space station.

"Have we died and just don't know it?" Liv whispered.

"This could be a dream," Sofia said.

Liv reached around Zach and pinched Sofia's arm.

"Ow! Whatddya do that for?" Sofia glowered at Liv and rubbed her arm.

Liv shrugged. "Now we know this isn't a dream."

Without another word, Liv ran down the slope and knelt on one knee at the edge of the water. She dipped her hand in and scooped up a handful of the liquid ecstasy.

"Stop!" Sofia shouted, running up behind her. "You don't know if that's safe to drink."

"It is," Liv replied confidently.

"Oh, so now you're a psychic, too?"

"You could say that. I've always been able to see things others don't. Like back in the pyramid, I knew you and Zach were there before he said anything to me." Liv brought the handful of water up to her lips, but Zach battered it away before she could take a sip.

"Damnit, Z!"

Liv spun around and thrust the palms of her hands out. A blast of energy lifted Zach into the air and threw him more than halfway up the slope.

He landed on his back with an *oopf*.

Liv's eyes rounded to the size of golf balls, and she rushed to where he was sprawled on the ground. "I'm so sorry. I didn't mean to do that. It just came out."

She reached out to help him up, but he recoiled and shot her a look that was cold enough to freeze her to the spot.

Then, on his own, he arched his back and flipped up to his feet in one swift move and brushed the dirt off his rear without saying a word to her.

"Let's go," he said, walking up to Sofia.

Liv opened her mouth as Zach took Sofia's elbow and started to walk away, but nothing came out.

"All water in Atlantis II is perfectly safe to drink," Elleci's voice called out. "Feel free to help yourself to this water or any other you find."

Sofia looked up at the middle of the bridge where Elleci was standing. At the same moment, the sound of slurping came from behind her. She turned back and saw Liv kneeling back on the bank of the aqueduct, gulping up the water.

How does *she do that?* The question sped through Sofia's mind, but her need for water overtook her need for an answer.

She ran to the bank, dropped to her knees, and joined Liv and Zach in scooping up handfuls of the sweetest water she'd ever tasted.

When her stomach could take no more, she wiped the water from her chin and sat back on her heels, eyeing the craggy ridge of rock on the opposite bank. As her gaze followed it off into the distance, she caught a flash out of the corner of her eye and turned her head to the left.

A dark shaft rose up through a layer of clouds hovering low over the tops of the trees.

"What's that?" she asked, craning her head back to follow the shaft up into the sky until it became a faint dark line.

Zach and Liv both followed Sofia's gaze.

A spark, like that of a giant bug zapper, briefly lit up the sky, revealing several linked hexagonal cells next to the shaft.

"What was *that?*" Liv exclaimed.

Sofia stared at the spot of the spark, but the pale, hazy sky now looked like an ordinary summer sky in Iowa.

Her gaze slowly moved around to the cliffs. *Did I just imagine the honeycomb cells?*

No sooner had that question crossed her mind then another spark flashed, lighting up several more cells, this time closer to the top of the bluffs.

"You saw that too, right?" she asked Zach, who was beside her.

"Yeah. It looks like we're inside some kind of artificial environment that keeps the temperature and humidity consistent for the trees. It's weird, though. I don't see any visible seams or joints."

"This whole place is weird, including her." Liv pointed to Elleci, who had moved to stand next to a tall statue of the lollipop symbol in front of the entrance of the temple. Her head was bent, and her palms were pressed together in front of her, the exact pose of the sculptures on both sides of the temple's doors.

"I hope she can tell us what's going on," Liv added.

Zach glared up at Elleci, his jaw squared and hard. "She better. I'm done getting fucked around. It's time we got the truth."

He got to his feet and held out his hand to help Liv up. He then offered his hand to Sofia.

The gesture brought back the memory of the kiss and her heart did a somersault.

She turned away and scrambled to her feet on her own, keeping her head down so he couldn't see the heat of embarrassment bloom on her cheeks.

God, I'm so pathetic. Why do I keep setting myself up like this? I can't imagine what he must think of me.

Out of the corner of her eye, she saw Zach and Liv walk off hand-in-hand toward the bridge, their heads bent together like two lovers.

More likely he's not thinking of me at all. And why would he? He's got his mom and dad and Liv to worry about. The kiss was a mistake. A distraction because we thought we were going to die here. I should forget about it ... about him. Besides, once we get back to Earth, I'll probably never see him again because the two of them will go back to Texas and I'll go to MIT.

She squeezed her eyes together and silently groaned.

How many more times am I going to be suckered into thinking someone could actually care for me? I'm smart enough to know better.

Or maybe I'm not.

SIXTEEN

Sofia trudged up the ramp to the bridge behind Zach and Liv, focusing on the intricate stonework to keep her mind off the loneliness that had filled every crevice of the empty cavern in her chest.

Like the temple façade, the bridge looked ancient, pyramid level ancient. It had been crafted with the same precision as the pyramids, too, in ways that had baffled archaeologists for decades.

"We're not going any further until you tell us what's going on." Zach shouted up at Elleci from the bottom of the steps leading up to the plaza.

Elleci didn't look up or respond but stood frozen in her prayer pose as if she hadn't heard him. Or was it that she didn't want to answer?

"Look, we've done everything asked of us. Just tell us …" Zach's words trailed off as Elleci lifted her head.

Elleci blinked at him as if she just realized someone was there. A serene smile spread across her face.

"I'm pleased to see you have been refreshed by the water. I will show you to your quarters now."

"No!" Zach bolted up the steps two at a time and grabbed Elleci's arm as she turned toward the entrance to the temple. "I want some answers now."

Elleci looked around. Her face showed no emotion, but her lime green eyes seemed to glow.

"Z!" Liv called, pointing to the steps behind him where a blinding white oval, three feet tall and just as wide, hovered in the air.

Lines of static fluttered through the oval. The light blinked out for a nanosecond, then blinked back on with a wavering image of Elleci with three men and three women standing in front of a long counter where several sophisticated microscopes and a rack of cork topped vials sat. Each of the women carried a small child with copper-colored hair in their arms.

In the group was the couple who had been coming to Sofia in visions from the time she turned thirteen—the ones she believed to be her real mom and dad.

Sofia's heart jumped into her throat.

Liv, too, seemed shocked and opened and closed her mouth several times before she could find her words. "I've seen some of those people before."

"Shhh," Sofia said, straining to hear what the man she thought was her father was saying.

But he was speaking in a language she didn't understand, so the silence did no good.

Sofia's mother gave her husband a stern look. "English please, Senki. That is our language now and we must fully embrace it, even in private. You know how dangerous it would be for all of us if someone on Earth heard you speak Pleiadian."

"Yes, of course, you're right, Miyana" Senki said in English and put his arm around his wife's shoulder. "I just wanted to savor the taste of our native language on my tongue one last time before I discarded it for good."

He turned to Elleci. "As I was saying ... the upgrades that Railue—" he nodded at a man who looked like an older version of Zach, "—developed for you have been installed. We also updated the life support and environmental monitoring systems and have reassigned them to Esos to oversee. That will secure the station and ensure it'll continue to run efficiently on the off chance we need to bring you down to Earth. You will still have full access to all systems while you're here, though, as well as the authority to step in and take over at any time should the need arise."

Elleci gave a slight nod. "I understand."

Senki looked to the third man. "Zodak, did you also have instructions for Elleci?"

Zodak stepped forward. "Yes. Elleci, I would like you to take over monitoring the solar activity. I expect Shamash's erratic flares—"

Sofia's mother loudly cleared her throat.

He chuckled and held his hands up as if in surrender. "Forgive me, Miyana, that was a slip. What I meant to say is, the sun's *erratic flares of late should settle down as it progresses through its cycle. But as the past has shown us, we can't entirely rely on it doing what it should. So, keep an eye on it and notify me right away if there are any irregularities that might affect Earth or the energy grid."*

Elleci gave another slight nod. "I will report all anomalies I note. As for Atlantis II, Esos and I will take care of everything until you and the children return."

"If all goes as planned, we won't be returning." Miyana smiled down at the child in her arms, who stared back with the biggest blue eyes. "But we all take comfort knowing you'll be here watching over our home away from home for us."

"We're going to miss you, Elleci," the woman next to Railue said as she juggled the squirming child in her arms. "I don't know how I'll ever get Garaile to sleep without you telling him a bedtime story."

"I have programmed stories into this for him, which should help." Elleci held up a round disk the size of a quarter.

"Whatever are we going to do without you?" the woman said, handing the child off to his father. "I so wish you could come with us now."

Elleci didn't acknowledge the statement but walked to the third woman. She pulled back the blanket and leaned in to kiss the sleeping child on the forehead.

"May you have strength, wisdom, compassion, and integrity to guide you, Alesandese. And may the watchful eye of Ea protect you and help you achieve all that you are meant to do."

Moving to Garaile in Railue's arms, she placed her palms on both sides of his face.

He instantly stilled and she gave him a kiss on the cheek, along with the same blessing.

Lastly, she stopped in front of Miyana. The little girl leaned forward with her arms outstretched.

Elleci smiled and took hold of the girl's hands. "All will be fine, Mirari. We will see each other again in the future. Until then, may your strength, wisdom, compassion, and integrity take you far, and may Ea watch over and protect you."

She kissed Mirari on the cheek, then stepped back and placed both hands over her heart and bowed her head before returning to her prayer pose.

"All right, then, I think we're ready," Senki said with a smile.

Alesandese's mother woke her, and Railue passed Garaile back to his mother. The parents moved into a tight circle and Zodak reached into his satchel, pulling out three golden chains with a stone pendant dangling from each.

Alesandese reached out with one hand and kicked her feet in excitement.

"Yes, my little Pūzeela, one of these is yours," Zodak chuckled and slipped a chain over her head. "But it isn't a plaything. You must take care of it and never lose it because it is your connection to us and to Atlantis II. It will also warn you when the Anunnaki are near."

He moved to Garaile, slipped a chain over his head, then put the last one on Mirari, and gave Miyana a nod.

Miyana smiled at the three toddlers. "Okay, children, do you remember me telling you that one day we would go to the big blue ball?"

The children nodded in unison.

"Well, how about we go now? Does that sound like fun?"

The three squealed with delight.

"Okay, then, remember what we practiced."

The toddlers reached for each other's hands as Zach's mom held up an open picture book.

For a brief moment, a bright light whited out the image. When the picture came back, a swirling whirlpool of iridescent light was behind the group.

"Good job!" Senki exclaimed, his eyes shining with pride. "I knew you were going to be great Guardians."

He smiled lovingly into Miyana's eyes and wrapped his arm around her waist, then turned back to Elleci. "You know what to do after we leave."

Elleci gave a nod of confirmation.

Senki and Miyana both put their hands over their hearts and bowed their heads toward Elleci, then turned and walked into the portal with their daughter.

The two other families did the same, leaving Elleci standing alone.

The oval, along with the video, vanished, but Sofia, Zach, and Liv continued to stare at the spot as if it was still there.

"Those people ... are they our real parents?" Liv choked out, clutching her pendant through her shirt.

"And those children were us?" Sofia softly asked, clasping her own pendant.

"Yes, to both your questions. You three were born here on Atlantis II on March 3, 2003."

March 3rd? The date floated in front of Sofia. She frowned. She'd been told her birthday was March 10th.

Elleci added, "Your parents stayed with you here for eighteen months after your birth before they took you to Earth."

"I don't understand, ma'am," Liv said in a small voice. "Why did our parents take us to Earth? Didn't they want us?"

Elleci's eyebrows drew together for a nanosecond, then smoothed back in place. "I do not have an answer to that question." She swung her arm toward the door once again and said, "Your quarters are waiting for you this way."

Sofia's nose was freely dripping tears on her t-shirt, but she didn't care.

This had once been her home where she and her parents were happy. She had seen it on their faces. But for some unknown reason, they had taken her to Earth. Then Daher found them and killed them.

The taste of rotten eggs flooded Sofia's mouth and a burning rage unlike anything she'd ever experienced erupted within her, sending hot lava through her veins.

If we had stayed here, they'd still be alive.

She wanted to scream, wanted to kick something or throttle someone, but what good would throwing a fit do? It wouldn't bring them back.

A rock from the cliff crashed to the ground with a reverberating thud.

I would've had a normal, happy life if Daher hadn't come along. She curled her hands into fists. *All this time I thought my parents left because of me. That I wasn't good enough for them.*

Another boulder rolled down the cliff.

But now that I know the truth and know who Daher is, no one is going to stop me from making him pay for what he's done. He thought taking over Earth would be a piece of cake, but he didn't know I'd be standing in his way!

With rage burning inside her, Sofia robotically followed Elleci through the door of the temple into a dimly lit, musty smelling room filled with glass cases on marble pedestals, holding a variety of items from artifacts to large colored rocks to open books. The walls were a splash with a circle vision video of an orange-colored sky and a landscape with strange flora and fauna that was most definitely not taken on Earth.

As she stepped through the back of the temple, the brilliant light of a setting sun hit her directly in the eyes. Shielding her face with her hand, she blinked until a rolling landscape and a domain as alien as it was beautiful came into focus.

A path of finely ground quartz sparkled in the light as it snaked around sleek metal and black glass buildings that could have been the setting for a sci-fi movie. Each building had its own unique shape: one looked like a giant crown, one was tall and cucumber shaped, one looked like a cruise ship, and there was even one that looked like an open bird's beak pointing to the sky as if waiting for food to be dropped in.

"Where is everyone?" Zach asked, breaking the silence.

"Currently, Atlantis II only maintains a crew of autonomous bots," Elleci answered. "The Pleiadians, except for your parents, left for Earth when the Anunnaki ships landed."

Sofia's stomach sank. She had hoped to talk to someone to find out more about her parents. She closed her eyes feeling exhausted and overloaded. If she didn't find a dark corner where she could curl up and process everything that had happened, she was going to completely shut down soon.

Elleci lifted her hand to the right. "This way to your living quarters."

Liv groaned out loud. "You promised us food."

"Food is waiting for you in your rooms a short distance farther," Elleci said and walked toward a building that looked like a black diamond in a silver setting engagement ring.

Sofia's strength was all but gone, but she forced her feet to take one step after another, focusing on the fact that she would soon be getting some nutrition.

As they walked, Elleci explained how to use the facilities and how to obtain what they needed, but the words buzzed around Sofia's head like an annoying gnat and didn't sink in.

They entered the diamond-shaped building and proceeded up a set of stairs to the second floor.

"This is your room, Olivia." Elleci pointed to a door in front of them. "That is yours, Zach." She pointed to the next door. "And Sofia, the third one is yours." Then, putting both hands over her heart, she bowed her head. "I will leave you now, so you can rest. Asenja."

She turned and walked away.

The three moved like zombies toward their rooms.

The minute Sofia stumbled over the threshold of hers, the rich scent of chocolate nearly knocked her to her knees. Her stomach growled painfully in response and her mouth began to water.

She looked around for the source of the torment and spotted a small niche in the wall next to the door. In it was a steaming mug and a dome-covered plate.

She tottered toward the niche on wobbly legs, picked up the cup with a shaky hand, and took a sip. Again, her legs almost gave out as the chocolaty concoction flooded her taste buds with pure happiness. She gripped the mug in both hands, closed her eyes, and took a longer swig.

After draining the cup, she lifted the plate cover and found an assortment of fresh vegetables arranged around a beige paste. She dipped a finger in, stuck it in her mouth, then moaned in ecstasy at the unexpected explosion of fresh flavors and a hint of citrus.

Wasting no more time, she wolfed down the entire plate in a matter of minutes, then picked it up and licked it clean.

With her stomach content, Sofia trudged to the bed, flopped down, and let out a long sigh of pleasure as the mattress automatically adjusted to the contours of her body. A dozen questions still swam in her brain, but the harder she tried to grasp onto them, the more they slipped away. It didn't help that her eyelids felt like dead weights and were determined to close.

She shook her head to try to disperse the mental cobwebs. *Get up! You've got to find a way back to Earth.* When her body didn't obey, she blew out a weary sigh. *Okay, I'll rest for a few minutes, but that's all.*

As if the room had read Sofia's thoughts, the ceiling lights dimmed and the glass wall across from the door turned dark, shutting out the light from outside. Then, a sweet tune began to play softly, triggering a long-ago memory of her mother. She smiled as her synesthesia sent waves of colors looping around her.

Seconds later, the colors as well as the rest of the world faded to black.

SEVENTEEN

Three-year-old Liv drew a card from the Candyland deck and let out an ear-piercing squeal. Then, grinning wickedly, she dramatically turned the cinnamon roll card over for Sofia and Zach to see.

"Ahh, no fair! You got that card last game," Zach cried, pushing out his bottom lip.

"Too bad," Liv crowed, wiggling her bottom back and forth on the floor as she gleefully moved her red gingerbread man along the trail to the top of the gameboard.

"Maybe you'll luck out next game," Sofia said, as she picked up the next card from the deck—a double purple.

As she reached for her green gingerbread man, the doorbell rang. Her skin prickled with a peculiar sense of danger and her hand stalled over the game piece. She looked over her shoulder toward the playroom door.

Muffled voices drifted down the hall from the front door. A minute later, her mother's fear hit Sofia like a wrecking ball.

Sofia jumped to her feet along with Zach and Liv, and the three ran to the door, straining to hear what was happening in the front room.

"Nooo!" Their mother's scream was followed by a muted pfft sound.

The three flinched and their eyes rounded like saucers as they took a step backward.

There was another quick pfft sound followed by a loud crash that made them all jump.

The three clutched each other's hands and tip-toed forward to peek through the crack of the door.

They could see their mother's head and shoulders lying on the floor. A tall man stood over her. He lifted his head and stared in their direction as if he knew they were watching.

Sofia sucked in a breath. The man looked like a reptile standing on two legs.

Sofia's body jumped clean off the mattress and her eyes flew open. The hairs on her arms were standing on end and her pulse was racing with the intense fear and agony of the dream. But the distressing images were already beginning to dissolve.

She rolled to her side and pushed her face into the pillow. The mattress conformed to her new position, but the crushing sadness that had settled over her was suffocating.

Ever since she'd gotten off the plane in France, she'd been having more and more dreams of herself as a little kid, but none had been as nightmarish as this one. The most disturbing part of it was, she knew in the back of her mind it wasn't just a dream. It was a memory of Abigail Smith, a woman she had totally forgotten about—a woman whom she'd once called Mommy.

Sofia rubbed her fingertips across her brow trying to erase the memory, but instead another one flashed behind her closed eyelids. She was snuggled up under the arm of the same woman, who was reading a bedtime story to her, Zach, and Liv.

Then, as if a flood gate had opened, memory after memory of Abigail and John Smith, who had been her family for a short time, poured in. But as with her biological parents, Daher had taken this family away from her, too. And not only had they been taken away, but the memory of them had been erased.

She curled into a fetal position and put a fist against her mouth to keep from screaming.

Why didn't you want me to have a family? she silently asked the air. *You don't want me to have Zach, either. Why? What have I done to deserve this?*

As long-lost memories shuffled through Sofia's mind, it became clear who had been controlling her life. She'd always thought it was some invisible entity, but it wasn't a supreme heavenly being at all. It was Daher and Will. Though technically, the blame could all be put on Daher. Will did what he did to keep her safe and out of Daher's grip.

Sofia covered her face with her hands and let an overwhelming sense of grief consume her. Exactly sixty seconds later, she sat up and blew out a long cleansing breath. She took another, then tilted her head back and looked up at the ceiling of the alcove above her bed.

"That's it, I'm done," she whispered. "No more letting Daher ruin my life and the lives of everyone I love. I'm taking charge now, and no one, not Will, not Zach, will keep me from doing what I have to do."

She laid there staring at the ceiling and thinking how she'd stop Daher until a nagging urge to relieve herself finally brought her back to the present. With a loud yawn, she stretched her arms over her head and scanned the room.

Thanks to all the explorations she'd done the past few days, she had gotten pretty good at detecting doors by their slight difference in color and their faint luminescent quality. On the wall across from the bed there appeared to be two doors.

Please let one of those be a bathroom, Sofia prayed as she gritted her teeth and swung her legs over the side of the bed, then wobbled like she was holding a basketball between her legs through the door that opened to a bathroom.

When finished, she stood in front of the mirror and stared at her reflection. Her pale skin looked dull, almost translucent in the soft bluish light of the room, and the permanent circles under her eyes were more like deep bruises.

"Gahhh," she scoffed in disgust, trying to comb her fingers through her ratted hair. "No wonder no one wants you. You're a mess! And you need a shower in the worst way."

As if the room had understood what she said, the wall to her left vanished, exposing what looked like a human-sized vacuum tube like what you'd find in a drive-up of a bank. The back and one side of the tube had two vertical rows of jets like a hot tub. A small, rectangular screen on the wall offered different options for sauna, shower, massage, and aromatherapy choices. There was also a bench seat, handheld sprayer, and a flat metal shower head on the ceiling.

All in all, it looked more like a control room of a rocket ship than a shower. But she prayed she could at least get it to wash away the grime of the past few days.

Thirty minutes later, Sofia strolled out of the bathroom with damp hair and a pinkish hue to her skin and an extremely soft, fluffy towel wrapped around her. The combination of steam and water with the scent of sandalwood mixed in had renewed her mind as much as it did her body, and she almost felt like herself again.

As she rubbed lotion up and down her arms, she thought about what her life might have been like if Daher hadn't gotten his ships through the energy grid. No doubt she'd be better prepared to stop him now.

She'd always done everything she could to avoid confrontations, but this was one she couldn't dodge even if she wanted to. Because as long as Daher was around, she'd never have the life she craved, or probably wouldn't have any kind of life at all.

Pressing her lips into a thin line of determination, she turned to the door next to the bathroom, which was a closet that contained several different pairs of loose-fitting pants and several martial arts style keikogi jackets.

Sofia hurriedly dressed, knotted her hair into a low bun and turned toward the door. Then jerked to a stop.

The niche beside the door where the food was sitting when she entered the room was no more.

She frowned and turned in a complete circle. Everything else was exactly as she remembered.

Sofia blew out a weary sigh and growled through clenched teeth, “Why can’t anything here be normal? I swear to God, I’m gonna be batshit crazy by the time I get out of here!”

With a disgusted shake of her head, she walked out the door and almost tripped over her own feet when Scarlett wished her peace throughout her day.

She pressed her fingernails into her palms, muttered a quick “You, too,” and hurried down the stairs.

A molded circular island sat in the center of the hexagon shaped common room. The island had computer monitors evenly spaced and embedded into its glossy top and pushed up before each monitor was a bar stool that looked like a large martini glass. The room also had a couple sofas and high-backed gaming type chairs that had clear hoods that curved over the back and came down in front of the seat like a scorpion tail.

There were several of the scorpion chairs scattered about the room, but Sofia’s gaze went straight to the one Zach was sitting in.

Her heart skipped a beat and for a moment she forgot to breathe.

She knew it wasn’t possible to avoid him forever—this wasn’t that big a place—but she wasn’t ready to face him just yet and had hoped to slip away before he or Liv came out of their rooms.

She longingly looked at the exit, judging the distance to see if she could make it out the door without him noticing.

“Hey, come see what I found,” Zach called out.

Her gaze shot to him, then back to the exit. Would it be lame to pretend she hadn’t heard him and leave?

Dammit. He’d know. Just play it cool and act like it’s no big deal.

Sofia sucked her bottom lip in between her teeth and shuffled toward Zach’s chair.

He didn’t look up. “Come closer, so you can see this.”

Zach scooted his body to the far side of the chair, giving her a small space to sit beside him.

The tips of her ears burned as she ducked her head under the hood and balanced on the wide padded arm of the chair. She held herself ramrod straight and pretended it was no big deal, but her racing pulse called her a liar.

But his nearness quickly became a non-issue as she focused on the video he was watching, which was one of her, him, and Liv playing tag in a beautiful garden of wildflowers.

In the video, the three of them didn't look to be much older than a year old, yet the way they were speaking and running around, they could have easily been taken for five-year-olds.

"Where did this come from?" Sofia whispered in awe.

"I found it in a folder labeled, Guardians."

"You were able to get into the file system?"

"Yeah. Elleci told us to ask for whatever we wanted. So, I did."

"Oh." Sofia had missed that part of Elleci's explanation.

"Several people have called us Guardians," Zach continued, "so when I saw that folder, I clicked on it. You wouldn't believe the number of videos they have of us from the time we were born until we left here."

"Can I see the list?" Sofia asked, hoping there were some of her and her parents.

Just as Zach raised his hand to the screen, Will's voice rang inside her head.

"Guardians, can you hear me?"

Sofia jerked up, hit her head on the hood, and almost fell off the arm before she found her feet.

"We can," Zach called out loud, scooting out of the other side of the chair.

Liv rushed out of her room and stood at the second-floor railing, wearing nothing but a towel. "Did you hear him?

Zach put his index finger over his lips to silence her.

"I was very happy to hear you've gotten some sleep and have been somewhat rejuvenated," Will went on. *"As I was saying yesterday —"*

"Yesterday? We talked to you a couple hours ago," Liv stated out loud.

"It feels like time stops when you're asleep, but I can assure you it's been over fifteen hours since we last spoke."

Sofia flinched. *Fifteen hours?*

"Who cares how long it's been, sir," Zach said. "You promised us answers, so let's hear em, starting with how do we get back to Earth."

"I understand you're anxious to get back to Earth, Garaile, bu—"

"Don't call me that. My name is Zach. And you understand nothing. Daher's men have my adopted mom and dad and I need to get back and find them."

There was a pause, then a sigh.

"I was hoping you hadn't learned of that situation." Will said. *"You have enough to deal with as it is. But don't worry yourselves about the Schultzes. The Sons are working on it and should have them safely back in our hands in no time."*

"The suns? Like the star?" Zach asked.

"The Sons of Ea are highly trained legionaries who have been fighting by our side and protecting this world for generations. Most are the offspring of a human/Pleiadian union."

"So, these Sons know where Daher has taken our parents?" Liv jumped in.

"Not specifically, but they know the Schultzes are somewhere in Cairo and Miss Lewis is in Nice."

"Maddie!" A panicky denial leapt to Sofia's throat. She shook her head. "That's not possible. Why would they take Maddie?" Even as she asked that question, the answer came to her. Maddie was as close to family as Sofia had.

"I can only assume it's because she's listed as the emergency contact on your application. And you have no one else they could use to bait you with."

The floor beneath Sofia's feet felt as if it'd been pulled away. She sank into the chair to keep from falling.

"As I said, you need not worry about your friend or the Schultzes," Will went on. *"Essol, or as you know him, Daher, took them to draw you out, so killing them would defeat his purpose. Plus, the Sons are not going to let anything happen to your loved ones."*

"Yeah ... that's a comfort considering what happened to our biological parents," Zach snarled.

"The Sons were not responsible for your biological parents' deaths." Will's sharp response held an edge of sadness. *"Your parents and you were supposed to stay in Atlantis II. But now is not the time to debate that. You need your full focus on training and developing and controlling your powers so you'll be prepared to defend yourself and Earth against the Anunnaki."*

Something snapped inside of Sofia. She jumped to her feet and shouted, "No!"

Zach and Liv turned to her in surprise.

"You keep saying you'll answer our questions, but then you never do. It's like you don't want us to know the truth of what's really going on."

"Well, well, the shrinking violet has some thorns after all," Liv said with a hint of approval in her tone.

"If you want us to cooperate, then you're going to have to give us some answers," Sofia added.

The tension in the silence that followed felt like a ticking time bomb.

"The last planet the Anunnaki invaded is now a scorched, barren wasteland." Will finally said, his tone laced with impatience. *"The few thousand inhabitants of that planet who survived the invasion are now scattered amongst several worlds doing their best to prevent the Anunnaki from annihilating other civilizations. I, along with the other Pleiadians who have persevered, are fighting*

that battle here on Earth with the Sons of Ea. So you'll just have to take my word that I don't have time to coddle you and tell you the tearjerking stories of your parents that you want to hear.

"You've grown up shielded from the war going on around you, but it's time for you to be the Guardians you were created to be and rise up and save the humans of this planet."

Zach threw his hands in the air, his fingers spread wide. "That's exactly what I want to do and why I need to get back there!"

The bar stools around the island flew across the room.

Liv gripped the railing and stood tall. "Me, too. I'm ready and willing to do whatever it takes to get Mom and Dad back."

"As commendable as that sounds, I can't allow that to happen. You're Earth's best hope, but as of yet, you've not mastered your powers. You don't even have the skills to stand up to the Nukiri, who are the Anunnaki's version of the Sons," Will said. "So, you must stay where you are and train with Elleci. With dedication and luck, maybe we can bring you back in six months."

"Six months!" Sofia, Zach, and Liv all yelled in unison.

"Our parents can't wait six months to be rescued!" Liv added, her voice cracking with emotion.

"And they won't have to. As I've said, the Sons will take care of your parents."

Liv's nose was bright red as she pleadingly looked down at Zach.

"This is fucked up. Y'all can't keep us here against our will," Zach said.

"I was hoping it wouldn't be against your will. Just as I was hoping you'd understand your limitations and the importance of learning to control your abilities. But either way, you will remain on Atlantis II until you're ready and able to defend yourselves."

"We—" Sofia started, but Will went on.

"Elleci will start your training immediately. I pray the cosmic power of the universe will see fit to unlock your minds and give you access to the wisdom and knowledge embedded there. In the meantime, the harder you train, the faster you'll make it back to Earth.

"Now, I'm sorry to say, I must tend to other matters. I'll check back in a few days to see how you're progressing." There was a brief pause before Will added, *"I know you think this unfair, but in time you'll see it's for your own good. Many Pleiadians have sacrificed much, including their lives, to keep you three alive and well. And the sooner you realize Earth's future depends on you becoming the true leaders your parents created you to be, the better for all of us. Think on that until we speak again. Asenja."*

Will was gone, but his words, "the true leaders your parents created you to be," continued to echo inside Sofia's head. He'd said that twice now. Both times he'd used *created*, which was an odd word to use.

"What are we going to do?" Liv asked meekly.

"What can we do?" Zach answered, his voice hoarse with barely contained anger. "We're fuckin' stuck here until Will decides we're ready to go back."

"No, we're not." Sofia pressed her lips together and slid around in the chair to face the display. "Show me the system files," she commanded. The screen immediately lit up. "We don't have to wait for Will. There has to be something in this system that'll tell us how to get home." She tapped a folder and skimmed the list of files that appeared.

After a few seconds, she looked around.

"Are you guys just gonna stand there or are you gonna help?"

EIGHTEEN

One week after the battle in the Pyramid

Tabari grabbed a bottle of water from the small refrigerator in his office and plopped down in the chair behind his desk. His hands were trembling so badly he could barely get the lid off. When he finally succeeded, he leaned his head back and poured the water over his face. The morphing skin that disguised his alien features soaked the water up like a sponge and only a few drops ran off his chin onto his shirt.

Daher had insisted Tabari ride with him in the limo from his villa to his office in the Katameya Heights Golf Club. Thankfully, it hadn't been a long trip, but being in an enclosed space with Daher for even a few minutes was extremely dangerous, especially as the Anunnaki leader was becoming more desperate by the day. Tabari had squeezed himself into the corner of the seat and kept his eyes on his tablet, taking notes as Daher spewed out one outrageous plan after another on how to locate the Pleiadians, all of which would surely expose who they were to the world and put their lives in jeopardy.

As of that moment, Tabari's offshore accounts held a little over fifty million from money he'd siphoned off Daher's accounts. He had hoped to get the amount up to at least seventy-five million before he disappeared, but with the way things were going, he wasn't sure he'd be able to wait. He hated to have to give up on the yacht he'd planned to go along with his island, but neither the yacht nor the island would do him any good if he were dead.

"Tabari, get in here!" Daher's thunderous voice came through the intercom on the desk.

Tabari reared up from his chair and looked around. Had Daher read his mind? His stomach felt like he'd swallowed a boulder and his hands trembled even worse as he picked up his tablet and hustled back down the hall of Daher's private wing.

He'd barely stepped over the threshold, when Daher spun around from the five foot tall window that looked out over the sixteenth hole of the golf course.

Daher's glare was sharper than ever, but his face shone with a strange expression that Tabari could only describe as excitement.

A small voice inside Tabari's head told him to run, but the boulder in his stomach had dropped, anchoring his feet to the floor.

"I have the perfect plan to get Gilamu and his motley group of Pleiadians to come out of hiding," Daher stated.

Tabari's dark bushy eyebrows came together to form a line that looked exactly like a bird's extended wings. He had literally just minutes earlier updated Daher on the Dracuzian's belief that the Guardians were off planet, and Daher had not mentioned a new plan.

"I want you to send one of the Nukiri to the ship to bring back a vial of the Cixotcus," Daher added almost gleefully.

Tabari visibly flinched and a cold shiver ran up his spine.

Cixotcus microbes from the Dracuzian's home planet were deadly to the Dracuzians and more importantly, to humans. They had been brought along to use as a last resort in case the humans refused to bow to the supremacy of the Anunnaki. If Daher released the microbes and wiped out the entire lot of homosapiens before the Anunnaki fleet arrived, there would be no one to manage the land, see to food production, and keep the planet's infrastructure up and running.

"Sir, I—"

"I will expose the Guardians' humans to the Cixotcus, then send them back to the U.S. to spread the pathogen. Since Gilamu considers himself the savior of this planet, he'll not be able to sit back and do nothing when he sees hundreds of thousands of his little pets start falling over dead. And the Guardians … I can't imagine them abandoning their family and friends either. So we'll get them, as well."

Tabari stared at Daher in disbelief. The Anunnaki leader had gotten more erratic over the last year, but this was downright deranged thinking.

"Sir, you do realize Cixotcus has no effect on Pleiadians. It is only deadly to humans and Dracuzians. And once it's released, there's no stopping it. It'll spread worldwide within a few months. Who will work in the mines, in the power plants, and grow the food then?"

Daher's giddy demeanor vanished as if a switch had been flipped off. He lowered his chin and drilled Tabari with a laser-like glare.

"Are you questioning my strategy?" Daher ground through his teeth. "I told you what would happen if you did that again." He leaned forward and placed his palms on the desk. "Must I give you a reminder?"

"No …" Tabari started, then gulped as an invisible force closed around his throat. He took a step back. "I-I wasn't q-questioning you, sir. You're the m-m-mastermind. I was only thinking of your comfort and how m-much you love Mulukhiyah for dinner. It would be a s-shame if we could n-no longer get the ingredients or have a c-chef to prepare it for you."

A bead of sweat ran down Tabari's temple as the Anunnaki leader narrowed his eyes. Several excruciating moments later, Daher blinked and the pressure around Tabari's neck ceased.

Daher turned and faced the windows.

After another long pause, he growled, "Instruct the lab to generate a virus from the Cixotcus. One that will only affect white-skinned, light-eyed humans. And tell them I expect it to be ready in two days."

"Yes, sir," Tabari croaked through his swollen throat and scurried back to his office as fast as his rubbery legs would take him.

He closed the door and pressed his back against the wood for a moment to slow his racing heart. He then staggered to his chair, collapsed in it, and gently massaged his neck.

It was pure luck he had been able to talk Daher down, but how much longer he would be able to do that was uncertain. The closer the fleet got to Earth the more desperate Daher became. The Anunnaki's insatiable thirst for power was going to ruin the entire mission, which was fine with Tabari, but not if it also ruined his plans to live out his life on this pristine planet.

"*Ezafak*!" Tabari hissed, knowing time was running out for all of them.

He closed his eyes and leaned back in the chair. Almost immediately an idea darted into his head. He sat up straight.

Ukani! He might help me thwart Daher.

The corners of his mouth curled up in a genuine smile. It was the perfect solution and really the only one. He could have Ukani stop Daher without risking his own life or even getting his hands dirty.

With a little luck, Ukani might even kill Daher in the process.

Tabari drummed his fingers on the desk in nervous anticipation as he thought about the message he would post on the dark web. Hopefully, Ukani still checked it and would be curious enough to hear Tabari out. If not, he may have to get his hands dirty after all.

Tabari glanced around to make sure no one was in the vicinity before he ducked around the corner of the breezeway. Wedging himself between two bushes, he held his breath and swiped the answer button on his cell phone.

He'd sneaked out of the compound in the wee hours of the morning, bought a burner phone, and gone to an internet café to send a message to Ukani, so there'd be no trace of it on Daher's servers. He had no idea when or even if Ukani would respond, but he hadn't expected a call back so quickly.

"Hello?" he whispered and cringed at the tremble in his voice.

"You have something for me?" asked a voice with a slight hiss.

"Ukani!" Tabari said louder than he intended. He twisted his neck around to see if anyone had heard him. The breezeway was clear. He lowered his voice and added, "I need your help in stopping Essol."

There was a long uncomfortable silence, and Tabari began to wonder if Ukani had hung up.

Finally, the Dracuzian spoke. “Why me?”

Tabari closed his eyes and breathed a sigh of relief. “Essol has sent the enforcers to hunt you, and we both know you’ll be found sooner than later and will be killed. The way I see it is, the only hope you have of staying alive is to disgrace Essol and remove him from power.”

There was another pause, but shorter this time. “Go on.”

Tabari rapidly summed up Daher’s plan to release the virus, leaving out the fact the virus was made from Cixotcus. “I know you have no fondness for humans, but I’m sure even you realize they are a necessity to keep this planet functioning for our continued comfort and benefit. Not to mention that the smell of eight billion decaying bodies would make it extremely unpleasant to live with for a very long time to come. But, more importantly, if the Guardians do turn off the grid, the Anunnaki fleet will land and neither of us will have the freedom to live out our lives as we wish.”

“And what do I get for doing this?”

Tabari knew Dracuzians had no sense of humor, but he couldn’t help himself. “The satisfaction of knowing you were influential in bringing Essol down isn’t enough?”

There was dead silence on the other end of the line.

“Then, how about this … I don’t tell anyone about the Pleiadian gold you stole.”

“Are you threatening me?”

Tabari tensed. “No, no, I wouldn’t do that. All I’m trying to do is make you understand you have everything to gain and nothing to lose. This is your chance to get a little payback for what the Anunnaki have done to your people. It’s also a once-in-a-lifetime opportunity for you and your fellow Dracuzians to live as free men on a luxurious planet.”

Ukani let out a low hiss, but after a few moments of silence, he growled, “Don’t try to contact me again. I’ll reach out to you when I have the virus.”

The line went dead.

Tabari closed his eyes and pressed his back into the wall. The call had gone better than he'd expected, but his pulse was still racing. He took a minute to settle his nerves before heading back to his office.

He had faith in Ukani, but even if the Dracuzian did get the Cixotcus, that only solved the immediate threat. And only the galaxy knew what other hair-brained idea Daher would come up with next.

Tabari sat down at his desk, brought up a photo of the private island he was negotiating to buy on the computer screen and drummed his fingers on the polished wood as he stared at the image.

He and the seller had been bickering over the price for months, but he could no longer wait the seller out. He needed to get his affairs in order sooner than later and be gone when Daher discovered the Cixotcus missing. If not …

He clenched his jaw and pushed that thought away. There could be no "if not" scenario. His luck had held out for him so far, but he knew it was time to pull back. He'd gone through too much to risk it all now.

Nineteen

Sofia felt like a disjointed marionette as she trudged back to the dorm from the brutal three-hour torture session, a.k.a Elleci's workout routine. The core workout, the weighs, and practicing new martial arts moves had not only pushed her, Zach, and Liv physically but mentally as well. It was like Elleci was trying to pound eighteen years' worth of training into a matter of days. Every muscle in Sofia's body, even ones she didn't know she had, felt like rubber. Holding herself upright and putting one foot in front of the other took every last ounce of strength she had left. But she'd be damned to give Liv the satisfaction of seeing her collapse on the floor.

Liv was a whole other pain in Sofia's side. No matter what Elleci and the two helpers, Sol and Uri, threw at them, Liv acted as if it was a competition and went overboard to make herself look more efficient and skilled than Sofia. It was almost as if Liv was getting extra one-on-one training on the side, but Sofia didn't know when she'd find time for that.

Too bad Sofia's BFF, Maddie, wasn't here. Maddie was a pro at handling mean girls and could turn the tables on them without them even realizing what had happened. Sofia, on the other hand, didn't have that particular skill set and had to just grit her teeth and try not to look like a fool.

A warm feeling rushed through her at the thought of her friend.

Sofia never had a true friend—a friend who accepted her for who she was and would stick by her no matter what—until Maddie came into her life. Of course, Sofia had no one to blame for that but herself. She was the one who'd built the wall around her to keep everyone out. But then Maddie came along and bored through the wall like a carpenter ant and took up permanent residency in Sofia's heart before Sofia even realized what was happening. Now Maddie was as essential as air to her, and Sofia couldn't imagine life without her friend.

Sofia staggered through the door of the diamond building and shuffled straight toward the stairs to the second floor.

Liv shrieked, "Ohmigod, Nick! Is that really you?"

Sofia jerked to a stop and looked up.

"When did you wake up? How are you feeling? Are you in pain?" Liv fired off a barrage of questions without taking a breath between as she hurried to Nick, who was sitting in a wheelchair in the middle of the common room.

Nick held his hand up. "Geez, take a breath already." His voice sounded as hoarse as a two-pack-a-day smoker. "I woke up yesterday."

He coughed and winced with pain.

The Segway robot standing behind the chair jerked to attention, wheeled around, and held out a cup. "Drink?"

Nick shook his head and waved it off. "D-O here thinks she's my mom."

The robot retreated and stood sentry behind the chair once more.

"Its name is D-O?" Zach walked up and stuck out his hand.

"That's what I call it," Nick replied, shaking the proffered hand. "You know, the droid from Star Wars? It moves around on a wheel like this one, 'cept it only has one big wheel, not two."

"This one looks nothing like D-O. The D-O from Star Wars has a cone-shaped head and no actual face," Zach said.

"True." Nick shrugged. "But it's my favorite droid from the movies, so I named this one after it."

He looked from Zach, to Sofia, to Liv, who had knelt beside the wheelchair. "So, you guys all got out clean? With no injuries?"

Sofia felt like a wrecking ball had slammed into her and her wobbly knees nearly buckled. She still didn't understand why her invisible shield had protected the three of them but not Nick.

"Yeah, we're all fine," Liv said, then looked down at the floor as if embarrassed. "I, um … I'm sorry I haven't been by to see you. I've been—"

"It's okay," Nick broke in. "You don't owe me anything. In fact, it's the other way around. I'd be dead if you guys hadn't brought me with you through that …" The creases in his forehead deepened. "What was that anyway?"

Liv looked over her shoulder at Zach.

He raised both eyebrows and shoulders in answer.

She chewed on her lip for several seconds as if trying to find the right words. Then, with a loud exhale, mumbled "Oh, what the hell" and lifted her chin. "That was a portal that brought us up here to … space."

Nick went still and stared at her with wide, rounded eyes.

Liv looked at Zach again, her eyes pleading for help.

Zach cleared his throat. "Look, bro …" He paused as if he too had to search for the right words. "This is gonna be hard to swallow, but I swear it's the truth. This place, where we're at right now, is called Atlantis II. It's a space station, a million plus kilometers from Earth, and we're kinda stuck here 'cause we don't know how to open the portal to get back."

Nick slowly lifted his gaze to stare up at Zach, but it took him another second to ask in a voice filled with awe, "So, this is an alien space station? Like the Death Star?"

Zach appeared stunned that Nick wasn't freaking out. "I guess you could say it's like that. It's a Pleiadian station, though."

Nick pursed his lips and nodded his head up and down. "Humph, that explains a lot. No place on Earth has the kind of tech I've seen around here." His eyebrows shot up. "So, those guys back at the pyramid, they're the Pleiadians?"

"Some of them were," Liv answered. "Daher's an Anunnaki."

Nick recoiled, his eyes growing even wider. "Whoa, Daher's an alien?"

Sofia, Zach, and Liv looked at each other with the same what-the-heck-do-we-tell-him-now expression.

"Wait a minute. I've heard those names before … Pleiadian and Anunnaki." Nick's face scrunched up. Then his eyes went wide again and shined with excitement. "I remember! There was an episode of Ancient Aliens on them."

"You watch Ancient Aliens?" Liv's snicker faded as the irony sunk in.

"What's wrong with that?" Nick replied defensively. "AA is a good show. And you just verified there are aliens on Earth, so it's a heck of a lot more credible than people think." His grin turned smug.

"Don't tell him any more," Zach telepathically said to Sofia and Liv.

Liv looked around, her eyebrows raised in question.

"He already knows too much. If he blabs what he knows when we get back to Earth, we'll be fucked," Zach added.

"So, which one are you guys?" Nick asked, oblivious to the telepathic conversation.

Liv swiveled back to Nick so fast, she almost fell over. "Which one?" The high-pitched squeak in her voice cancelled out her attempt to look confused.

"Pleiadian or Anunnaki. Which one are you?"

Sofia glanced at Zach out of the corner of her eye and saw the tic pulsing in his jaw.

"I'm going to guess you're Pleiadian since Daher is Anunnaki," Nick continued when no one answered. "That's why he was trying to capture you, isn't it?"

"Look," Zach started, but Liv held up her hand and stopped him.

"Come on, Nick … really?" Liv tilted her head and pushed her shoulders back, making her top stretch tight across her breasts. "Do *I* look like an alien?"

Nick's cheeks turned pink, but he didn't back off. "Well, you're not a Gray, that's for sure. But that doesn't mean you aren't alien. Daher doesn't look much like an alien, either, and you said he's an Anunnaki."

Sofia's stomach dropped. She couldn't believe how fast he was putting it all together. It had taken her eighteen years, and she still wasn't a hundred percent down with it.

"I'm not as stupid as I look," Nick added. "And remember, I was there in the pyramid when you shot that light out of your hands. No human can do what you did."

Sofia pressed her lips together and spoke to Zach and Liv, ***"Look guys, I don't know about you, but I can't lie to him. He's seen what we can do and knows who we are. Maybe if we explain to him what's at stake, he'll understand."***

She waited for one of them to say something, but Zach just balled his hands into fists and glared at Nick, and Liv sat on her heels with her chin tucked to her chest.

Great. So, again *it's up to me to do the dirty work.* Sofia heaved a sigh and dropped to one knee beside Nick's chair. But before she could open her mouth, Liv spoke up, "You're right. We're Pleiadians."

Zach recoiled and his alarm and anger hit Sofia like a blast oven.

Nick let out a guffaw, which immediately turned into a moan. His hand went to his right side, and his breath came short and fast. The robot woke up and rolled closer as it tapped something on a wristband on its arm.

"Are you okay?" Liv put a hand over Nick's. "Can I get you something?"

Nick took in a huge gulp of air as if he'd just come up from underwater. But within seconds, the pain etched on his face began to recede.

"I knew it!" he wheezed through clenched teeth.

Liv got to her feet and turned to Zach. Sofia could tell they were fighting by the looks on their faces, but it was a private exchange that neither she nor Nick were privy to.

"Guys, it doesn't matter now," she said out loud. "After what happened in the pyramid, a five-year-old could figure out we're aliens."

She squeezed Nick's arm. "You can't tell anyone about us, though, okay? Our lives depend on it, and I'm not just saying that. It's for real. Everyone in the world would be out to get us if they knew who we were."

Nick shifted to sit up a little straighter. "You think I'd rat you out?" His shocked gaze moved up to Zach and Liv. "Man, that hurts." He hung his head and mumbled, "I thought we were friends."

"We are." Liv dropped back to her knee so she could look him in the eye. "But you have to understand, this is new to us, too. I mean … imagine how you'd feel if you were told you're an alien?"

"That would be so awesome!"

Liv scoffed. "Easy for you to say. You don't have some uber rich dude out there trying to kill you."

Nick sobered. "Yeah, about that. Why does Makin Daher want you dead? Does it have something to do with that power grid he was yelling at us to turn off?"

Sofia answered, "The grid he was referring to is an energy grid the original Pleiadians built around the planet after they won the battle for Earth. They put it up to keep the Anunnaki from coming back."

Nick pursed his lips and again slowly nodded. "Daher got through, though, so I guess the grid doesn't work all that great, huh?"

"No, the grid does work." Sofia went on to explain about the solar blast that had taken it down for a time. "So now Daher's trying to get the grid turned off so he can bring down the rest of his men. But we three," she gestured to herself, Zach, and Liv, "are the only ones who can turn the grid off."

Sofia could almost see the wheels in Nick's brain whirling to process everything he'd heard, and she knew exactly what he was feeling.

"I guess it's lucky we're up here in space then," Nick finally said.

His face suddenly paled. "Daher can't get in here, right? We're safe as long as we stay where we're at?"

"Yeaaah, that's the thing," Liv said. "We can't stay here. Daher has taken our parents and Sofia's friend."

Her voice caught and she lowered her head, unable to go on.

Sofia put a hand on Liv's shoulder and picked up where Liv left off. "That's why we have to go back. The only problem is, we don't know how to get back. And Will, the other guy from the pyramid, won't help because he wants us to stay here. He thinks if we go back, we'll be captured again. But we're not letting that stop us. We've been searching through the system files for information that will tell us how to open the portal. We haven't made much progress yet, though, because of the strict training schedule Elleci's got us on."

"I could help," Nick said eagerly. "Back home I'm kinda known as a computer geek. And I'd rather do that than lay around and stare up at the ceiling."

Sofia and Liv both perked up and turned to Zach. His anxiety level had scaled down some, but it was still in the red zone.

"I don't think that's a good idea," he said telepathically. *"We don't know the kind of personal stuff that's in those files. He may dig up something we don't want him to know."*

"Couldn't we password protect the personal files and only let him into the ones we want him to see?" Liv asked.

"Yes, we could," Sofia answered, then winced as Zach's anxiety spiked again.

For a second, his feelings threw her off, but she pushed ahead before he could object further.

"Look, the longer we stay here, the longer Daher has your parents and my friend. And Lord knows what he's doing to them." She swiped away a drip from her nose with the back of her hand. *"Obviously, we can't train and go through files at the same time, so Nick's the perfect solution. And with him doing the computer research, we'll have time to explore more of this place. Who*

knows ... the answers we're looking for might be in one of the other buildings."

"Sofia's right, Z," Liv added, teaming up on him. *"I know Nick comes across as kind of a loser, but he's not a bad guy. And he already knows we're aliens, so what else do you think he'd find that could hurt us?"*

Zach raked his fingers through his hair and walked away a few steps, then flipped back around. *"He can't have access to any of our family or personal files."*

"That shouldn't be a problem," Sofia said. *"We'll instruct Scarlett on what he can and cannot see."*

Liv jumped to her feet and gave Zach a quick hug, then turned to Nick. "We'd really appreciate your help in digging through the files." She pointed to the scorpion-tail chairs. "Do you think you can get into one of those? That's how you access the system."

Nick looked around. "I think so."

"Awesome! After you pull the shield down in front of you, ask Scarlett to show you the system files. A touch screen will come up right on the shield. You'll want to look for any information that'll help us get back to Earth."

Nick frowned. "Aaand ... who's Scarlett?"

"Oh, yeah, sorry. That's what we call the AI that runs the internal systems—you know, the voice that comes out of the air? The one that kind of sounds like Scarlett Johansson."

"The voice?" Nick asked, looking completely perplexed. "I guess I haven't heard it yet. Or maybe only you Pleiadians can hear it. Like the telepathic thing you guys do with each other, so I can't hear what you're saying."

"What makes you think we do that?" Liv tried to sound hurt, but the lop-sided grin Nick gave her said he wasn't buying it.

"Ha, your face just confirmed it!" he gleefully replied. "I could tell you were doing it, anyway. Like I said, I'm not stupid."

"This isn't a game, Nick." Zach's voice was low and menacing. "It's serious business. We're depending on your help to get home and to keep our identity a secret. If you double-cross us—"

"Z! What the hell?" Liv cut him off. "He's not going to double-cross us. And if he does, it'll only be because you're being a dickhead."

"Don't mind him," Sofia said to Nick. "He's a little overwhelmed. We all are. But I know you'll do what's right, and that's all we ask."

She rose and started toward one of the chairs to get it set up for him.

"You don't have to tell me how serious it is," Nick said, looking directly into Zach's eyes. "The Anunnaki almost killed me. So I'll gladly do whatever I can to get us back and help take down those shitheads. Just promise me this: you won't leave me out when the time comes to face off with them."

Sofia stopped mid stride and looked back.

Like hell you're going to help! At least not if I have any say about it. I'll not have your death on my conscience.

TWENTY

Sofia stepped into the shower tube, but instead of turning on the water, she hit the infra-red sauna and sat on the bench to let the heat do its work on her sore muscles.

She was physically drained, but an odd nagging feeling that something was about to happen squirmed in her abdomen. She didn't know if that something was good or bad, and she was afraid to get her hopes up that it was good. She'd been let down too often.

But then again, if she had listened to her gut in the first place, she wouldn't be in the mess she was in now.

She slumped against the wall, closed her eyes, and thought about her weird new ability to feel Zach's emotions. It had never bothered her to see people's auras, which often told their emotional state, but this was different. She could feel his actual raw emotions, which made it so much more personal and felt kind of wrong. Like an invasion of privacy.

Oh, God! She reared up straight as another thought came to her. Could Zach tell she was feeling his emotions? She put her hands over her face and wilted back into the wall.

Please, please, don't let him know. He doesn't need another reason to hate me.

Why did these kinds of things keep happening to her?

Her whole life she'd had one hurdle to jump over after the next. No wonder she was so exhausted all the time.

Sofia rested her head against the shower wall and focused on the heat of the sauna as it seeped into every part of her body. Little by little, her thoughts melted away, and as her eyelids drifted shut, the video Elleci had shown them on the steps of the temple replayed in her mind.

"As for Atlantis II, Esos and I will take care of everything until you and the children return," Elleci said in the replay.

"E-s-sews," Sofia whispered the name out loud as she heard it. "Who is that I wonder? And why haven't we met him yet?"

"I am here," Scarlett's voice rang out.

Sofia sat up straight, her eyes wide open. "What?"

"You called me?"

She frowned. "You're Esos?"

"Yes."

It took Sofia's brain a second to process this new development. "Are you a person?"

"I am the Environmental Support and Operating System of Atlantis II."

The crease in her brow deepened. ESOS. "Sooo you're not a person?"

"I am the Environmental Support and—"

"Okay, I get it," Sofia cut in. "We've been calling you Scarlett."

"That is not my name," Esos said matter-of-factly.

"Sorry, we didn't know that. I'll be sure to let the others know, so we won't make that mistake again."

Well, this is something new, anyway. What else have I missed?

Sofia cocked her head to the side and brought up the video again. As it had during the first time she'd watched it, the picture whited out at the point where she, Zach, and Liv joined hands and she couldn't see what was happening in those few seconds.

"Esos, you know that video that was taken of us right before we left for Earth? Can you tell me what happened after the three of us joined hands?"

"I know of no such video."

"What do you mean?" Sofia asked skeptically. "How can that be? You keep a record of everything that goes on here in Atlantis II, don't you?"

"I do. There are daily recordings going back to the time the system was turned on four centuries ago. But there is no video of your departure in the database."

Sofia's frown deepened. *That doesn't make sense.* "You do know we went to Earth, right?"

"I know you have not been on Atlantis II for the last sixteen years and three months in Earth time."

Sofia stared into space. How could Esos not have a record of them leaving? Could the video have been erased from the system?

"Esos, can you tell if a file has been deleted?" she asked.

"There is no way to delete a file from the system other than to destroy the system."

Aghh. "Then how can you not have the video?"

"I do not have an answer to that question."

This is crazy. I know the video exists. I've seen it. So, it's got to be here somewhere. We were all in a room with a countertop and some microscopes ...

Sofia sucked in a sharp breath.

Could it have been taken somewhere other than Atlantis II?

"Esos, is there a Pleiadian spaceship here on Atlantis II, or another base somewhere?"

"Atlantis II has many spacecrafts, mostly used for mining water from asteroids," the AI replied. "As far as Pleiadian stations and bases, there are many on and around different planets in different galaxies. Earth has two operating bases: Atlantis II, located one point five million kilometers from Earth, and *Anides*, located in the city of Istanbul."

Istanbul? Sofia shook her head. *That can't be it. We hadn't gotten to Earth yet in the video. Wait a minute. Elleci was in the video, which means she has to know where it was taken.*

Sofia jumped to her feet so fast the blood rushed out of her head. She leaned against the glass and closed her eyes until the room stopped spinning, then hurriedly showered and dressed, and bolted out the door.

"Hey, what's up?" Zach called as Sofia whizzed past him.

She slid to a stop and looked around in surprise. She hadn't noticed him sitting in a chair pushed up next to Nick's. "Oh, I, um … I think I may have discovered something."

Zach's eyebrows raised in question. He pushed the scorpion chair hood up and leapt out of the chair in one swift move.

"Remember that video Elleci showed us on the steps?" Sofia asked.

"Yeaaah?"

"Well, Esos doesn't have a record of it."

Zach held a palm up. "Whoooa … who's Esos?"

"Oh, that's Scarlett's real name. It means Environmental …" She scrunched up her nose, trying to remember the rest, then waved her hand in the air. "It doesn't matter what it means. What matters is I think there's a secret room here in Atlantis II. And I think it might have the answers we're looking for."

"A secret room! Cool," Nick exclaimed.

"What makes you think that?" Zach snorted, giving her a what-have-you-been-smoking kind of look.

"I'll explain later. Right now, I've got to find Elleci," she said and headed out the door.

Sofia heard Zach yell, "Wa—" before the door closed behind her, but she kept going. Something in her gut told her this was important, and she wasn't going to ignore it this time.

She had almost reached the training center when Zach caught up to her.

"Hold up a sec," he said, taking hold of her arm and pulling her to a stop.

She yanked her arm free. "I can't. I need to find Elleci."

He grasped both of her upper arms and turned her to face him. "You're not making sense. Tell me what's going on."

"I don't know yet. That's why I need to—"

Without warning, he pulled her into his chest and covered her mouth with his.

Caught by surprise, Sofia stood rigid for a nanosecond. Then his tongue slipped between her teeth and her resolve evaporated in a flame of desire that quickly jumped the firewall in her abdomen and spread through her like a virus.

As she leaned into the kiss, a small voice in her head screamed, *No!*

She put both palms on his chest, and it took all her willpower to push back.

Zach started and in a flash, his expression went from one of ecstasy to one of horror. He dropped his hands to his sides and lowered his gaze to the ground as confusion and embarrassment poured out of him.

"I … I didn't mean," he muttered barely loud enough for her to hear.

Her cheeks burned with desire, but in the next heartbeat that desire transformed into indignation.

"What the hell, Zach?" Icicles dripped from each word. "I'm not a toy you can play with whenever Liv's not available."

Zach grimaced but had the decency to remain silent.

Humiliation and outrage warred inside Sofia.

"I don't have time to play your stupid games. I need to find Elleci and figure out how to get us home."

Before her bravado could incinerate in the heat coming off Zach, she turned and dashed off.

Zach raked his fingers through his hair and watched Sofia race away.

Christ, what the hell was I thinking? He hadn't meant to kiss her. He'd only intended to slow her down and find out what she'd learned. But every time he got close to her, his brain turned to mush, and he could only think of two things: how soft her lips were and how sweet they tasted.

Dammit! Somewhere along the way he'd become an addict, and she was the drug of his choice.

Fuck! He kicked at a nonexistent rock. *What am I supposed to do now? Apologize? Tell her it meant nothing?*

He knew he couldn't do that—he couldn't lie.

Zach hung his head and rubbed the back of his neck. What was it about her? No other girl had ever had this kind of effect on him. And he'd gone and blown it good this time. She had the perfect reason to hate him now.

But maybe that wasn't such a bad thing. If she hated him, she'd keep her distance and he wouldn't have to worry about losing control and making an ass of himself every time she was around.

A sharp pain tore through his chest. He bent in half, put his hands on his thighs, and slowly breathed in through his nose and out through his mouth.

After repeating the exercise three more times, he turned his head to the side and stared at the training center. Staying away from Sofia was going to be harder than anything he'd ever done, especially since they were cooped up in here together.

"But I can't let her down again," he said under his breath. "She needs someone to take care of her. I owe her at least that much."

He winced, knowing that he needed her a whole lot more than she needed him. But he also knew he had to push his feelings aside and focus on her happiness, because her happiness was the most important thing to him right now.

Twenty-One

Elleci was setting up a row of large, tubular-shaped bags at one end of the gym when Sofia stormed in, breathing heavily—but not from running.

"Esos says there's no record of the video taken of us the day we left for Earth but I know there is one 'cause you showed it to us and you were in it so you have to know where it was taken and I want you to take me there right now," Sofia gushed out in one long breath.

Her emotions were roiling inside her like steam inside a pressure cooker, and she was trembling so hard she didn't notice the ground beneath her feet was also shaking. The quake quickly spread across the room. Weights, targets, lasers, and weapons went crashing to the floor from racks and hooks on the walls.

A calming voice whispered in Sofia's ear, "Do not fret, *wudala*. I am here. All is well."

Sofia started and a long-forgotten memory flashed through her mind. It was that same strange word being cooed in her ear as her mother cradled and rocked her to sleep.

She gasped out loud and the quake stopped as quickly as it had started, leaving an eerie silence in its wake.

Sofia blinked at Elleci, then grabbed onto Elleci's arm as her legs threatened to give out.

At that moment, Zach burst through the doors and slid

to a stop. "What happened? Did we get hit by an asteroid or something?"

He looked around at the equipment and furnishings that had been haphazardly strewn about the room as if a tornado had swept through.

"Did you do this?" he asked Sofia, his eyes wide with wonder.

Sofia pushed back from Elleci, her eyebrows pinched together as she surveyed the damage.

She slowly shook her head. *No … I couldn't have done this.*

"It appears the special abilities your parents gifted you with are beginning to develop." Elleci answered for Sofia.

Sofia recoiled and looked at the chaos around her. "Are you saying I was the one who threw all this stuff around?"

"Your energy did. When you three were still embryos, your parents enhanced your genes and DNA and gave you extra tools to help you fulfill your role as Guardians."

Zach looked as if he'd seen Freddy Krueger. "They gave us the ability to create earthquakes?"

"It is called vibration manipulation. So far, Sofia is the only one who has shown to have this ability. You and Liv may or may not develop it. I was not involved in your gene therapy, so I cannot say for sure what abilities you have."

Zack let out a loud disgusted snort and threw his hands in the air, his fingers spread wide. "That's just fuckin' great! We have special powers, but no one can tell us what they are. So what … when we accidently destroy a room, we're supposed to just shrug our shoulders and say, "Whoops?""

"It is unfortunate your parents are not here to explain their thinking, but these abilities were not meant to be a burden. They were a gift. And though you do not fully understand your parents' reasoning, you are fortunate that they had the forethought to provide you with these tools. Because by law, Pleiadians are not allowed to openly use advanced technology weapons on Earth. So having these abilities will make a difference when you face off with the Anunnaki."

Liv burst into the room and stopped short just inside the door. As she took in the state of the room, her face turned into a mask of bewilderment. "What happened here?"

"They changed our DNA," Zach replied gruffly.

Liv's eyes grew wider. "They what? Who did?"

Instead of answering, Zach turned and stalked away.

Sofia, still grappling with the idea that her DNA had been altered, looked into Elleci's eyes. She'd never noticed how cold and vacant they were until that moment. Had Elleci's DNA been altered, too? That thought led to another: Did Elleci also have special powers?

She realized how little she knew about the woman.

"Who are you?" Sofia hesitantly asked. "Are you a Pleiadian?"

"Technically, I am. Although I do not have living organs or DNA."

Sofia's jaw fell as Zach and Liv jerked around and stared at Elleci with the same look of bewilderment.

"How do you not have DNA? Is that a Pleiadian thing?" Zach stammered.

"No. All natural-born Pleiadians have DNA the same as all living things. I, however, was created by Pleiadian technology."

Created? There's that word again. Elleci's strange quirks—her lack of an aura and body vibrations, her face and skin that sort of radiated and hadn't changed one iota in the sixteen years since that video was taken—rushed to the forefront of Sofia's mind.

Sofia swallowed hard. "Are you ... real?"

"That is a rhetorical question. If I were not real, would I be standing here? I can assure you everything about me is real: my brain, my emotions, my ability to make decisions, my ability to evolve."

"Wait ..." Liv stammered, looking at Elleci strangely. "Are you saying you're an AI?"

Sofia's spine went rigid. *Ohmigod!* She had totally missed it, and it was so obvious. And here she'd always thought she was good at reading people.

"I am not familiar with the term AI. I am an Evolutionary

Computational Intelligence designed to serve and protect you Guardians."

Sofia knew she was being rude, but she couldn't stop staring. The woman looked so real, felt real, and acted just like a living, breathing person.

"Are Sol and Uri from training, Evolutionary Computational Intelligence beings too?" Liv squeaked.

Elleci nodded.

The three stared at her with the same astonishment they had when she'd told them they were in a space station.

Zach was the first to find his voice. "Sooo … you were created to serve us? Like you have to do what we ask and get us what we need kind of thing?"

"I have been specifically assigned to see to your needs and well-being, as well as your training and education, which I have waited a long time to begin. Now that you have returned to Atlantis II, I will be able to catch you up on all that you have missed."

Oh no! Sofia's stomach sunk with a sudden realization. *Elleci thinks we're going to stay here!*

She shot a sidelong glance at the others, who were still staring at Elleci in awe.

She looked back at Elleci. *Damn, if only I could read her emotions like I can Zach's.*

She cleared her throat. "I think you misunderstand. We're only here because it was either this or be crushed under a couple tons of bedrock. We had no idea we'd end up in space when we jumped through that portal."

Zach snapped to attention and added, "That's right, and we're not planning on sticking around. Daher kidnapped our parents, mine and Liv's adoptive parents that is, and Sofia's friend. We have to get back and save them."

Elleci pressed her palms together in the prayer pose that had become very familiar. "I am aware that Essol has taken your family. I am also aware he did this to lure you into a trap, which is why your training is so important. You must be prepared before you go face-to-face with him and the Nukiri."

"That may be true, but we can't just sit here!" Sofia cringe. That sounded like a whiny little kid. She took a breath and leveled out her voice. "Daher could be torturing our families for all we know."

She took Elleci's hands in hers. "Please understand. You have to open a portal and send us back."

"It is technically a wormhole. Will and the others refer to it as a gateway. And I am not programmed to create one."

Sofia dropped Elleci's hands and clenched her teeth to hold in the scream rising in her throat.

"I don't believe you." Zach's voice held a hard edge. "There has to be a way for us to get back to Earth."

Elleci remained calm. "I did not say there was no way to Earth." She turned and moved toward the door. "Come with me."

"Where's she going?" Zach mumbled to Sofia, then called out to Elleci, "Where're ya going?"

"To your parents' laboratory."

Sofia's spine went straight. "Is that the secret room where the video was shot? You know where it is?"

"Of course." Elleci stopped and looked back. "You did want me to take you there, did you not?"

Sofia's mouth opened and closed like a goldfish before she could get out, "Yes!"

Zach eyebrows rose in question. "Is this the secret room you were talking about earlier?"

Liv's head swiveled back and forth between Zach and Sofia as if she was watching a tennis match. "What the hell is going on?" she yelled in frustration.

Too many facts were shuffling in and out of Sofia's mind for her to answer. A second later, she inhaled sharply and spun around to Zach.

"*She* was the one who did it! Elleci wiped all the metadata of the room from the system."

The facts started to all fall into place.

Sofia turned back to Elleci, who was waiting by the door. "The last thing my dad said to you in that video was, 'You know what to do.' Was he telling you to delete the metadata in the system so no one could find the room."

"Yes. I was instructed to delete all references to the laboratory after you departed. I am the only one who has knowledge of it, but I cannot access it. Only you three can do that."

The bubble of excitement bouncing inside Sofia's chest stilled for a moment as Elleci's words sank in. Then she let out a whoop and whirled around to Zach. "I told you so!"

Without thinking, she threw her arms around him, then jumped back when he stiffened.

Oh crap, I did it again.

Sofia took another step back and snuck a sidelong glance at Liv before she hung her head, her cheeks burning with embarrassment. "I'm sorry. I didn't mean …" She couldn't continue.

She turned and started to walk away, but after only two steps she stopped.

This is ridiculous. I shouldn't have to walk on eggshells and be scared of what I might do or say around them.

Steeling herself, she turned back. "Look … the three of us obviously have a connection that's more than just being Pleiadians. I can't explain it and I doubt you can either. I just know that it's there and it's stupid to try and deny it."

Sofia stood strong as a wave of Liv's antipathy slammed into her. She ran her tongue around her mouth to bring back some moisture so she could go on.

"I understand you two have always had each other, and now, here I am a third wheel. But I want you to know, I'm not trying to come between you. I just want to get Maddie back and go home to my life the same as you do. But it looks like we're going to have to work together to do that."

She squared her shoulders. "So … how about we forget about what's happened and start over? Then, once we get everyone back safe and sound, you can go your way and I'll go mine. … Deal?"

Liv's eyes narrowed suspiciously as she looked from Sofia to Zach, whose face was as red with embarrassment as Sofia's.

Zach released a long, weary sigh. "I'm so—"

"Don't," Sofia said sharply. "There's nothing to apologize for. As of this moment, the past is forgotten, and we all have a clean slate. Got it?"

His jaw hardened and his tic pulsed like a heartbeat. "Got it. We're all in for this one mission, then it's adios."

His words tore through Sofia's heart, but she held her back straight and gave a curt nod. The daggers of jealousy coming from Liv stabbed at her. She clenched her jaw and stiffly walked away, praying Liv and Zach didn't have the same ability to read emotions that she did.

"Can you please take us to the room now?" Sofia asked as she approached Elleci.

Elleci nodded and headed out the door. "This way."

Sofia bit down on her bottom lip and followed, fighting the urge to run away as fast as she could.

Before the door closed, she heard Liv ask Zach, "What happened between you two?"

"Nothing," Zach replied. "Just drop it."

The harshness of his tone took Sofia's breath away and the bridge of her nose began to burn with unshed tears.

Obviously, Daher wasn't the only one who could completely destroy her.

TWENTY-TWO

Daher's voice boomed down the hall, rattling the windows in his private wing at the Katameya Heights clubhouse, "Tabari!"

A chill ran up Tabari's spine and his hand froze midair over the briefcase where he had just packed the last of his personal items from the office. Hours earlier, he had electronically signed the paperwork that finalized the purchase of his private island.

Had Daher somehow discovered his plan?

Frustration and resentment oozed from every pore until it occurred to him there was no way the Anunnaki could know. Not this quickly, anyway.

Tabari exhaled the breath he'd been holding and wished the end of the day would hurry and get there so he'd never have to jump at Daher's command again. Until that time, he had no choice but to play the part of the trusty assistant and act as if everything was fine.

With a deep sigh, he grabbed up his tablet from the desk and headed for Daher's office one last time, his head already in a beach chair on his island sipping Mai Tais.

Steps from Daher's office door, a strange, malignant vibe in the air made the hair on the back of Tabari's neck stand on end. He gripped the tablet tighter against his chest to keep his hand from shaking and cautiously walked into the office.

The usually impeccable room was in shambles. All the furniture was upended except for the desk Daher was standing behind. Some of it was even smashed to pieces. The priceless artwork from the wall was on the floor in shreds, and Daher's treasured artifacts, vases, and bookcases had been reduced to splinters.

Three Dracuzian enforcers were standing at the side of the room, their hands positioned atop their weapons.

Tabari gulped back the panic inching up his throat.

Daher placed his palms on the desk, leaned over them menacingly, and hissed through his teeth, "Where's my virus?"

Tabari jumped, then silently cursed himself for doing so.

The virus was the last thing he'd been worried about, for he'd assumed Ukani would wait to intercept the courier. And he'd been counting on those couple extra days to disappear in. But if Ukani was already in possession of the virus, he must have broken into the lab instead.

Damn.

Tabari squared his shoulders and pushed his fingernails, which were really more like eagle talons, into the palms of his fists, in a concerted effort to keep his composure.

"I'm not sure, sir."

Daher's murderous glower made it clear he wasn't buying Tabari's answer.

Tabari could feel the artery in his neck pulsing with his heartbeat and prayed the Anunnaki leader wouldn't notice. "I'll go check with the lab—"

"No," Daher said in a voice as deadly as a cobra. "I already know the Cixotcus isn't there."

Tabari opened his eyes as wide as he could in an attempt to look outraged. "It's not? Where is it, sir?"

Daher pursed his lips and narrowed his merciless eyes as he walked around the desk, stopping less than a foot in front of his assistant.

"That's what I'd like to know. Isn't it strange that neither you nor they," Daher tilted his head to indicate the enforcers, "know where it is, even though the full extent of your job is knowing what is going on?"

Tabari fought through his rising panic to keep his expression blank.

"Why must I constantly remind people what happens to those who fail me?" Daher added.

Before Tabari could blink an eye, one of the Dracuzians made a gurgling sound and crumbled to the ground in what seemed like slow motion, the short handle of a blade sticking out between his wide-set eyes.

Tabari's stomach lurched, and its contents moved into the back of his throat as the smell of swamp gas permeated the room. He hadn't seen Daher move, but Daher was the only one who owned daggers with unique zuamsi handles embossed with the Anunnaki crest.

"Now, is someone going to tell me where my virus is?" Daher said, his voice dangerously calm.

Tabari threw a sidelong glance at the two remaining enforcers. They had shifted their stances and looked prepared to fight, but neither said a word.

"I …" Tabari's voice cracked, but he went on. "I don't know, sir."

That wasn't a lie. He had no idea where Ukani was. He wasn't even sure it was Ukani who had taken the virus.

A low growl rumbled in Daher's throat and a second Dracuzian collapsed on the floor with a knife protruding from his neck.

"One of you has to know something about the virus's sudden disappearance," Daher stated without acknowledging another man had gone down.

"I wasn't aware Cixotcus had been brought to this planet," the lone Dracuzian said, his voice low and raspy.

Daher scrutinized him for several seconds, then turned back to Tabari and drilled him with a stabbing look that went straight to the bone.

Tabari opened his mouth to defend himself, but before he could get a word out, an invisible force clamped around his throat.

"Are you really going to waste your final breaths lying to me? You think me a fool?" Daher tsked. "Your deception is as tangible as the sweat gathering on your forehead."

He let Tabari struggle to catch his breath another minute, then sighed. "I didn't want to believe you would betray me, but I should have guessed. You were against me using the Cixotcus from the beginning."

"I w-wouldn't ..." was all Tabari could choke out.

Daher snorted in disgust and walked back to his desk. After righting his chair, he sat down, put his elbows on the top, and steepled his fingers.

"I am certain of one thing, though." Daher tapped his index fingertips together as if keeping beat with Tabari's pulse. "You have neither the strength nor the skills to take out my maid, let alone a Nukiri warrior. So, how did you do it? Who do you have working with you?"

Tabari felt like his head was about to explode, and even if he wanted to confess, the pressure squeezing his windpipe and vocal cords made it impossible to speak.

"I can't imagine anyone other than a Dracuzian would be able to get in and—" Daher reared to his feet, flipping his chair over backwards.

"Is it Ukani working with you?" His voice sounded incredulous.

Tabari couldn't hold back his startled reaction. He never thought in a million years Daher would be able to put him and Ukani together.

"The enforcers have been scouring this planet for that traitor and you're the one to find him?" Daher released the pressure to allow Tabari to answer.

At that moment, a Dracuzian appeared in the doorway.

"The virus was not in his office," the enforcer said.

"Humph." Daher rounded the desk and leaned his butt against the front edge. "So, what did you do with it? It isn't in your office or apartment. Though I'm told your belongings were all packed." His eyebrows turned down into two sharp slashes. "Were you planning on going somewhere?"

Tabari whimpered something inaudible.

A slow, malicious grin crept across Daher's face. "You of all people should know there is no place to hide from me. But I tell you what. Tell me where Ukani and the virus are, and I'll consider making your death a quick one."

A bead of sweat ran down Tabari's temple. He didn't know where Ukani was. But if he could convince Daher he could get a hold of the Dracuzian, he might live long enough to escape. He opened his mouth and tried to force the words out, but all he could produce was a croak.

Daher seemed to enjoy Tabari's discomfort, but after a few seconds, he straightened his back with a huff and started for the door as if bored with the whole thing.

As he passed Tabari, he lifted his right hand and slowly bent his fingers into a fist one by one.

Tabari made a small squeak as he fell to the floor and flopped around like a fish out of water.

Flashes of his life passed behind his eyelids: scrounging food from garbage piles in the outer wastelands, sneaking into the inner city and joining the Nibiruian army to keep from going to prison, working his way up to a negotiator and go-between for a young and nefarious diplomat named Essol.

He had existed back on Nibiru, but had never experienced an ounce of joy until he came to Earth and found the small, secluded island. *His* island where he would have been free at last. He could see it now—the sparkling blue waves gently rolling up on the beach, rocking his chair.

He stilled and watched the peaceful scene until the blue faded and the world went black.

Stopping in the doorway, Daher snarled over his shoulder toward the last Dracuzian in the room.

"Dump the bodies in a volcano. And find Ukani!" He turned

down the hall and yelled back, "No more excuses. If you can't produce him, you and the rest of your unit will swim in the lava alongside these three."

Daher stormed into the lobby like a bull charging a muleta in a bull ring.

"Have the Falcom ready for takeoff at dawn," he barked to the Dracuzian standing in the entryway.

The enforcer didn't flinch. "The pilot will want to know where you're going."

"I'm going to take care of the situation since your lot doesn't seem to be able to," Daher growled and barreled out the door to his waiting car.

He slumped in the rear seat and stewed.

Damn you, Tabari. I wish I could kill you all over again. You thought your traitorous deed would stop me, but you were wrong. I'll get the Guardians to show themselves even if I have to personally kill every single human they've ever associated with!

TWENTY-THREE

Zach shook off Liv's hand and followed Sofia out the door. It didn't seem possible that a little over a week ago he was bagging groceries in Texas and his only worry was how to pay for his college tuition.

Now, he was stuck in space, training to take on a powerful alien race, and the only girl he'd ever felt a real connection with hated him—all because he'd let Liv talk him into signing up for a stupid TV reality show.

No, that wasn't fair. He couldn't blame Liv. Daher would have eventually found them one way or another. And if they hadn't gone on the show, he wouldn't have discovered who he really was.

It was ironic, really, that as a kid he used to tell anyone who would listen that he was going to save the world when he grew up. It was a dream that never left him and was the reason he'd decided to major in geoscience. He wanted to develop a way to reverse global warming, the biggest threat to the planet.

He clicked his tongue. Global warming almost seemed trivial now that he knew the real threat was alien invaders. Unfortunately, there was no college degree that dealt with how to defeat the Anunnaki.

Zach involuntarily shuddered at the thought of being an alien.

He used to think he was some kind of mutant freak since he could run faster and jump higher than any other person in the history of the world. But never once had it occurred to him that he wasn't from Earth. Then again, why would it? He didn't look like an alien. At least not the big-headed, bug-eyed ones depicted in the movies.

He balled his hands into fists. If Will had come forward with the truth sooner, everything would have been so much easier for him growing up. They might have even been able to avoid this whole mess and taken steps to ensure their parents' safety. He'd also have found Sofia sooner, and she wouldn't have had to grow up alone.

He grimaced as he remembered the three of them swearing they'd stick together forever and always. Not only had he failed to live up to that promise, he'd forgotten Sofia even existed. It wasn't totally his fault, though. He was just a toddler then. Still, he'd never forgive himself. And now, more than ever, he was determined to protect her.

She might balk at that—she thinks she can take care of herself—but like it or not, he wasn't going to abandon her a second time.

The artificial sun was lowering in the pale sky as Elleci led them down a walkway Sofia had never been on before. The air was infused with floral scents as the path wound through flower gardens and around buildings and out to a tunnel drilled through the rocky ridge. The tunnel spilled out to a patchwork of terraced fields three levels high and stretching as far as the eye could see. Some of the fields were plain, plowed dirt. Others had neat green rows of crops in varying stages of maturity. Every so often a piece of machinery could be seen moving through a field, but they were all too far away to tell what they were doing.

"We turn a lot of what we produce here into biopower to help sustain the station," Elleci commented as they walked. "We also keep a small supply on hand to accommodate anyone who takes refuge here."

They walked on to the end of a field planted with soybeans, then took a well-worn path that circled back toward the rocky ridge.

At the base of the cliff, Elleci motioned for the three to come closer. "I need one of you to press your palm right here, please," she said pointing to the rock face.

Liv lunged forward before the other two could make a move and pressed her palm over three dime-sized, raised circles that wouldn't have been noticeable if Elleci hadn't pointed them out.

Soundlessly, the edge of a large rectangular section of rock separated from the rest.

Elleci took hold of the edge and swung the slab out as if it weighed no more than a piece of cardboard.

"After you," she said, gesturing toward a dimly lit elevator car.

Once they were all piled in, a metal door slid across the entrance. Sofia waited for the feeling of movement, but none came. All that happened was three small squares above the door lit up one at a time. When the last one was lit, the door slid open, revealing a large, dimly lit room and a slight chemical smell.

Excitement bubbled up Sofia's throat at the sight of a long counter holding several sophisticated microscopes and a circular rack of vials along the wall straight across from the elevator. This was it. This was where the video had been shot.

She stepped out of the elevator and scanned the room. On one wall was a row of wire mesh cabinets holding dozens of rack servers that appeared to be functioning, if their blinking lights were any indication. The other side of the room had all kinds of laboratory equipment and instruments, many of which she didn't recognize, and in a dark back corner sat three miniature sized MedPod capsules like what Nick had been in in the ER. A shiver ran up her spine.

Elleci stood at a small, square table where a 3-D list of files floated in midair above the surface. She rapidly tapped one file after another until she found what she was looking for—a video showing a group of figures huddled on a bench in what appeared to be the back of a van. Deep shadows obscured the scene and the video bounced as if the vehicle was driving along a dirt road.

"My children," a weak voice said in the video. "It pains me to have to say this, but it must be said ... we have failed you."

Dad! Sofia's heart leapt into her throat. She rushed to the table and strained to find her father's face in the shadows.

At that moment, a vehicle passed the van and a stream of light from the oncoming headlamps rolled over the figures, illuminating Senki sitting between Zach's mother and Liv's mother, who was leaning heavily against her husband's shoulder. They all looked disheveled and had smudges on their faces.

Senki continued, "We knew before we brought you to Earth that several Anunnaki vessels had landed during a coronal mass ejection event that had disrupted the energy grid. But we felt it important for you to experience life on the planet and form a bond with its species. You are, after all, the next generation of Guardians and will be in charge of protecting the human race. And we weren't overly concerned because we knew that only a few Anunnaki ships got in.

"Unfortunately, what we didn't know at the time was that the Anunnaki had brought with them a battalion of the deadliest hunter-trackers in the galaxy. When we did discover the Dracuzian enforcer were here, it was too late and many of our people were already lost."

Another stream of light rolled over the four adults and Sofia noticed their wrists were bound with a wide band, edged with a thin strip of red light. She also saw a large, dark stain covering the front of Liv's mother's shirt.

Sofia made a small noise as her breath hitched in her chest. At the same time, Zach inhaled sharply and slipped his hand into hers, entwining their fingers together.

"Miyana and a friend were able to slip you three away before you were captured," Senki added. "They're making arrangements at this moment to ensure you are kept well-hidden. We all pray for Ea's blessings that you will stay safe and be able to fulfill your destinies."

He bent forward and held his stomach as he lapsed into a coughing fit. When he raised his head, a spot of blood sat on his bottom lip.

"We expected to have more time with you to explain your unique capabilities and train you on how to use them, but it seems—"

The side door opened, cutting off his words.

An overhead lamp bathed the four in light and illuminated the blood splattered over their clothes, faces, and hands.

A muscular arm covered in blue ink tattoos reached in, grabbed Liv's father by the neck, and hauled him out of the vehicle.

Liv's hand flew to her mouth and a strangled squeak escaped her lips.

"All the knowledge you need is inside you," Senki frantically added.

Another arm pulled Liv's mother out of the van.

"Trust your intuition and rely on each other and Elleci. She'll be the one now to teach and train you in all that you need to know.

"We didn't intend for it to be this way, but we have faith in you and lov—"

The video went black before he could finish.

A suffocating silence pressed in around Sofia and her chin began to tremble. Then, without thinking, she turned and crumbled into Zach's shoulder. Liv joined in and the three clung to each other for several, long minutes before Sofia sniffed and pulled back.

"We can't allow Daher to hurt anyone else. He has to be stopped," she said.

Zach's nose was as red as Sofia's, but his eyes were churning like a dark storm. He shot Elleci a glare, the tic in his jaw pulsing. "We need a gateway opened now."

His tone made it clear he was done messing around.

"As I have said before, I cannot do that."

"But we can," Zach stated. "We opened one in the pyramid. Tell us how to do it."

Elleci pressed her palms together as she so often did, but instead of bowing her head, she stared straight ahead, her eyes twitching back and forth ever so slightly.

Sofia's heartbeat pounded in her ears as she waited for Elleci to say something.

After what seemed like an eternity, Elleci blinked and focused on the three of them. "It is not safe for you to return to Earth at this time. You have not yet learned how to control your abilities, and you are not trained for combat."

"You sound like Will, but I don't care if it's safe or not!" Zach shouted, the power of his anger rocking the equipment in the room.

Elleci was undeterred. "My directive is to see to your training and ensure you are able to defend yourselves."

Zack opened his mouth to respond, but Sofia placed a hand on his arm.

"We understand we need more training," she said. "But there's nothing that says we have to do it here. Right? We could do our training just as easily on Earth."

Elleci's brow creased then smoothed so quickly that if Sofia had blinked, she would have missed it.

"Without an understanding of your abilities and how to use them, you would be vulnerable on Earth," Elleci doubled down.

"But we don't have time for that!" Zach said, his anguish adding an edge to his voice. "You just showed us what Daher's men did to our biological parents. Now he has our other parents, the ones who've raised me and Liv, and we can't let him kill them too."

Elleci stared straight ahead again.

Zach squared his shoulders and lifted his chin. "I order you to tell us how to open the gateway."

Sofia faced Elleci and placed a hand on each of the woman's shoulders. "Our parents took us to Earth even though they knew the Anunnaki were there. They did that because above all else we're the Guardians of Earth, and it's our duty to protect it and all humans. Just like it's your duty to protect us."

She ran her hands down Elleci's arms and enclosed Elleci's hands in her own. "If our parents hadn't believed we'd be able to survive on Earth once they were gone, don't you think they would have sent us back here right away? But they didn't. They made special arrangements for us to be raised with the humans instead, because they knew we belong on Earth. So help us do what we were born to do. Help us become the Guardians our parents wanted us to be … please."

Elleci hesitated for a long moment. “I am not allowed to impede on your duties as Guardians, but I, too, have a directive. That is to protect you.”

“Come with us then. We welcome your protection.” Sofia squeezed Elleci’s hand to emphasize her words.

“To Earth?”

“Yes,” Sofia and Zach responded simultaneously.

“If we were to go to Earth, would you agree to continue your training and listen to my and Gilamu’s directions? And will you not engage with the Anunnaki and Nukiri before you are ready?”

All three eagerly nodded their heads.

Elleci considered this for a moment more.

“All right, I will consent to go with you. Earth will be in the proper position for our arrival at 3:00 a.m. Meet me in the training center at that time. In the meantime, I will reprogram and repurpose the transmitters used to block your memories into a GPS tracker and communication link between us. I suggest you use this time to get some nourishment and rest.”

Liv let out a whoop and Sofia covered her mouth with her hand. They had done it!

But before Sofia’s elation could even settle in, a barrage of questions flooded her head. What do they do now? Daher wasn’t going to just give up Maddie and the Schultzes. They didn’t even know where he was keeping them. And what if they failed? What would happen then?

Sofia’s head began to throb. She squeezed her eyes shut. So much was counting on the three of them being someone they didn’t know how to be.

Her parents had put their faith in Ea to watch over her. She didn’t know who Ea was, but she assumed it was the Pleiadian God. She herself had never been a religious person, though she always felt there was a higher being controlling her life and not for the better.

A spark of anger flared in her stomach.

Ea, are you the one who's been messing with me all this time, making me fight every day to survive?

She caught herself and made an effort to push her resentment back. Now was not the time to bring up the past. They needed help that only a higher being could supply.

Look, my parents believed in you, and I deserve a break for once. So, help us defeat Daher or at least help us get Maddie and the Schultzes back. You owe me that much for all that you've put me through.

If that isn't something you can do, then please just do me a favor and stay the hell out of my way!

TWENTY-FOUR

Sofia silently walked back to the dorm with Zach and Liv as they babbled about their return to Earth. But as soon as she crossed the threshold and caught sight of Nick working in one of the scorpion chairs, her stomach dropped.

"Holy crap! We forgot about Nick," she said telepathically to Zach and Liv. *"What are we going to do with him?"*

At that moment, Nick looked up. "Oh, hey guys …" His eyes widened and an oh-shit-something's-happened look spread across his face. "What's going on?" he asked, his voice rising at the end.

"I'll handle this," Liv said under her breath, and instantly curved her lips into a flirty smile. "Hey, Nicky," she purred as she seductively swayed up to his chair. "Nothing much is going on." Her Texan accent was extra thick, as it always seemed to get whenever she was trying to manipulate someone. "We're just fixin' to go away for a bit."

"Oh. Where ya going?"

Liv flipped her hair and knelt beside his chair, letting her breast brush against his arm. "We're just gonna pop down and pick up our parents and Sofia's friend. Nothing you need to worry about."

His eyes widened. "But aren't they on Earth?" he croaked, looking from Liv to Zach and Sofia.

"Well, yeah, we're —" Liv started.

"If you go, I'm going too." He lifted the display screen out of his way and swung his legs around to rise. An involuntary moan escaped his lips.

Liv reached out and clasped his arm to the chair to hold him in place, her siren persona gone. "Nick, please … you're in no shape to go anywhere. And honestly, you'd just slow us down. Plus, I … we …" she quickly corrected, "don't want you to get hurt again."

Nick pulled his arm free and scrambled out of the chair, standing as straight as he could, which was still partly hunched over. "I won't get in your way. I swear. I could do surveillance or whatever you needed me to do."

Liv looked over her shoulder at Zach and Sofia for help.

"Nick—" Sofia started.

"Or you could do your thing and heal me. Then I won't slow you down," Nick cut in.

Liv looked at him as if he'd gone mad.

"I know you have the power to do it. I read it in the files," he added.

Liv spun around to Zach; her eyebrows raised in a question. "What's he talkin' about?"

Zach gave her a two-shoulder shrug in answer, looking as stunned as she was.

"What did you read?" Sofia asked.

"It said that Pleiadians can use energy to heal."

Sofia's jaw dropped and her mind whirled. "What else did it say?"

"That's all. Just that you have the power to heal some injuries."

There was so much they still didn't know about being a Pleiadian, but the ability to heal?

Oh!

Sofia turned to Zach. "Remember the cut I got on my head in the cavern at the maze?"

His brow puckered, but he nodded.

"And remember it was gone when I woke up in Cairo? There wasn't even a red mark to show where it had been."

Zach's eyes widened in recollection. "Yeah, I remember. The catch in my knee was gone after that, too. So, what? You think Will fixed us while we were out?"

"There ya go. Proof. Now do your magic so I can go with you." Nick's face shined with the hope of a young boy asking for a puppy.

"Bro, just because someone else can heal doesn't mean we can." Zach's voice held an edge of actual regret.

"But I saw you shoot energy from your hands and throw Daher across the room. How different can it be?"

A long moment of silence followed before Liv hesitantly spoke. "Maybe we could give it a try?"

Zach turned on her as if she'd suggested they announce to the world they were aliens. "Are you kidding? This isn't like trying out a new cheer routine. We have no idea how to do something like that."

Sofia listened to the two argue for a second, then turned to Nick. "I've never tried this before and I don't know if it'll work, so don't get your hopes up."

She vigorously rubbed her palms together and placed one hand over the front of his wound, the other hand over the back. Then, after releasing the air from her lungs, she closed her eyes, consciously relaxed her muscles, and concentrated on collecting the energy in the room. The fiery ball in her abdomen instantly came to life and started to expand until it was pressing against her ribs.

Beneath her hands she could feel heat coming from his wound as well as from the incision where he'd been cut open. In her mind's eye she saw a blurry dark mass of injured tissue deep inside him that had not yet healed.

Focusing on that mass, she released her energy.

A woozy feeling rippled through her and the hair on her arms stood on end as the energy surged out of her.

She did her best to let just a little out at a time, but it quickly became too much for her to control. Within seconds, the room began to spin. Then, a blinding light exploded in her head.

"Sofia!" Someone called her name from far away.

"Sofia, are you okay?" A hand softly shook her shoulder.

She struggled to open her eyes, but she didn't have the strength to lift her eyelids. A warm hand pressed against her forehead, and an electric current ran down her spine, reawakening her body.

She opened her eyes to find Zach's scowling face hovering inches above hers. His closeness startled her. She recoiled and tried to scoot back, but he stopped her with a hand on her shoulder.

"Just relax and be still. You're gonna be all right," he said tenderly.

She frowned and looked around. Liv and Nick were also bent over and staring at her.

What's going on? Why am I on the floor?

She brushed Zach's hand off and pushed herself up to her elbows, forcing the others to retreat. "What happened?"

"You fainted," Liv said.

Sofia blinked in disbelief.

"Yeah, you were healing me, then just keeled over," Nick added.

"Oh, God, Nick ..." The memory of what she had done came back in a flash. She sat up too fast and the room tilted again. "Did I hurt you? I'm so sorry. I thought I—"

"No, no, don't be sorry," he cut her off. "I'm healed. Look!" He stood up straight and beamed as he held his arms out to the side. "I won't slow you guys now."

The Segway robot came racing through the door pushing a scaled-down version of the CDT chair. Without saying a word, it took Nick by the arm and forced him into the chair.

"Hey!" Nick yelled, struggling to pull his shirt down as the bot lifted it to retrieve a cord from a small device attached to his chest. But he was no match for the bot, who inserted the end of the cord into a slot in the chair.

A 3-D image of Nick's body materialized in the air above a wide band he wore on his wrist. A small, shaded box moved up and down the length of the image scanning it, but nothing flashed as an issue and no warning bells went off. And only one of his vital numbers to the left of the diagram blinked red—his heart rate.

"Your pulse rate is elevated," the robot said, poking around his side. "You need to rest."

Nick slapped its hand aside. "Stop it! I'm fine. Let me out of this thing."

"You are not yet one hundred percent. You need rest," the robot persisted.

Nick's cheeks turned pink, and he avoided looking at the three watching. He yanked the cord connecting him to the chair and stood. "I'm good enough. Go back to your closet and leave me alone."

The robot quieted but did not leave.

"So, are we going to Earth or what?" There was determination written all over Nick's face.

Sofia struggled to her feet with Zach's help. She felt weak and completely drained. What had happened was a blur, but like Nick, she put on a brave face so the others wouldn't know.

"Since we don't leave until 3:00 a.m., I'm going to get some rest," Her voice sounded weak even to her. "I'll meet you guys down here at 2:50."

She steeled her back, but her knees buckled after one tentative step.

Zach took hold of Sofia's arm to make sure she stayed upright.

"I think getting some rest sounds like a good idea for all of us," he said, keeping a firm grip on Sofia's arm.

As he helped her up the stairs, he whispered, "What happened back there? Did you really heal him?"

"I seriously don't know. He wants us to believe I did, but he could just be saying that so we don't leave him behind. But one thing I do know is I might've done some real damage to him if I hadn't blacked out. The energy was totally too much for me to handle."

Liv bounced up behind them. "Can you believe we actually have the ability to heal people? That's so cool."

Zach shot a disgusted look over his shoulder. "Didn't you hear what Sofia said? She could have seriously hurt Nick."

"But she didn't, and with more practice —"

Zach spun around at the top of the stairs. "Are you fuckin' kidding me? What if we end up killing someone while we're *practicing*." He added air quotes to the word practicing.

His words hit Sofia like a slap.

God, what was I thinking? What if I had killed Nick?

Elleci was right. They needed more training to learn how to control their powers. They also needed to know what powers they actually had.

Sofia grimaced. It wasn't likely that Daher would just idly sit by until they got up to speed. And who knows how much time Maddie and the Schultzes had before Daher did something drastic … if he hadn't already.

Crap!

The weight of the world suddenly felt as if it was riding on Sofia's shoulders. And even worst, she felt as if she had completely lost control of the situation and had no idea what to do. But the thought that froze the blood in her veins was that she would let everyone she cared about down.

How would she be able to live with herself if that happened?

TWENTY-FIVE

The bridge of Sofia's nose burned with unshed tears as she listened to Zach and Liv bicker. After a second, she swiped her hand under her nose and staggered toward her room.

Zach looked around, "Hey, you okay?"

Sofia nodded her head as she stepped through the door and went straight to the bed. She fell onto it and covered her face with her hands. The mattress automatically adjusted to her body and a faint smell of lavender wafted over her, but she had too much on her mind to calm down.

With a groan, she rolled to her side and pressed the pillow over her ears to muffle the words that were running on a loop through her head —*I could have killed him.*

Even the thought of being the cause of someone getting hurt made it hard to breathe.

To take her mind off Nick, she pictured Daher's face. Supposedly, she had the tools to defeat him, but would those tools be enough? And more importantly, would she learn how to use them in time?

She squeezed the pillow tighter around her head, but the doubts kept coming.

Sixty seconds later, Sofia's internal alarm went off and her eyes shot open as if someone had yelled her name.

Her parents hadn't given up and neither would she.

She filled her lungs and whispered to the air, "I was born to do this job. And I have the knowledge within me to succeed. Dad said so, and he can't lie so it has to be true."

Sofia rolled to her back and stared up at the ceiling as her brain churned with a barrage of *what ifs* and *should haves.*

Minutes turned into hours, and all too soon it was time for her to get up, even though she'd gotten very little rest. She stumbled her way into the shower and came out a short time later wrapped in a towel. A pile of clothes had been delivered while she was showering and were sitting on the bed next to a pair of ankle-high boots.

She walked over, picked up a small rectangular box of contacts. "I don't wear contacts, so what are these for?" she wondered out loud.

"The box contains micro-computing lenses that will conceal the color of your eyes," Esos answered. "They are also equipped with zoom capabilities, a compass, and the ability to read heat signatures. To activate the different program options, look up to the left corner and use your eyes as a mouse to scroll down, then squint to select."

Sofia stared at the box and shook her head, feeling very much like Alice stumbling through a wonderland of Pleiadian technology with no idea of what was going to be revealed around the next turn.

Setting the box to the side, she lifted a deep teal top lined with a golden film that was as thin as plastic wrap.

"The clothes are protective gear made for your journey. I also sent you a drink to renew your energy and give you nutrients that will sustain your body," Esos said.

Sofia looked over her shoulder. The niche by the door was back and in it sat a tall glass filled with an unappealing-looking green liquid.

She blew out a sigh, let the towel drop to the floor, and slipped the top over her head. Next she pulled on a pair of ordinary-looking skinny black pants, and lastly, she put on a collarless, form-fitting black biker jacket. Both pieces were lined with the same golden film as the shirt and looked like they were made of leather, but the fabric was actually a lightweight, very comfortable synthetic.

None of the pieces looked like they would provide much protection, but she'd seen enough of the Pleiadian technology to trust that they would.

After putting in the contacts, Sofia zipped the jacket halfway up and stood in front of the mirror. The image that looked back at her was pretty badass and looked nothing at all like the nerd who'd left Iowa a week ago.

That thought made her blush even though she was alone.

If only I was as badass as I look.

She cocked her head. Maybe her look would fool Daher and his men long enough to give her an advantage.

She snorted. Who was she kidding?

"It is 2:50," Esos said, breaking into her thoughts.

Sofia turned away from the mirror, tugged on the hem of the jacket, and mumbled under her breath, "Well, here goes nothing."

She descended the stairs, feeling very much like she was walking to her doom.

Zach and Nick were already waiting by the door arguing.

Zach, dressed in black with a jacket like hers, turned to her in exasperation as she approached. "Will you please tell him we aren't going to a Comic Con, and this getup he's got on is gonna draw too much unwanted attention."

"There's nothing wrong with what I've got on!" Nick shot back, holding his arms out to show off his belted V-neck tunic, loose pants tucked into boots, and a long, hooded cloak.

Sofia bit down on the side of her cheek to hold back a laugh. If she didn't know better, she would have thought Nick had come straight off the set of a Star Wars movie. The only thing missing was a lightsaber hanging off his belt.

"Umm, you look really good, Nick, but don't ya think the cloak is a little much?"

Nick opened his mouth to reply, but his attention got diverted by Liv, who at that moment came down the stairs.

Liv's sleek, shiny hair was pulled over one shoulder, and unlike Sofia, she looked hotter than a supernova in her skinny black pants and biker jacket. And the air in the room seemed to evaporate in her heat.

Liv smiled coquettishly when Nick whistled under his breath and seductively swayed her hips up to the boys.

"Ya'll ready?" she purred, threading one arm through Zach's, and the other one through Nick's, who was practically drooling.

Without even looking at Sofia, Liv led the boys out the door, leaving Sofia standing there by herself.

Lord help us, Sofia thought, rolling her eyes to the ceiling as she followed after them.

TWENTY-SIX

Elleci was waiting for them at the training facility, dressed in a similar black outfit as the Guardians instead of in her usual blue robe. She scanned the three from head to toe, giving each a nod of approval.

To Nick she simply said, "Get rid of the cloak and tuck your shirt into your trousers."

Nick's face fell, but to his credit he did as she asked without arguing.

She handed each of the three Guardians a wide black band for their wrists.

"This is how you will communicate with me when we are apart. Push the center of the Atlantean symbol and speak out loud. My responses will come through the microchip in your head."

She motioned for the three to come closer together. "Earth is in position. Are you ready to proceed?"

Sofia moved up next to Zach and Liv and silently prayed this wasn't a mistake.

"Join hands, please, and make a circle," Elleci said.

"We've already tried the circle thing. It didn't work," Liv said, her voice high with anxiety.

"You must have been trying to return through Khufu, which has collapsed and is no longer accessible. Any other functional gateway would have worked."

Liv gave a disgusted tsk. "What other functional gateway?"

"There are many gateways on Earth. To travel to one you must have it in mind when you join hands," Elleci patiently replied.

"We weren't thinking of Atlantis II when we came here," Zach fired back. "We didn't even know this place existed."

"From Earth, all gateways lead to Atlantis II," Elleci explained. "It's only when you return to Earth that you have to make a choice."

"So, we can go right to where Daher is holding our families?" Sofia asked, her voice edged with a mixture of awe and hope.

"You could if Daher, as you call him, were holding the hostages at a gateway, which is highly improbable," Elleci said. "Plus, we do not currently know the location where the hostages are being held."

"They're in the Sahara Desert," Nick declared.

Four intense stares darted to him, but Zach was the one who spoke up first. "How do you know that?"

"There's a video of them on the net. I'm assuming it's them, anyway. It's titled, '*Three American tourists held captive in the Sahara Desert.*'"

"Ohmigod, Nick! Why didn't you tell us?" Liv screeched, grabbing onto Zach's arm as if he was her anchor.

"I was going to. But then you came in and told me you were leaving, and then Sofia healed me, and ..." Nick shrugged his shoulders. "I forgot."

Sofia looked at Elleci. "Is there another gateway in the Sahara?"

"No, Khufu was the only one. The next closest would be the original Pleiadian base of Atlantis. It is the one I was going to suggest we use."

"Atlantis? As in the Lost City of Atlantis?" Zach scoffed. "That place is just a myth. No evidence of its existence has ever been found."

"Of course it has never been found," Elleci said. "Pleiadians would not be so irresponsible as to leave their technology somewhere a human could discover it. But I assure you, the abandoned city does exist and is located in a hidden valley at the bottom of the Atlantic Ocean off the western coast of Spain."

Sofia's breath froze in her lungs. *We're going to jump into the Atlantic Ocean?*

"When it became clear the ocean would be reclaiming the city, a spherical shell was built around the data and communications center to preserve it as a gateway. A transport tunnel linking the sphere to the mainland was later added."

Sofia released the breath she was holding.

"That's great, but I wouldn't say the Sahara Desert is close to Spain," Zach said.

Elleci waved off his concern. "It is only a few hours flight away."

"We have no money or passports, though!" Liv sounded near panic.

"That will not be a problem. My contacts will take care of everything," Elleci assured them.

Zach's eyes narrowed. "Contacts? Are you talkin' Will? 'Cause I don't want him to know we're back on Earth. He'll try to stop us."

"I am sorry, but Gilamu already knows you are coming. Esos reported to him as soon as it was agreed upon."

"Fuck!" Zach turned away and raked his fingers through his hair.

"It's okay," Sofia said. "We'll figure it out. Right now let's just concentrate on getting there."

"Sofia's right. We're wasting time. Time Mom and Dad might not have," Liv added.

Zach shook his head and looked around. "So many things have already gone wrong. I just don't want to see this one go south too."

"It won't," Sofia stated with a confidence she wasn't really feeling. She then wiped her hands on her pant leg and took Liv's hand, and held her other out to Zach.

He let out a sigh of resignation, pressed his lips into a thin line, and took both Sofia and Liv's hands. Three beams of light shot into the sky, joining together a few feet up to make one brilliant ray.

Sofia closed her eyes and thought *Atlantis*. A watery image of three rings popped into her head like a long-lost memory. But before she could get a clear impression of it, a loud whoop broke her concentration.

She opened her eyes to find a large wavering oval of iridescent light hovering a few feet away.

Liv's face was a picture of pure elation as she threw her arms around Zach's neck. "We did it, Z!"

Elleci stood to the side of the gateway. "After you."

Zach peeled Liv's arms from his neck to take her by the hand, then held his other hand out to Sofia. She took it without hesitation and reached for Nick's hand.

"Okay, on three," Zach said.

Sofia inhaled deeply on the count of two and held it as the four teens walked into the gateway together.

Frigid air whipped around her, and streaks of lights flashed by. It felt like she was being pulled in all directions at once. In the next heartbeat, she was standing in darkness, dizzy and disorientated, her hands numb from clutching Zach and Nick's hands so tightly.

Elleci walked out of the portal right behind them, and called out, "Emlura."

Soft lights flicked on, showing a good-sized circular room filled with servers. A counter stacked with consoles and control panels encircled the entire room.

Nick stumbled to the closest chair and flopped into it, burying his face in his hands. Sofia, Zach, and Liv leaned heavily on the counter to keep from falling over.

"Put this under your tongue," Elleci instructed, handing each a small, flat pill. "It will help your bodies readjust to Earth's gravity."

Sofia took the pill and closed her eyes. Within moments the dizziness stopped, but she waited several seconds more before she opened her eyes and looked around.

A streak of silver darted past her. She flinched and stood stock still, moving only her eyes. Several more silver streaks zipped by, then another going in the opposite direction.

Fish! She was seeing fish swimming in the murky water outside the sphere, which was completely transparent.

Sofia giggled and spun around to the others.

At that moment, a video of the five of them lit up a twelve-by-twelve section of the clear wall. Another square right next to the first, lit up with a different scene, then another, and within a minute, there were four rows with six videos in each row.

After the video of them inside the sphere, the next four showed different sections of the underwater city. Rays of sunlight cutting through the water distorted the images and created wavering shadows, but she could still make out majestic marine-encrusted columns, structures, and statues of the legendary city.

The other nineteen screens featured landscapes, buildings, and rooms in other parts of the world, one of which showed Will and a group of people huddled around a table.

"Found it!" Zach called, drawing Sofia's attention away from the images.

"Yup, that's it," Nick said over Zach's shoulder. "'*Three American Tourists held captive in the Sahara Desert.*'"

Sofia's heart skipped a beat as she hurried to the computer terminal where Zach was standing and squeezed in between Nick and Liv.

The monitor showed a dark, grainy picture of the Schultzes sitting on the ground next to Maddie. Maddie's head was bent over her lap and her hair was hanging down in front of her face.

The floor of the sphere in Atlantis began to shake, rattling the chairs and equipment.

"Guardians!" Elleci called out sharply. "You must not lose control of your emotions. If the seal breaks on this sphere, we will all be doomed, as will your family. Breathe in and out through your nose and focus on the rhythm of your heart."

Nick turned to Liv, his eyes as big as saucers and his face so pale he could have passed for a goth. Timidly, he put one arm over her shoulder, and rubbed his other hand up and down her arm, frantically whispering, "It's okay. They're going to be okay."

Liv screwed up her face like she was going to lash out, but instead, a small sob came from her throat as she turned and buried her face into his shoulder.

For an instant, Nick looked shocked and unsure of what to do. Then, he wrapped his arms around her and cooed, "It's going to be okay."

Zach leaned against the counter and blew breaths out through his clenched teeth.

Sofia was also devastated, but more so for Zach and Liv for having to see their parents like that. She reached out and placed a hand on top of Zach's.

A charge of electricity ran up her arm.

He turned his head to the side and locked eyes with her. The blaze of the gold ring around his pupils was hidden by his dark contacts, but she could feel his pain and knew he was struggling to reign in his anger.

Sofia put an arm around his waist, pulled him in, and pressed her forehead to his.

"We got back to Earth on our own. We're going to get your parents back, too," she whispered into his mouth that was an inch away from hers.

His hands went to her waist and a tingling sensation fluttered to life in her stomach even though she tried to squelch it.

The memory of his lips pressed against hers replaced all other thoughts in her head. What she wouldn't give to feel that euphoria again right now. But deep down inside she knew kissing him again would only make matters worse.

"A plane has been arranged to take us to Cairo. It leaves in an hour," Elleci said, breaking the spell.

Sofia jumped back and held onto the counter as she struggled to restart her heart.

Liv turned away from Nick, her chin still trembling. "I want to go home, Z," she said and moved into his arms. "We gotta get Mom and Dad and get out of there."

A cold emptiness filled Sofia. It was probably for the best that she, Zach, and Liv would go their separate ways once this was done.

But leaving Zach was going to be hard—like leaving an arm or a leg or half her heart behind.

TWENTY-SEVEN

Sofia turned back to the video of Maddie and the Schultzes.

The three were sitting on copper-colored sand under what appeared to be some kind of canopy. Behind them were several black-capped mounds. The three looked dirty and exhausted, but at least they were still alive.

Look up, she mentally projected, hoping Maddie could sense her. But her friend remained slumped over, her face completely obscured by stringy strands of her hair.

Sofia leaned closer to the screen for a better look.

Maddie's hair looked so much longer than it had a little over a week when Sofia left. Sofia squinted at the image.

Were those purple streaks in Maddie's hair?

Her chest tightened. Maddie thought putting unnatural colors in hair was gross. But another girl Sofia knew always had purple streaks …

She inhaled sharply. *Holy shit!*

Sofia's gaze shot to the girl's left wrist. The arm was turned in a way she could only see the curly S of a tattoo, but it was enough to make her pulse race.

"Ohmigod, could it be?" she looked around for Elleci. "Is there a phone in here? I need to make a call."

"No—" Elleci started, but Nick cut her off.

"I can help out with that." He nudged Sofia aside and tapped a few keys of the onscreen keyboard. "Who d'ya wanna call?"

"Madeline Lewis in Urbandale, Iowa." Sofia's mouth was so dry, she had trouble getting the words out.

"Got it," Nick said and stood back as the sound of a phone ringing filled the air.

The invisible python around Sofia's chest was back and squeezing so hard she could barely fill her lungs. "Come on … come on. Pick up."

On the fourth ring, there was the sound of rustling, then a meek, "Hello?"

Sofia flinched as if she'd been punched in the stomach and her shoulders slumped.

"Hello?" Maddie repeated.

Sofia jerked up and glanced at the video of the three hostages to make sure the girl didn't have a phone up to her ear. "Yes, Maddie, I'm here!"

"Sofia? Ohmigod, is it really you?" came a squeal from the other end. "I was beginning to think you'd forgotten all about us! How are you? Where are you?"

Tears from Sofia's nose splattered the back of her hands splayed out on the countertop. The words she wanted to say got stuck behind the lump in her throat and all that came out was a hoarse half laugh, half sob.

"Sofia, are you there?" Maddie asked. Then, in a distant voice as if she was holding her phone away from her mouth, she added, "Oh, no, I think I've lost her."

"No, no, I'm here." Sofia swallowed hard. "I'm … oh, God, it's so good to hear your voice. I thought you'd been …"

The reality of the situation hit her like a sledge hammer.

Daher had taken Meredith, *not* Maddie.

But why? It didn't make sense … unless he'd somehow mistaken

Meredith for Maddie. Which meant Maddie might still be in danger.

"Maddie, where are you right now?" she asked.

"Ethan and I are on our way to the movies to see—"

"Ethan Newburg? You're dating Ethan Newburg?" Sofia blurted out before she could stop herself. Then realizing what she'd said, she added with as much enthusiasm as she could muster, which wasn't much. "Um … that's great. But I need to know if you've seen Meredith lately?"

Maddie let out a loud snort. "Thank God, no! She quit work a couple days ago, though I don't know why. I was doing the majority of her work. She's such a—"

"Maddie, listen," Sofia interrupted. "I need to know if you know where Meredith is *right now*?"

"No, I don't. She just up and left and no one's heard from her since. And, you know, she doesn't have any friends, so no one really cares what she's doing. But why do you want to know about Meredith?"

An unexpected hollowness filled Sofia's chest. She and Meredith had been archenemies the entire time they'd lived together in the foster home. But it wasn't until this moment she realized Meredith was more like her than she thought—unwanted and unloved.

"Oh … um, I thought I saw someone who looked like her," Sofia said to brush Maddie's question off. It wasn't a lie.

"Really?" Maddie inhaled sharply. "That's weird, because before Meredith left, she told Ella she was going overseas to start a new life. But none of us believed that 'cause you know … well, it's Meredith."

"Yeah," Sofia mumbled, guilt filling the hollowness in her chest. "But listen … if someone comes up to you and offers you a trip overseas for free, don't take it."

"Why would someone … wait a minute, what are you saying? Is that what happened to Meredith?" She didn't give Sofia a chance to answer before she added, "Ohmigod, she took my nametag when she left. Is someone coming after me?"

"I didn't say that. Just be careful. Okay? Don't trust any stranger who approaches you. And *definitely* don't go anywhere with them no matter what they promise."

"Oh-kayyy, this is getting weird. You're kinda scaring me."

"Look, I gotta go. Promise me you'll be careful. Don't go anywhere by yourself, and don't trust anyone, especially if they mention me."

"Sofia, wait! Are you in trouble? Is Meredith in trouble?" Maddie's voice was hoarse with fear.

"I gotta go. I'll call ya later," Sofia said and motioned for Nick to disconnect.

Sagging against the counter, she hung her head and tried to tamp down the emotions raging inside her before they erupted and did some real damage.

Knowing that Maddie was safe didn't cancel out Sofia's guilt. It was still her fault that Meredith was being held captive. And though Meredith wasn't her favorite person, she didn't deserve this.

God, I'm like a human accident waiting to happen. Everything I touch gets messed up and everyone close to me gets hurt.

Zach was watching Sofia, waiting for her to explain. When she remained silent, he asked, "What was that all about?"

She swiped her hand under her nose. "Daher doesn't have my friend, Maddie."

"Yeah, we got that," Liv interjected.

Sofia pointed to the video. "That girl's name is Meredith. She's my old roommate from the last foster home I was in. She's one of those people who'll stab you in the back to get what she wants." She shook her head. "I have no idea how she pulled it off, but she somehow talked Daher's men into taking her instead of Maddie. She must have thought that she could weasel some money out of him, him being a billionaire and all. And I bet you anything that he doesn't know who she really is."

"Wow, she sounds like a great friend," Liv sneered.

"We aren't friends."

"So … since that's not your friend, does that mean you're not going to help us get her and our parents back?" Zach asked.

His words stabbed right through Sofia's chest. "My God, do you really think I'm that shallow?"

Zach had the decency to look embarrassed. "No, of course not. I didn't mean it that way. It's just … everything is so fucked up right now." He blew out a long breath. "I'm scared."

Sofia's indignation dissolved as fast as it rose. "I'm scared, too, but we can't let Daher hurt anyone else."

Liv put two fingers under Zach's chin and forced his head up to look at her. "Dad always said we were an invincible team once we put our minds together. And he's right. We've always been able to figure out our problems. This one's no different. We don't need anyone else's help."

"You are wrong, Olivia," Elleci interjected. "You and Zachary are not prepared to face the Anunnaki or even the Nukiri on your own. It would be reckless and dangerous for you to try."

Liv's cheeks grew pink. "I wasn't saying we should go in there by ourselves. I was just reminding him that when we're together, we've always been unstoppable."

"And don't forget about me," Nick piped in. "I'll be right there with ya."

Liv's cheeks grew pinker.

"I'm with you, too," Sofia said, though she doubted that was what Liv wanted to hear. But like it or not, she was going to be a part of bringing Daher down. And if she had to give up her own life to do it, so be it.

There was only one person who would care if she didn't come back, and Maddie would get over it quickly.

Twenty-Eight

Elleci walked up to a large round hatch in the wall and held her wrist up to a panel next to it. "Come, we must be going."

The whine of a machine starting up broke the silence. The sound of something shifting—something large—followed, and with a hiss, the hatch sprung open. Beyond the opening was a short platform leading up to what appeared to be a sleek train car.

"This tram will transport us to the mainland. From there, a shuttle will take us to the plane," Elleci said and motioned for the four to enter.

"Come on." Sofia said to Nick and walked across the platform onto the tram.

There were two single seats, one in front of the other, on both the right and left side of the door and a row of single seats on the other side of the car. Sofia took the seat to the right of the door. The minute she sat down, an over-shoulder safety harness lowered and locked her in place.

Elleci stepped in last and handed each of them a mask that looked like something a jet pilot would wear. After explaining how to hook the air tube into the side of the chair, she took the seat at the front of the tram behind an instrument console.

Without warning, the tram took off like a rocket, and Sofia

gripped the arm rests with white knuckles as the g-force pushed her back into the seat. To add to her discomfort, Liv, Zach, and Nick's emotions were hammering at her like a battering ram.

What had her parents been thinking when they gifted her this ability? Not only was it terribly distracting, but it made her more anxious. She gritted her teeth. If there was only a way to block it or turn it off.

My shield! The thought hit her so suddenly, she jumped. She had no idea how the shield worked, but it did stop things that would hurt her from getting in. Maybe it could also stop the emotions from getting in.

Holding her breath, Sofia closed her eyes, and pictured her shield descending over her.

As she envisioned it coming down, the weight of the others' emotions receded little by little until they were completely gone.

Ohmigod, it worked! She slumped in her seat, feeling a hundred pounds lighter.

But though she no longer felt the others' fears pressing on her, she still had her own, and they were just as bad.

Zach was lost in thought as the tram sped across the ocean floor and started up an incline that grew steeper by the minute. One scenario after another flipped through his mind as he tried to piece together a plan for rescuing his parents without involving Liv and Sofia. So far, his efforts had been fruitless, and his desperation was beginning to show as the clock ticked down.

He refused to give up, though. The mere thought of Daher getting his hands on Liv or Sofia made his lungs seize and he couldn't breathe.

Liv and Sofia would be furious if he did manage to keep them from going along on the rescue, but they were both unhappy with him now as it was, so not much would change there. And if it came down to a choice between dealing with their fury or the gut-wrenching guilt he'd feel if something happened to one of them, he'd take the fury any day.

The hiss of the hatch opening broke into Zach's thoughts.

Elleci slipped out of her harness and stood. "We have a short distance to go on foot to get above ground. I hope no one is claustrophobic."

Zach waited for the others to file out before he stepped into a tunnel barely wide enough to walk in a single file. The air was thick with humidity, making each breath challenging and droplets of water dripped from the low ceiling onto his head.

He wasn't claustrophobic, but he was thankful when the tunnel opened into a small landing of a spiral staircase. He was the last one up the stairs, which emptied out into a dark space no bigger than a closet. He walked through a door into a large, cavernous room that looked like it had been abandoned for years, going by the debris and dust littering the floor and the graffiti spray painted on the walls.

Elleci was standing in a doorway to the outside talking to someone Zach couldn't see.

As he walked toward her, a hot breeze swept in, swirling up the dust. The smell of seaweed and fish that accompanied it took him back to the family vacations they used to take every summer to the Gulf of Mexico.

At that moment, Elleci stepped aside and Kemen, Will's sidekick who had been at the pyramid with them, entered.

Zach narrowed his eyes and growled, "What's he doing here?"

Kemen put both of his hands over his heart and bowed his head. "It's good to see you again, Guardians. You're looking well."

Zach squared his jaw. "I'm fixin' to get my mom and dad out of that hell hole and there's nothing y'all can do to stop me."

"I'm not here to stop you," Kemen replied. "I'm here to help."

"Oh, yeah? Like the last time when you lied to us and then delivered us straight to Will!"

"I apologize for misleading you. It was a desperate time, and you had no understanding of the danger you were in."

"Who is this guy?" Liv whispered to Zach.

"He's a guy Sofia and I met on the streets of Cairo. He pretended to be a tour guide and said he could get us into Khufu. But he really only intended to deliver us to Will."

"You're not being fair, Zach," Sofia cut in. "He did take us to Khufu, and we wouldn't have gotten out of there alive if he and Will hadn't been with us."

Elleci held a hand up silencing them. "Kemen is not your adversary. He is a loyal Pleiadian and has taken an oath to keep you Guardians safe. He is here now to take us to Cairo, and it would be wise to get moving. According to the latest intelligence, Essol is preparing some kind of cataclysmic event to get your attention."

Sofia's gaze snapped to Elleci. "A cataclysmic event? One that involves Meredith and the Schultzes?"

"I cannot say. The details are not yet known."

Kemen stood to the side so they could exit the building. Zach followed Liv out and gave Kemen another scowl as he passed, but the Pleiadian's eyes were on the sway of Liv's hips as she walked away.

Zach clicked his tongue and opened his mouth, then closed it as inspiration hit him—Kemen's attraction to Liv might be something he could use to his benefit.

"Hey," he said as Kemen came out the door. "I was thinking … this rescue could end up going south pretty fast. You know, like in the pyramid when all the shooting started, and that other girl got killed. It was pure luck that Liv or Sofia didn't get hurt too."

Kemen's eyebrows pinched together as he shot Zach a sidelong glance.

Zach tilted his head toward Kemen and lowered his voice. "Liv is super close to our mom, and there's no telling what she might do when she sees Mom with the Anunnaki. I'm afraid she might do something stupid, which would put us and the entire rescue mission in danger. So I was thinkin' it's probably best if Liv doesn't go into the Anunnaki camp. I would suggest that to her myself, but, of course, she's not going to listen to me. She might listen to you or Will, though.

"And if she stays back, then we'd also have to keep Sofia back, or else we'd have a whole helluva lot of drama on our hands. And trust me on this … you don't want to have to deal with that."

Zach waited for Kemen to say something, but the Pleiadia remained quiet.

"Well, think about it. I know we all want this rescue to go smoothly with no one getting hurt." He gave Kemen's shoulder a pat and slowed his pace so Kemen could go ahead of him.

As he watched Kemen's back, an uneasy feeling settled in his stomach. He didn't like going behind Liv and Sofia's backs. But sometimes you had to do the hard things to take care of the ones you loved.

And he would do just about anything for the two of them.

TWENTY-NINE

Liv's emotions felt like a pile of worms, wiggling over and through each other. One minute she would be worried sick about her parents. The next she would be trying to sort through the being an alien thing. On top of that, this trip, which she had planned on being the turning point in her and Zach's relationship, had become a total disaster. Instead of them becoming closer, Zach seemed to be drifting further away.

And then there was the whole Sofia thing.

Liv wanted to hate her, she really did, especially at those times when it appeared something was going on between Sofia and Zach. But she couldn't. There was something about Sofia that tugged at Liv's heart, and the memory flashes of them as toddlers weren't helping.

At least once they rescued the hostages, Sofia would be going back to Iowa, which would remove her from their lives and solve the problem. Though every time Liv thought of Sofia leaving, an uneasy feeling pricked the back of her mind—a feeling that Liv would lose a vital part of herself.

She shook her head to clear her thoughts. Sofia wasn't the priority at the moment, rescuing her parents was, and that's what she needed to focus on.

They'd been talking about the rescue for days but had yet to come up with a plan on how to pull it off. The biggest issue was that

Daher was holding them in the Sahara Desert. And unfortunately, they weren't wizards and couldn't magically apparate into the camp, grab the hostages, and pop back out. Sneaking in was also a no-go because the Nukiri would be able to see them coming from miles away. Even at night, the moonlight reflecting off the sand acted like a low wattage light bulb, which, of course, was probably the reason Daher had picked that location.

Liv wrapped her arms around her stomach as a sudden wave of guilt washed over her. If she hadn't been so intent on getting Zach alone on a romantic get-a-way, her mom and dad wouldn't be in this mess. Now it was her responsibility to fix it and make everything right.

She shuddered at the thought and closed her eyes. In the background she heard the sound of the waves splashing against the seawall. Then all of a sudden, an overwhelming dusty, earthy smell of sand engulfed her, and the world faded away as a vision moved in.

The dark of night had begun to fade, and the horizon was a clear line between heaven and Earth as Liv raced across a barren landscape inside a human-sized hamster ball equipped with side-by-side stationary chairs. Zach was ahead of her in his own clear ball, and Sofia was directly behind her in another. Two-man hamster balls flanked the three of them on each side and Kemen brought up the rear, in a ball by himself.

"Olivia, increase the strength of the wind and intensify the sandstorm if you can," Will said inside her head. "The cloud needs to be thick enough to completely cloak us. And stay close to Zach's tail so you don't lose him. He's got the map in his head and is the only one who can guide us in."

Lines of concentration creased Liv's forehead under the tinted face shield of her helmet. Her Zurit shuddered as the force of the wind and sand accelerated. She pushed the throttle forward until she could see the faint glow of Zach's vehicle's instrument panel through the swirling brown cloud.

"Livy, listen to me," Zach said telepathically. "I don't care what Will says. I'm going in to get Mom and Dad. But you stay in the Zurit … that's an order. I can't risk Daher getting—"

A hand landed on Liv's shoulder and a charge of electricity shot through her, jolting her out of the vision. She squeezed her eyes tighter together and tried to bring it back, but the vision was gone. Clenching her teeth, she opened her eyes and blinked Kemen's face into focus.

"Are you okay?" he asked, his features dark with concern.

The bright sun and the sound of the ocean and people laughing disoriented her for a second.

She looked around and frowned. "Where are we?"

The crease in Kemen's brow deepened. "We're in Cadiz, Spain on our way to the airport to get a plane to Cairo."

Zach came up behind them. "What's going on?"

The sound of his voice brought back his words from the vision. Liv lifted her chin and replied coldly, "Nothing's the matter. I'm fine."

"Livy," Zach said, catching her by the arm as she turned to walk away. "What happened?"

Liv glared at his hand for a heartbeat, then yanked her arm free. "What makes you think something happened? And even if something did, I can totally handle it on my own."

She stormed off, giving him a scowl that would have made a polar bear shiver.

Zach recoiled and exchanged a what-the-hell-was-that look with Kemen, who responded with a shrug and a shake of his head.

"What was that all about?" Sofia asked, joining the two.

"I have no idea," Zach replied, then added in a louder voice so Liv could hear. "But when her claws come out like that, you want to stay clear."

Liv winced and the fire in her belly expanded.

You think it's okay to risk your life, but because I'm a girl, I have to sit back and do nothing. Well, I've got news for you, mister … I'm the only one who knows how this is gonna go down, and I'm fixin' to make damn sure Will knows that if he wants my cooperation, he has to keep you out of the fight.

This is my mistake and my mess to clean up!

THIRTY

Meredith ground her teeth and swiped at a trickle of sweat running into her eyes. Her once-in-a-lifetime chance to grab the lifestyle she'd always felt she deserved had turned into a true Steven King kind of nightmare. And she didn't even know why.

One minute she had been flirting with the most gorgeous boy in the whole French Riviera and the next she was sweating her butt off in the middle of fucking nowhere.

Her cell mates, Scott and Martina Schultze, insisted that the TV reality show, Road to Riches, was the reason they were all there, but Meredith refused to believe that theory. Though it wouldn't surprise her at all if this was all Sofia's doing. Sofia had probably found out Meredith had impersonated Maddie and had done this in revenge.

"Uh oh," Martina exclaimed, jolting Meredith out of her musings. "Something's going on out there."

Meredith sat up and peered through the strands of greasy, sweaty hair hanging in her face. The Yappers, as she called the guards who reminded her of the little yappy dogs that would just as soon bite you as look at you, were spazzing out and running around. The Rottweilers, who were taller than the others guards and looked like they could have been MMA fighters in a previous life, also seemed more agitated than usual. But the Poodles, who walked around like they were royalty, looked as bored and unimpressed as ever.

She pushed herself to her feet and walked to the line she'd drawn in the sand to designate the boundary of the invisible electrical field that held them prisoner. She'd learned the hard way that though it looked like nothing was there, if she got too close, it would zap the shit out of her. And she had the burn marks to prove it.

Rising onto her tiptoes, she tried to see over the crowd that had gathered at the opposite end of the camp, but all she could see was a large cloud of dust billowing into the sky.

"Looks like someone's arrived," Scott said from behind her. "Either that or it's a dust devil. 'Cept I don't think the guards would get so worked up over something as trivial as a dust devil."

"It must be someone important," Martina said, joining her husband. "Even the big, bald brutes are standing at attention."

After a couple of minutes, the crowd parted to let a camouflage painted 4X4 vehicle pass through. It headed toward a large geodesic domed structure that was three times bigger and sitting away from six other domed structures. The vehicle turned down the side of the larger dome and disappeared behind it.

Two of the Rottweilers moved to the door of the dome and stood guard, though Meredith couldn't imagine why. They were in the Sahara Desert for God's sake. A place that no one in their right mind would come to.

"Well, that was anticlimactic," she mumbled under her breath and walked back to her canvas cot. It and two others were the only pieces of furniture they'd been provided in their prison cell.

"I don't know about that," Martina said. "I have a feeling someone important was in that Jeep. Maybe even Makin Daher himself."

"You really think so?" Meredith jumped up and rushed back to the barrier. "Do you think he knows we're here?"

"*Pfft.* Of course he does. Who do you think put us here?"

Meredith twirled around, her jaw set. "Why do you keep saying that?"

Martina's expression softened. "Ahh, honey." She raised her hand to brush Meredith's hair away from her face.

Meredith recoiled.

Martina's hand fell back to her side. "I know you don't want to believe it, but I'm telling you, that man is the reason we're all here," she added. "He's not who you think he is. He's a bad person. And it's not a coincidence we were brought out here right after I had a run-in with him at the golf clubhouse."

"You're wrong. You'll see." Meredith crossed her arms, stomped back to her cot, and threw herself down, covering her eyes with her forearm to let Martina know she was done listening to her nonsense.

However, the doubts that had been simmering in the back of her mind started working their way to the forefront. They festered there for a moment, before she pushed them away.

No! Mr. Daher's a billionaire. What would he gain from kidnapping the three of us? It's got to be someone else. Someone Sofia's pissed off and who wants a chunk of the show's prize money.

Her cot suddenly pitched, and a raspy voice said, "Get up!"

She peeked one eye out from under her arm. One of the Yappers was standing over her.

Meredith shot to her feet so fast the world tilted to its side. She put her hand on the guard's arm to keep from falling over.

He yanked it away, gave her a look of disgust, and snarled, "Come with me."

"Where're you taking her?" Scott asked, stepping in the guard's way.

The Yapper shoved Scott to the side with a sneer and took Meredith by the arm, dragging her out of the cell.

"Don't you hurt her!" Martina yelled after them, her voice trembling.

Meredith looked back over her shoulder. Scott's arm was around Martina's waist and the legitimate worry on both their faces sent a strange, unfamiliar feeling fluttering through Meredith's chest. No one had ever cared enough to worry about her before.

She raised her hand in an awkward wave and gave them a weak smile. "I'll be all right."

She bit down on her bottom lip, hoping that wasn't a lie.

As hot as it was inside her cell, it was ten times hotter outside in the sun, and the walk across the camp was almost unbearable. By the time they got to the large dome structure where the Rottweilers stood guard, her skin felt like it was beginning to blister.

She preceded the Yapper through the door into a small entryway blocked by another door. He pushed her through the second door.

"Hey, watch it!" she scolded.

Cool air hit her parched skin. She tilted her head back and let out a long sigh of relief.

"Don't just stand there. You're letting the cold air out," said a stern voice with an unrecognizable accent.

Makin Daher himself sat behind a large, polished wood desk, one that looked like it belonged in a palace not in the middle of the desert.

"Mr. Daher!" she gushed and scurried forward. "I'm so glad you're finally here. These horrible men have—"

"Sit!" Daher cut her off.

The harsh coldness of his voice froze her words in her throat and a tiny alarm went off inside her head.

Daher looked her over, the contempt in his eyes sending a shiver up her spine. "I said, sit."

Meredith took a shaky step to the side and sat down on the edge of a padded brocade chair facing the desk, then assumed the pose she used whenever facing a judge: back straight, knees pressed together, and hands folded in her lap.

He steepled his fingertips on top of the desk and drilled her with a penetrating stare.

Oh God, he knows I'm not Maddie.

Tears began to gather behind her eyes.

"Need I remind you who paid your way to France, put you up in a luxury hotel, and gave you credit to buy personal items to the tune of over three thousand euros?"

Fortunately, Meredith was sitting, which was the only thing keeping her stomach from dropping to the floor.

"In return I asked only one thing: that you be here for Sofia when she arrived," Daher continued. "But instead of gratitude for my generosity, you've done nothing but complain about having to put up with a little inconvenience."

"Oh, no, no … you've got it wrong," Meredith stammered. "I'm eternally grateful for all that you've done and for your generosity. I didn't know that Sofia was going to be coming here. No one told me that."

"Eternally grateful, you say?" Daher pursed his lips and raised his eyebrows. "What would you be willing to do to show that gratitude?"

It felt like all the air in the room was suddenly sucked out. She opened, then closed her mouth, not sure what he was alluding to or, for that matter, what exactly she would do to live like a princess again.

A deafening silence hung between them.

Daher blew out a heavy breath and beckoned to the guard at the door. "I guess I made a mistake. I thought Sofia and I could count on you." He gestured to the guard to take Meredith out.

"No, you can … count on me, that is," Meredith said anxiously as the guard stepped up beside her. "I'm here for Sofia, and I'll do whatever you want if you'll send me back to France when this is over."

Daher studied her for a moment, then nodded knowingly. "The Riveria made quite an impression on you, I see. Can't say I blame you. It's a lovely place." He leaned over his elbows on the desk. "I'll tell you what … I'll agree to send you back to France and do you one better. I'll provide you with a stipend of three thousand euros a month for one year, which should get you settled into a nice little apartment and money to spare for food and whatnot, under one condition … you help me out with the show."

Meredith sucked in a sharp breath. Was she dreaming or was this really happening?

"Well?" Daher asked when Meredith didn't answer.

Still too shocked to speak, she nodded eagerly.

The corners of Daher's mouth turned up in a smile, the kind a predator gives its prey. "I'm expecting Sofia and the other two contestants to arrive shortly for the last challenge in the competition. The goal of the challenge is for them to rescue three hostages." He held his hand out. "You and the Schultzes being said hostages."

Ohmigod! She could barely hold back her squeal of delight. "Am I going to be on the show?"

Daher nodded. "You are. And your part is very important. If they do succeed in rescuing you, I want you to signal me from whatever location they take you to."

He handed her a gold chain with a pendant in the shape of two small golden wings joined in the center with a red gem.

"When you arrive at their final destination, push the ruby there in the center, but only after you get inside. That will alert me to your location. My men will then come and take care of the rest."

She stared at him, expecting there to be more, but he just stared back waiting for her reply.

"That's it?" she asked. "I just have to let Sofia rescue me, then signal you where we are, and I get the money?"

Daher spread his hands wide. "That's it."

"Will I have to pay it back?"

"No, it'll be yours free and clear."

She slumped back in the chair and looked down at her hands and the dirt beneath her nails. Her gaze darted back to Daher. "Will I get to shower? I don't want people to see me looking like this."

She lifted a strand of hair and let it fall back.

"If you clean up, it won't look very authentic now, would it?"

"But—"

"Tell you what, we'll tape it with you looking this way first. Then you can take a shower and we'll do a second take and decide which we think will get higher ratings."

A smile spread across her face and grew so wide her dry skin felt like it was going to split. Was this really happening? It seemed too good to be true, but a billionaire like him wouldn't lie. And what was thirty-six thousand euros to him? That desk he was sitting behind probably cost more than that.

"Ohmigod, I can't believe this!" In her whole life she'd never been so lucky. "Thank you so, so much. You don't know what this means to me."

"One more thing."

Meredith's breath caught in her throat. Was this the part where he put an insurmountable stipulation on it?

"You must not mention any of what we've talked about here to the Schultzes or anyone else, especially not to Sofia, Zachary, or Olivia. No one can know about the necklace. Understand?"

"Oh, absolutely. My lips are sealed." She made a key locking motion over her lips. "You can count on me."

"So, it's understood then, that if you so much as hint about anything I've said—France, the money, everything—is off the table." Daher waited for her to nod again, then signaled the guard to take her out.

Meredith walked out in a daze, and it was all she could do to wipe the smile from her face. Luckily, the heat helped with that. As did the thought that her suffering in this god forsaken oven was all because of Sofia.

By the time the Yapper pushed her inside her cell, her resting bitch face was back, and she didn't even have to pretend to be pissed off.

THIRTY-ONE

The shuttle van pulled up to a nondescript hangar outside the main terminal of Jerez International Airport in Cadiz, Spain.

Kemen immediately jumped out and ran to two men and a woman who were coming out of the building as everyone else piled out of the van. After a few minutes, he walked the three to the van and introduced them to the group.

"This is our pilot, Raul."

The man put one hand on top of the other over his heart and bowed his head. "My Guardians."

"And this is Oriel, and Dosha," Kemen said.

The two bowed in the same manner as Raul.

"They will be escorting Nick to Anides, our base in Istanbul," Kemen added.

Nick's eyebrows shot up in surprise, but before he could voice a protest, Kemen went on, "Elleci informed us of your skills, and we feel you would best serve us in monitoring the camp. The latest report has Daher on the move, so you'll have plenty to do keeping track of him and informing us of any new developments."

Liv stepped forward and slipped her arms around Nick's neck. "Kemen's right … computers are your thing and you're really good at it. I'm gonna feel so much safer knowing you're watching over us."

She planted a sweet kiss on his cheek.

Nick froze and appeared to stop breathing.

"Come, our planes are ready." Kemen pointed to two Gulfstream 550 jets sitting on the tarmac.

Zach stepped up and gave Nick a quick one-armed hug. "Thanks bro, I'll owe you one." He looked like he wanted to say more, but instead he gave Nick a pat on the back and walked to the plane.

Sofia ran up next and gave Nick a quick hug. "Thanks for your help. We'll see you soon," she said and hurried after the others, leaving Nick standing there looking forlorn.

The plane ride was uneventful and quiet, which gave Liv a chance to think of how to get Will away from the others so she could talk him into keeping Zach out of the camp. The problem was she didn't really know Will and had no idea how to best approach him. Though she seldom had trouble getting men to do her bidding, something told her Will was different and her usual tactics weren't going to work.

But before she had come up with a solid plan, the plane landed in Cairo.

Unlike the laid-back atmosphere of the Jerez airport, Cairo International was a bustling madhouse. Thankfully, Kemen was with them or they would have been in real trouble, especially when they got to customs. But somehow, though Liv didn't know how Kemen managed it, the five of them were hustled out of the terminal and into a panel van waiting at the curb in no time at all.

The temperature was already sizzling hot and traffic on the streets was bumper to bumper even though it was just a little past eight in the morning. A thick cloud of exhaust and manufacturing fumes blanketed the city, adding a dingy haze over everything and partially obscuring the tops of the modern skyscrapers a few blocks away.

Liv had hoped to sit next to Kemen in the van to gather information about Will, but he climbed into the front passenger seat, and she was stuck in the back.

The driver didn't wait for everyone to get buckled in but took off like he was racing in the Indy 500, swerving around cars to the blare of horns and other drivers yelling obscenities.

Liv was a bundle of nerves when the van finally pulled over to the curb in the old section of the city, letting them spill out onto a street that would be considered an alley in America.

"Stay close," Kemen yelled to be heard above the buzz of the crowd making its way toward the world-famous Khan el-Khalili street bazaar.

The scent of lemon, cinnamon, and cloves infused the air, competing with the foul smells of rubbish piled along the street and in front of buildings where many of the street vendors were still in the process of setting up their stalls.

The small group followed Kemen through the chaotic maze, dodging the hawkers who aggressively thrust their wares at them as they passed.

By the time he turned down a side alley, Liv's patience had waned and if one more peddler had shoved a statue of Bastet or an engraved brass tray in her face, she would have unloaded a string of profanities that would have made a rapper blush.

Kemen seemed oblivious to the onslaught and led them to a newer-looking building and up to a second-floor apartment. Inside were seven people gathered around a table covered with large sheets of paper. An older man with a weathered face turned his head toward the newcomers.

At the same time, a wave of anger erupted from Zach and the tic in his jaw began working.

Liv perked up. *So that's Will?*

In the pyramid, she'd been too focused on Daher and the goon pointing a gun at her to get a good look at the Pleiadian.

Will was tall with broad shoulders, and his auburn hair that brushed the top of his collar had streaks of silver throughout. His eyes were a sapphire blue with golden rings like hers, only the bags under them were deeper and darker and more like someone had given him a good beating.

Will gave each of the Guardians a quick nod, then threw a stern look at Elleci before turning back to the printout and picking up where he'd left off.

"Out of the twenty guards, these three look to be Dracuzians."

Elleci and the Guardians joined the group at the table and stared down at two large aerial photos, one a thermal image and one in black and white. The images showed a camp sandwiched between two large rock masses. At the north end was a grouping of six small domed structures. A seventh dome that was three times bigger than the rest was sitting a ways off from the others. The south end was blocked by a line of parked vehicles. Butted up against the eastern mound at about midpoint sat a panel truck next to a large black square.

"The other guards seem to be a combination of Anunnaki and Nukiri, the bulk being Nukiri. This," Will pointed to the black square, "is where they're holding the hostages. It's been reported they're using a force field as means of containment and that the generator supplying the power is in here." He pointed to the panel truck. "Kemen, it'll be your job to take out the generator."

Kemen nodded.

"We go in at first light tomorrow morning, which should hopefully catch the guards before they're fully awake," Will continued. "Guardians, you'll each have a Zurit to yourself and will transport one of the hostages out in the extra seat."

Sofia and Zach's expression showed their confusion, but Liv nodded her understanding.

A deep crease appeared between Will's eyebrows. Without taking his eyes off Liv, he added, "Zurits are spherical vehicles that can easily traverse the sand dunes in the desert. And since they camouflage themselves by reflecting the surrounding environment, we should be able to get within a half kilometer of the camp before being detected. Isn't that right, Olivia?"

Liv reared up. Everyone was staring at her. She quickly looked back at the images on the table to hide the guilt heating up her cheeks.

"How would she know ..." Zach started to ask, then whipped around to face her. "Did you have a vision?"

She shifted from one foot to the other but kept her head down. She hadn't planned to reveal anything until after she'd made a deal with Will so she wouldn't lose her bargaining power.

"What did you see, Olivia?" Will asked calmly.

She looked up through her lashes. "I … um, I'd like to speak with you in private, please, sir."

Will raised his eyebrows, then pushed off the table without saying a word and limped toward the hall.

Liv threw a sidelong glance at Zach and started to follow, but he caught her arm as she passed him.

"Whaddya doin'?"

"I need to talk to Will for a sec."

"Livy …" Zach said accusingly.

"It's okay. I just need to straighten out a couple things." She pulled her arm free and hurried after Will before Zach could question her more.

Thirty-Two

Will entered a room that was barely big enough to hold a full-sized bed, small bedside table, and wooden chair that were crammed into it.

He eased himself onto the chair and Liv came to a hard stop in the doorway as an agonizing sense of pain punched her in the chest.

She held back a gasp and stared questioningly at Will who was leaning at an odd angle on his right hip with his right hand holding his left arm across his chest. His skin had a yellowish tint to it and his aura was more of a burnt orange color than golden.

"Are you sick?" Liv blurted out, then realized how rude that sounded. "I'm sorry, I …"

Will waved his hand in the air in dismissal. "I'm fine. It's nothing for you to worry about."

Liv moved to the end of the bed and sat down so she could look him in the eye. His pain was literally making it hard for her to breathe.

"Forgive me for saying this, sir, but you're not fine. I can feel your pain."

Will's eyes dilated in surprise. "You can feel my pain?" His shocked expression transformed into one of understanding. "Ahh, yes … Elleci informed me that your parents had gifted you three with special abilities. That is against our laws, you know?"

Liv sat up straighter, but Will gave her a wink and added, "I won't tell anyone if you won't."

"I didn't¬—" she started, but he again waved his hand in dismissal.

"That's a discussion for another day. What's important right now is that you tell me what you saw in your vision."

Liv pressed her lips together and studied him. It was obvious her usual tactics were not going to work, but his pain was making it hard for her to think. She blew out a weary sigh and crossed her fingers, hoping he would understand the position she was in.

"Before I tell you, I need to ask a favor. You know Zach and I grew up together, but what you probably don't know is that we have a special kind of bond that's more than brotherly and sisterly. More than even friends, and I don't …" her voice cracked. She licked her lips. "I wouldn't be able to cope if something happened to him. I mean that literally. It would kill me. So, I'm asking you, please … order him to stay out of the camp."

"Is that what you saw? Something happens to Zach?"

"No, no, nothing like that. But I was interrupted and didn't get to see the whole thing. I know Z, though. He would run straight into a fire to save someone if he thought they were in danger. And for Mom and Dad he'd be even more reckless. There's no limit to what he would do to protect them. That's why I need you to order him to stay back and not leave his Zurit. Lie to him if you must. Just keep him out of the fight."

Will stared at Liv, his look tender, almost fatherly. "You know I can't lie to him even if I wanted to."

Liv opened her mouth to protest, but he held his hand up and continued.

"I can truthfully say I don't want anything to happen to him any more than you do. Actually, I don't want to see any of you get hurt, but this isn't just about Zach, you, and Sofia. This is about keeping the Anunnaki from destroying this world."

Her stomach sank and the air in the room became heavier.

"But I will guarantee you this … the Sons of Ea and I will

continue to do everything in our power to keep you all safe, as we've been doing since the day your parents brought you to Earth," he added.

Liv dropped her gaze to her hands in her lap.

Will tenderly placed two fingers under her chin and lifted her head until their eyes met. "Many people have already sacrificed their lives to keep you three alive, and every one of those men and women in the other room will do the same if the situation demands. But let me remind you that you are a Guardian … the best of us. And, together with Zach and Sofia, you could save worlds if you trust in each other and use the powers your parents gifted you."

Trust in each other. That was what Sofia's father had said in his last video. But that's easier said than done. Especially when none of them knew what they were doing.

Will leaned back in the chair and grimaced. "Now, tell me what you saw in your vision."

Liv bit down on her lip, then related her vision, only leaving out the part where Zach ordered her to stay in the Zurit.

When she was finished, Will stared off into space for a minute.

"What is this map you mentioned that Zach has in his head?"

"I'm not sure what it is," she replied. "He doesn't really know either. The way he described it to me when it helped him win the Texas State Basketball Championship was it was like a diagram laid over his vision that showed him where the plays were going to happen and where he needed to be to get the rebounds."

Will nodded. "And you have control over the wind?"

Liv shrugged. "I guess. I didn't know I did until the vision, so I've never tried to do anything with it. Are there other Pleiadians who can control the wind?"

"I personally have not seen another who could, but I believe there have been one or two mentioned in our history."

Another silent minute passed before Will slapped his leg and rose. The agony from that effort was like a needle jab to Liv, but other than a tightening around Will's mouth, he hid it well.

"This is good and just what we needed. I must tell the others." He turned toward the door.

"Wait," Liv said, stopping him. "Are you going to order Zach to stay out of the camp?"

Will turned that fatherly look on her again. "If I had my way, none of you would go anywhere close to that camp. But again, if I had my way, you would still be in Atlantis II. You insisted on choosing your own path, so how can you deny that same choice to another?"

"But he could get hurt!"

"That is a risk we all take on every day. And you must understand, this is a war. There are no guarantees in war."

With that said, he turned and hobbled up the hall. When he got to the doorway of the main room, he exclaimed in a loud voice to the group, "Olivia has found us a way in!"

Liv sheepishly walked up to the table and tried her best to ignore Zach's glare and the disappointment radiating from him as Will relayed her vision to the others.

"Why didn't you tell me?" Zach asked in her head as the others were discussing a new plan.

Her chest grew tight with guilt, but what could she say … that she didn't have enough faith in him or that she didn't think he could take care of himself?

"I was going to tell you as soon as I clarified a couple of things with Will," she replied without taking her eyes off the table.

"Zach, from what Olivia says, you're able to bring up a map of sorts that will guide us into camp?" Will asked, unaware of Zach and Liv's conversation.

Zach jerked up as if caught doing something he wasn't supposed to be doing.

"Can you tell us how that works exactly?" Will added.

"I, um … I don't know," Zach stammered. "It's only happened twice and both times it just appeared on its own."

"You weren't specifically thinking about the situation or trying to picture what to do or anything?"

"No."

"Hmmm, interesting."

"Do you think it's wise to count on Zach to guide us in?" Kemen asked. "What if the map doesn't appear to him?"

"It will," Liv answered, her tone sharp with conviction. "My visions have never been wrong."

Murmurs and grumblings went around the room until finally Elleci spoke up.

"I have spent the better part of the last six days with the Guardians and have personally witnessed some of their unique powers. It is true they are not one hundred percent proficient in controlling their abilities, but if you allow me to work with Zachary, I can get him ready."

Will studied her for a moment, then said, "See what you can do to get him up to par." He turned to one of the women at the table. "Alazne, you go with Liv and make sure she'll be able to produce a sandstorm. The rest of us will sort out the final details."

Elleci nodded her head. "Do you have a room where we can work in private?"

Will tilted his head toward one of the men at the table. "Show them to the apartment next door."

Liv wanted to run after Zach and tell him she was sorry, but she really wasn't, and she couldn't lie. All she'd been trying to do was keep him safe. And she'd do it all over again even if it meant he'd be mad at her for as long as he lived. Because the only thing that mattered was him being alive.

THIRTY-THREE

Sofia remained at the table, but instead of listening to the discussion, her mind churned with thoughts of the impending raid. She had hoped to convince Will to assign Zach and Liv some duty that would keep them out of the Anunnaki camp, but Liv's vision had changed all that.

So, now she had to figure out another way to keep them safe, because she was pretty sure her shield wouldn't extend far enough to cover them in separate vehicles.

An intense swell of anguish suddenly engulfed her, jolting her out of her thoughts. She looked up. The room had emptied except for Kemen and Will, who was leaning on his hands on the table, his chin resting on his chest.

Sofia stepped closer and put a hand on his arm, then yanked it back as a sharp, knee buckling pain shot up her arm. "Oh my gosh, are you okay?"

"I'm fine," Will replied through clenched teeth.

"No," she shook her head slowly. "You're not fine. You're in a lot of pain."

He grimaced. "You can feel others' pain, too?"

Sofia turned to Kemen, and with the sharp tone of a mother defending her child, asked, "Why haven't you healed him?"

Will answered before Kemen could open his mouth. "Some things can't be healed by our energy. But don't worry about me. Once we get your friend, Maddie, and the Schultzes back, I'll have this taken care of."

"She's not my friend."

Will craned his neck to look at her, his eyebrows raised in surprise.

"Daher took the wrong girl," Sofia went on to explain. "The girl at the camp's name is Meredith."

An amused look wiped out the pain on Will's face. "Daher made a mistake? Interesting." He looked over at Kemen. "Another sign the pressure is getting to him. Too bad we can't be there to see his reaction when he learns of his error."

His gaze returned to the images on the table. "But it makes no difference that he has the wrong person. She's a human and we have a duty to protect and rescue her."

Sofia bit down on her lower lip.

I hope he feels as strongly about protecting Zach and Liv.

She swallowed hard. "While we're talking about protecting people, I wanted to ask you about Zach and Liv."

A knowing smile tugged on the corner of Will's mouth. "Let me guess. You want me to keep them from engaging with the Anunnaki?"

"Well, yeah … but for a good reason."

His wry smile was disconcerting and the rest of the words she had prepared vanished.

Will walked around the table and gingerly sank onto a chair. "I worried that separating you from the other two at such a young age would diminish the bond you three had forged in the few short years you had together. But I can see I had no need to worry. Your connection is as strong as it ever was."

His lungs rattled with a cough, and he winced. Sofia and Kemen both started forward, but he waved them off and went on.

"From the moment you were born, you three have been protective of one another. Or so I was told. I wasn't there. But it lightens my guilt to see that attribute has stayed with you. It will greatly help you fulfill your destiny, which, as I tried to explain to Liv, is the reason why I'm not so much worried about you three as I am about the human race and this planet. Humans have no one to stop the Anunnaki but us. If we don't succeed, the Earth will be decimated the same as Pleiades was."

Sofia inhaled sharply. "The Anunnaki destroyed our planet?"

An inexplicable sense of loss swept over her, even though she'd never been to Pleiades.

"Not completely, but they tried," Kemen replied. "They took advantage of a time when our military was at its weakest—right after we sent replacement troops out for those that were patrolling other worlds. They snuck in a small platoon of their agents, but not to go to battle with our people. To poison our waters and air and make our world uninhabitable." His tone dripped with contempt. "It was cowardly. But that's the way of the Anunnaki. If they know their brute force can't overpower the militia of a planet, or if they see no chance of obtaining new slaves and resources, they destroy the planet.

"They plan to do the same thing here on Earth if we don't stop them. And we can't stop them without your, Olivia, and Zach's help," he added.

Sofia put her hand over her mouth, feeling more lost than she'd ever felt.

"But as far as your request, my dear, you can rest easy," Will said, "We have no plan to send any of you into the camp. If you had completed your training, it would be a different story. But as it is, and with Essol's presence in the camp, the risks are too high. Though I know the time is coming sooner than we would all like when you Guardians will have to step up and fulfill the purpose for which you were created."

There's that word again.

"You keep using the word *created*. What does that mean exactly? I know for a fact we aren't AIs like Elleci because we have real flesh and blood. So are you saying Pleiadians don't have ... um, you know." Her cheeks felt like they were on fire. "Um ... do they not make love?"

Will let out a loud guffaw, which brought on another coughing fit.

When he was able to speak again, he said, "Yes, we have the birds and the bees, and we couple the same as humans. Where we differ is that we remove the eggs from the mother, externally fertilize them, and gestate them in a birthing pod instead of the woman's womb. We find it safer for both fetus and mother that way. I used the term created only in reference to your parents altering your genes. By doing that, they virtually created the most powerful Guardians to have ever lived."

A shiver ran through Sofia at the thought of Pleiadians being born in a pod. It sounded so Hollywood B movie kind of thing.

"Now if you'll excuse me." Will pushed himself up to his feet with a great effort. "I'm going to get some rest while I can. I suggest you both do the same. You're going to need all your strength tomorrow."

Sofia watched him limp down the hall and lowered her voice so only Kemen could hear. "What's wrong with him?"

Kemen looked up from tapping something into a wide wrist band and gazed at Will's back. "He was caught in the collapse of the cavern in Khufu. It took us over twenty-four hours to find him trapped under a large slab of bedrock. By then he was close to death.

"We were able to heal his leg enough that he can walk with a splint, but his liver is damaged beyond repair. He needs a transplant but won't agree to surgery until you and the hostages are all safely back in *Anides*."

Sofia was too shocked to speak. She had no idea Will's injuries were so serious.

She balled her hands into fists, pushing her fingernails into her palms to keep from screaming. The light above the table flickered off.

Crap! That was all they needed right now—for her emotions to bring the whole building down.

She filled her lungs and pictured her powers, which she imagined to be a mini sun in her abdomen, and willed them to grow smaller. It took several seconds of intense concentration and deep breaths before the blazing ball of energy began to respond and she no longer felt as if she would explode.

As her heart rate slowed, a new resolve took form.

The Anunnaki had already taken so much from her. She couldn't let them take Earth too. It was still hard to wrap her mind around the idea that she, Zach, and Liv had special powers, but denying them had done nothing but cause trouble. The same with denying that the three of them were bound together. Nothing good had come of that, either, and nothing would until they fully accepted the fact that they were the *three* Guardians.

A new sense of purpose swept through Sofia.

She didn't always see eye to eye with Zach and Liv, but they were as much a part of her as she was a part of them. And they were the only family she had now.

And families stick together.

THIRTY-FOUR

Dawn had begun to nudge the darkness away as Sofia crouched behind an outcropping on a mini volcano shaped mound alongside Will, Kemen, Zach, and Liv. The camp was over half a kilometer away, but thanks to their high position and their contacts, the yellow and orange thermal images of figures milling about in the camp were clearly visible.

"There's a lot of activity down there for this early in the morning," Kemen said from Sofia's right. "I don't like it."

As she shifted up to get a better look, Nick's voice came into her head. *"Come in Rogue One. This is Red Leader. Over."*

"Nick?" Liv asked. "Is that you? …How am I hearing you?"

"Dosha hooked me into the microchip in your heads so I could directly communicate with all of you," Nick replied. *"She linked me into Will and Kemen's comms, too. Over."*

"So, who's Rogue One?" Zach asked.

"I've given your team that call sign, 'cause, you know, you're out there to stop the evil Empire like the Rebel Alliance did. Over."

Zach rolled his eyes and shook his head.

"I saw that. Over."

Sofia looked around to find Nick.

"Look up, over," Nick added.

All eyes turned skyward and toward a speck about the size of a dragonfly hovering above their heads. Its wings dipped right, then left, then leveled out as two miniscule UV lights blinked on, then off.

"Is that a drone?" Liv asked.

"Yup. State of the art, baby. I'm heading over to the camp to monitor things up close for you. Over."

"You don't have to say over every time, Nick," Will said. "Do you have news for us?"

"Yeah, but you're not gonna like it. A truckload of men are heading toward the camp. They left Daher's compound about two hours ago. Ov …"

Sofia and Liv simultaneously jerked around, their tension literally crackling in the air.

"Do you think he knows we're here?" Sofia asked, pushing the words out through her heart, which had jumped into her throat.

"Thank you, Nick," Will said absentmindedly and stared off into the desert.

"Does this mean we'll have to trash our plan?" Zach asked.

Will didn't respond.

"Will!" Zach yelled to get his attention. "Are we still doing this or what?"

The older Pleiadian gave a slight shake of his head as if coming out of a daydream. "We're not changing the plan. Kemen, go let the troops know we move out in ten."

Kemen scrambled to his feet and scurried down the rocky mound to where the thirteen Zurits and a Defiant X stealth helicopter were waiting.

Will wiped his hand down his face. "I don't know how Essol would know you're back on Earth, unless …" He let his words trail off and stared back out at the desert. "It can't be a coincidence that he arrived at the camp yesterday and is now bringing in more men."

Liv put a hand over her mouth.

Zach spun around, his ire making Sofia flinch. "What the fuck! Daher's in the camp and you didn't tell us?"

"You had enough on your plate, learning to control your abilities. You didn't need to worry about anything else. Besides, Daher being there changes nothing. You three never were going into the camp."

Will pushed himself to his feet, which seemed to take a great deal of his strength.

Zach jumped up, too, his fists clenched ready to fight. "Whaddya mean we aren't going into the camp? You can't get there without me and Liv."

Will studied him for a moment, his expression turning sad as if he was saying goodbye to a long-lost friend. "You're so much like your father."

He then added in a tone of authority, "This is how it's going to go down. You're going to take us to the camp, then wait with the Zurits for someone to bring your parents out to you. End of story."

He turned to start down the hill, but halted and turned back to face the Guardians, regret rolling off of him in waves.

"Your parents charged me with looking after you three and making sure the Anunnaki didn't find you. I know I've made mistakes and I own them, but I got you a full fifteen years to grow and develop. That's not bad considering Essol had every Dracuzian out looking for you." He suddenly looked exhausted.

"I hadn't planned on exposing you to the Anunnaki and all of this for a few more years, but the reality show changed all that. Now the best thing I can do for you is to let you go and have faith that you will do the right thing and accept the mantle of Guardian that's been bestowed upon you.

"And I do have faith in you because I know you have a wealth of knowledge in your DNA from centuries of Pleiadians who have come before you. More importantly, you have each other. And I cannot stress that enough." His voice became a little desperate. "You are each one-third of a whole, and though you have your own unique powers, you'll never be as strong or as effective apart as you are together. That's why you must train and put your differences and insecurities aside or the future of Earth is lost."

His words were a slap across Sofia's face. Not only did they sting, but she knew in her heart they were true.

Will looked as if he wanted to say more, but instead he took a deep breath and proceeded down the hill, calling back over his shoulder. "We leave in eight minutes."

Sofia reached out and entwined her fingers with Zach's and Liv's. A surge of energy ran up both her arms, sending a tingle throughout her body. She squeezed their hands. When Zach returned the gesture, her emotions swelled, then swelled even more when Liv did the same.

Liv started to pull away without saying a word, but Sofia held her back.

"Guys … wait …" Sofia sniffed back the tears gathering in the bridge of her nose. "They wiped my memory when I was little, making me forget you, but my heart always remembered. And … well, I know there have been some tough times over this last week and a half, but I'm really glad I had the chance to get to know both of you again," her voice quivered. "I hope we can stay friends."

She pulled them both in for a hug to hide the embarrassment that was heating up her cheeks.

"I know what you're doing," Liv whispered in Sofia's ear. "But you can save your energy for the Anunnaki, 'cause Zach's already taken."

The spark of hope inside Sofia deflated like a balloon. She pulled back with denial on her tongue, but she knew it would do no good.

Oblivious to what Liv said, Zach put his arm around both their shoulders. "We're more than friends. And we're gonna show Will that we're not as useless as he thinks. But right now we better get down there, 'cause I wouldn't put it past him to leave without us."

Sofia wasn't sure how she made it down the hill, but before she knew it, she was in the midst of activity at the bottom.

Will was talking to Kemen off to the side and motioned Liv over.

Liv held up a finger to say just a minute and faced Zach. "Promise me you won't do anything stupid."

The tic in his jaw began to pulse and his lip pressed into a thin line.

She stepped up until they were practically nose to nose. "I mean it, Z. You don't need to go and be the hero, 'cause if you get hurt, I'll kick your ass when we get back." She threw her arms around his neck and gave him a peck on the lips, then leaned back. "I love you."

"I love you, too," he said in return.

She gave him another quick kiss, then flashed Sofia an I-told-you-so look before she ran to Will.

A dull ache ricocheted off the empty cavern of Sofia's chest as she turned to walk away. Zach caught her hand and stopped her, and a tentacle of his fear snaked around her arm. The hairs on the back of her neck stood on end. She raised her eyebrows in question.

"Do you believe Will's excuse for not telling us Daher's at the camp?" he asked.

The question caught her by surprise. She frowned. "Yeaaah … why wouldn't I?"

"I don't know, it's just … he said himself it's not a coincidence that Daher found out about the raid."

"What? You think Will told Daher?"

"Yes … no …" Zach ran his fingers through his hair. "I don't know. There's too much stuff I don't understand. I don't know what to think. But it pisses me off that he treats us like little kids and keeps things from us. I know there's more stuff that he's not telling us."

"You're right. He's not telling us he's dying."

Zach jerked up straight. "What?"

"Kemen told me," Sofia said. "Will was seriously injured in the pyramid and needs surgery, but he insists on completing this raid first."

Zach's mouth dropped open.

"Zach, Sofia come," Elleci called. "You need to get in your Zurits."

They both looked around.

Sofia turned back to Zach. "Look, I know Will hasn't always been one hundred percent up front with us. But I think he really does have our best interest at heart. After we get back, we'll sit down and ask him all your questions. Okay?" She could feel Liv's glare on her back. "Right now, though, we've gotta go. They're waiting on us."

She squeezed his hand, then released it.

"Sofia," Zach said in a rush as she started to move away. "Don't get in a Zurit. Stay here. It's too big of a risk for you to go into the camp. Besides, there's no reason for you to go. We'll get your friend out and bring her back for you."

She clicked her tongue and opened her mouth to respond, but he cut her off.

"I know what you're going to say … that we're stronger together. But I can't lose you again. Not after I just found you."

Sofia's heart skipped a beat and for a moment she was at a loss for words. Did he really care for her after all or was he just being a good guy? She so wanted to believe it was the former, but their relationship had been such a roller coaster she was afraid that it could just be her wishful thinking. Even so, there was no doubt the longing and love she felt for him.

She put a hand on his chest, hoping he could feel it the way she could feel his emotions.

"I don't want to lose you, either," she whispered. "That's why I have to go. I'm the one who has the shield that'll protect us."

"Let's go!" Kemen shouted, cutting off Zach's reply.

Sofia knew her nose was probably beet red, but she held his gaze, wanting him to read in her eyes what she couldn't say aloud.

"Z, come on!" Liv yelled, breaking the spell.

His head swiveled to Liv, then turned right back to Sofia. "Promise me, then, you won't go anywhere near Daher and won't take any risks."

"Ditto," she said, and though she wanted more than anything to press her lips against his, she turned and ran to the Zurit that Krogen waved her to.

With Krogen's help, she climbed up and strapped in. Then,

after giving her a brief lesson on how to use the controls, which were similar to a joystick in a video game, Krogen hurried off to get into his own vehicle.

As Sofia lowered her helmet over her head, Zach's words replayed in her mind. She smiled to herself and lifted her eyes to the stars that were visible through the clear shell of the Zurit.

Darkness was waning fast, and every second left fewer stars dotting the sky. But the star she really wanted to see wasn't there anyway. The Seven Sisters constellation was always hidden by the sun during the summer months. But she knew it was still out there somewhere, even though she couldn't see it.

Pleiades, you've always helped me figure things out in the past, and now more than ever I need your magic to help clear my mind and see what I need to do.

She closed her eyes and pictured the constellation of three thousand stars that encompassed her home planet. All at once, Rachmaninoff's *Rhapsody on a Theme of Paganini* began to play in her head and her synesthesia sent waves of color dancing around her. Within seconds, the tension in her muscles began to ease.

The fog in her head then began to lift, and an image of her mom and dad materialized behind her eyelids. Their smiling faces shining with love and pride gave her the boost she needed.

And for the first time, she began to believe they really *could* do this.

THIRTY-FIVE

Will's voice came through Liv's helmet, "Final check. Everyone ready?"

One by one the Zurits responded with "Check."

Liv squeezed her eyes shut and squelched the small voice in her head that had nagged her most of the night, filling her mind with doubts.

My visions have never been wrong. I can do this, she told herself, then said out loud, "Check."

"Okay, Olivia, start the sandstorm," Will said, then added, "Zach, head out on my signal. Olivia, stay close to his tail, and Sofia, you stay on Olivia's. Our goal is to get in and get the hostages out before the Nukiri even know we're there. Stay safe, and may Ea be with us all."

Liv bit her lip and stared at the horizon, now a stark line in the glow of the rising sun.

"You can do this, Livy," Zach said encouragingly inside her head.

The world seemed to come to a standstill as she inhaled a deep breath and envisioned a powerful magnet at her core, drawing in all the energy around her and pulling down the cold air from the troposphere.

Seconds later, a low-pitched rumble broke the silence, then

rapidly grew louder as if a train was drawing nearer. Puffs of sand began to stir, then lifted into the air.

When the rumble had become a roar and the horizon had disappeared behind a thick red cloud, Will called, "Move out!"

Zach's Zurit lurched forward. "Sorry," he mumbled through the comm in his helmet, then rolled off smoothly, picking up speed as he rounded the end of the mound.

Liv clenched her teeth in determination and took off after him and the others followed, except for Elleci.

Will was concerned the sandstorm might force tiny particles of sand into Elleci's internal workings and cause damage. Plus, all the seats in the Zurits were taken, so she was the logical choice to stay with the helicopter and have it ready to take off as soon as the others got back with the hostages.

Liv had traveled a short distance when four Zurits sped past her to flank Zach, two on each side. Four more zoomed up and flanked her in the same way.

She had lost all sense of time when Will's voice came into her head. *"Olivia, increase the strength of the wind and intensify the sandstorm if you can. The cloud needs to be thick enough to completely cloak us. And get closer to Zach's tail so you don't lose him. He's got the map in his head and is the only one who can guide us in."*

A rush of déjà vu hit her, and her confidence soared.

She concentrated harder on pulling down more air.

A sudden gust of wind pushed her toward the Zurit on her right. She yanked the joystick to the left and gripped it with both hands to hold the vehicle steady, then pushed the lever forward until she could detect the faint glow of Zach's instrument panel.

"Livy, listen to me," Zach said telepathically. "*I don't care what Will says. I'm going in to get Mom and Dad. But you have to stay in the Zurit … that's an order. I can't risk Daher getting his hands on you again."*

Liv smiled to herself. She knew this was coming and had prepared for it. *"There may be another universe out there where you can boss me around, but this is not it. And you're not the only Guardian, you know. There are three of us, remember?"*

"I'm not kidding, Liv. I don't want you—"

"Save it for the Nukiri, Z. I'm going in, and there's nothing you can do to stop me."

Sofia squinted and leaned as far to the side as the seat belt allowed, trying to see past the vehicles the Anunnaki had lined up between the two rock mounds. Blocking the view of the camp was a logical tactical move on their part, but the thought they had done so because they knew the raid was coming twisted the knot in her stomach.

"The camp's just up ahead." Zach's voice came through the comm in her helmet. "The diagram says to go around to the back of the hill on the east side. From there we can climb over the top. That'll bring us down right beside the hostage cell."

Sofia veered her Zurit to the right, made a wide sweep around the hill, and pulled to a stop at the base of the rock. The minute she opened the hatch, a hurricane strength gust blasted her with sand. She hurriedly jumped out and slammed the door shut, but a layer of sand still covered everything inside.

She hunched her shoulders and started forward, then realized she had no idea which way to go. She turned in a full circle, looking for the others, but the groups' battle gear, even the helmets that were equipped with a full-face shield, were made to mask their heat signature, and she could see nothing through the red cloud.

As a small seed of panic began to take root, she noticed a faint UV glow of a lollipop symbol that was on all of the helmets a few yards away.

She gritted her teeth and pushed against the wind to inch toward it.

"Nick, come in. Are you there?" Will said through the comm.

There was a crackle of static, then Nick's voice. "That's Red Leader to you."

Sofia felt Will's annoyance just as she reached the group huddled behind one of the Zurits.

"Are you in position, Red Leader?" Will asked, sounding like he was speaking through clenched teeth.

"Affirmative. I ducked the drone into the truck next to the hostage cell to keep it from being blown into the rocks, but I still have a good view of the camp. It looks like the guards are expecting you. They're lined up at both ends of the camp."

Kemen threw his head back and spit out a word Sofia had never heard before. From the venom in his voice, she guessed it was the Pleiadian equivalent of the F word.

Will replied in the same language. Kemen grunted something else and sprinted off with two other dark-clad bodies.

"The rest of you come with me," Will said in English. "We'll go in through the south end and draw the guards away from Kemen's group, who are going over the top. Guardians, you wait here for us to bring out the hostages. Then load them up and high tail it back to the chopper."

"I'm going in with you," Zach said, stepping up.

Will straightened his shoulders and turned to Zach. "No, you're—"

"They're my parents!"

"This is not up for discussion. You have your orders. If you can't abide by them, I'll have you locked in a Zurit."

Zach's chest puffed out, but Liv stepped forward, putting a hand on his arm. "You don't have to lock him up. We'll stay put."

Will paused for a moment, then turned to one of the Sons of Ea, who looked to be in his mid-twenties. "Eneko, stay with them and do whatever it takes to keep them here."

Will waved to the rest to follow and they disappeared into the red cloud of sand.

"This is fucked up!" Zach yelled after them, then spun around to Liv and Sofia. "You guys stay. I'm going in to get Mom and Dad."

Before either Sofia or Liv could issue a protest, Eneko stepped in front of Zach to block his way. He was holding a gun with both hands in front of him, the barrel pointed to the ground.

Zach flinched, momentarily taken aback at the sight of the weapon. "You fixin' to shoot me?" He snorted a laugh. "I don't think so."

He stepped to the right.

Eneko mirrored the move.

"Zach," Sofia said, "don't be stupid. He's not playing around."

"Z, please," Liv added.

Kemen's voice came through Sofia's helmet. "We're in position above the hostage cell and ready to drop in on your signal."

Eneko must have heard it, too. He looked up.

As quick as a striking cobra, Zach lunged and grabbed the gun out of Eneko's hand.

Eneko wasn't as fast as a Pleiadian, but he was well trained in martial arts, and without hesitation, he swung his foot around, catching Zach's leg right behind the knee.

Zach went down hard, and the gun went flying. But he instantly rolled and trapped Eneko's leg between his feet. Then with a twist, he brought Eneko down beside him.

The two sprang back to their feet and faced off.

Zach raised his fists and danced from side to side, then lunged forward, feinting a punch as he kicked out.

Eneko wasn't fooled. He caught Zach's foot in his hands and with a hard twist, sent Zach once again to the ground.

Zach instantly arched his back and jumped right back to his feet.

But before either of them could make another move, Sofia jumped between them. "Stop it right now!"

The two men, both breathing heavily, glared at each other, but held their ground.

"What are you doing?" Sofia said, putting a hand on both of their chests. "You're on the same team for crying out loud."

A loud explosion suddenly shook the ground. Everyone froze.

Then Will's voice came through their helmets, "Kemen, get the hostages out of there now!"

Zach looked over his shoulder. "Something's … wait. Where's Livy?"

Sofia looked around to where Liv had been standing just seconds earlier. She was gone.

Eneko forgotten, Zach frantically yelled, "Livy!" The wind blew her name away as soon as it left his lips.

Black smoke and the muffled sounds of mini explosions rolled over them from the camp.

Zach turned to Sofia. "Where'd she go?" His voice was sharp with panic.

She shook her head. "I … I don't know. She was right there a minute ago."

Eneko glared at Zach. "Was this all a distraction so she could sneak away and go into the camp?"

"Fuck, no! I don't want her anywhere near that camp or Daher." Zach scanned the area again. "Dammit, Livy."

Kemen's voice rang through the comm. "Olivia! Get down!"

The words were like a shot of adrenaline to Sofia. Thinking only that Liv was in trouble, she took off in a run in the direction Will had gone. But running against the wind was like running through water.

Before she'd gotten far, Zach rolled up to her in a Zurit. "I'll get her. You stay here."

"Like hell I will!" Sofia ran to the next closest vehicle and yanked the hatch open.

Eneko caught up to her just as she reached for the joystick. He waved his arms in the air and yelled, "Stop!"

Sofia pushed the joystick forward and didn't look back.

THIRTY-SIX

Liv's heart stalled at the sound of the loud explosion.

Then Will's voice came through her helmet. "Kemen, get the hostages out of there now!"

The words were like a punch in her gut. *Mom! Dad!* She clutched the pendant under her jacket and turned toward the rock mound.

In the next heartbeat, she was standing in the midst of thick, black smoke. Voices yelling things she didn't understand were coming from every direction. She whirled around and sucked in her breath at the sight of complete chaos and the orange and yellow heat signatures of men dashing about, randomly firing guns at seemingly nothing.

"Olivia!" Kemen yelled. "Get down!"

As she started to turn back, a linebacker—at least that's what it felt like—tackled her to the ground.

"Get off!" she shrieked, kicking her legs as her upper body was pinned down.

"It's me," Kemen said in her head.

Liv instantly went still. *Kemen? How ... no, that's impossible. He's in the camp.*

"You aren't supposed to be here," Kemen yelled.

All at once, the facts fell into place and her lungs froze. She'd teleported into the camp, just like she had that time at Daher's villa.

The line of vehicles she'd seen earlier from the mini volcano were about fifty yards away, except now they were all ablaze. Through the thermal lens of her contacts, the flames appeared more white than yellow and danced wildly in the wind, sending white sparks flying into the air. The heat signatures of Daher's men melded with the heat, making them invisible against the backdrop of the flames.

The Pleiadians' heat signatures were masked by their suits, though, so they stood out as black shapes in front of the raging fire.

"Come on," Kemen said. *"I have to get you out of here."* He pulled her to her feet. *"Hurry, this way."*

He started toward the panel truck a few feet away, then stopped and pulled Liv down to a squat with a *"Shhh,"* as a group of Nukiri appeared from behind the truck.

Remembering the truck was right beside the cell where her parents were being held, Liv's pulse raced. But when she twisted to look around, her stomach dropped. The only things under the square canopy were three canvas cots.

The hostages were gone.

Liv reared up to scan the area. "Where's Mom and Dad?"

"Get down!" Kemen yelled, tugging on her arm.

"Olivia, what are you doing here?" Will shouted through the comm.

"I have to find my parents!" she replied.

At that moment, two dark figures from the Pleiadian team ran up. One reached for Liv's free arm, but she spun away and wrenched her other arm out of Kemen's grip as she yelled, "Zach!"

"Livy, where are you?" Zach said in her head.

"I'm by the hostage cell. Mom and Dad aren't here!"

A wave of hatred suddenly swept over Liv, sending what felt like ice shards through her veins. She spun around to see a tall, mostly orange figure with an abnormally large head standing about ten feet to her right.

Daher!

The taste of spoiled milk filled her mouth and she nearly gagged.

Daher's voice thundered through the smoke. "Guardians … come out, come out wherever you are."

Behind Daher stood a group of at least ten of his minions. The three Dracuzians were a head above the others, and each held a hostage before them.

Liv's mom and dad weren't putting up a fight, but the third hostage, Meredith, was wrestling with her guard, struggling to get free. The guard gave her a hard tug, but she didn't stop struggling until he put a gun to her head.

"You have ten seconds to show yourself," Daher added. "Or you can say goodbye forever to one of your humans." He lifted a hand.

The guard on the end pushed Liv's father forward. He feigned a stumble, then twisted and rammed his shoulder into the brute.

The Dracuzian wasn't fazed, but her father bounced off him and fell to the ground. The enforcer kicked him in the ribs and roughly yanked him back to his feet.

Liv's mother's cry of "Stop it!" was muffled by the scarf she had over her mouth and nose.

The ball of energy at Liv's core flared and the wind howled louder. She started forward, but Kemen grabbed her around the waist and held her back.

At the same moment, Will removed his helmet.

"You might want to tell your men it's not a good idea to abuse the hostages," Will said calmly as if discussing the weather. "The Guardians won't like it if you harm their family."

"Well, if the Guardians were the least bit concerned about their humans, they'd show themselves," Daher replied just as nonchalantly.

"What makes you think the Guardians are here?"

Daher's voice carried a smile. "You always did have a good poker face, but I'm going to place my bet that you're bluffing this time."

He whipped a knife out of his loose, ankle-length cloak and threw it. The blade flashed in the light from the fire right before it embedded itself in Liv's father's shoulder.

Her father let out an agonizing cry and fell to his knees.

For a moment, Liv was paralyzed and couldn't even breathe.

In the next heartbeat, though, she found herself on the top of the rock mound. Before she could get her footing, a gust of wind slammed into her, pushing her dangerously close to the edge. She squatted down, grabbed hold of a jutting rock, and looked around.

The camp was three hundred feet below her.

Oh shit, did I jump again? Why does this keep happening to me?

Liv's mind was racing with so many thoughts it took her a moment to feel a strong ominous presence close by.

Cautiously, she turned her head and spotted a heat signature of a large being lying on the ground, not fifteen feet from her. The being was looking through the scope of some kind of a strange weapon that was aimed down at the camp.

Her mouth went dry, but not because of the sight of the gun. Because she had felt that same foreboding energy before.

It was Reptile Man. And he was going to shoot Will.

Forgetting about the wind, Liv jumped to her feet and had to fight to keep from being blown over.

"Attack!" Kemen shouted through the comm.

She twisted her neck to look down at the camp.

At the same moment, a white beam shot down from the top of the mound just as Daher turned toward the Dracuzian holding her father.

"Nooo!" Liv flipped around to the Reptile Man and thrust her hands out.

Her blast of energy hit him in the middle of the chest just as he was rising. He let out a small *oof* as he was knocked backward and disappeared over the side of the mound.

A part of her brain couldn't believe what she'd done, but she didn't take the time to process it. She had to get back down to the camp. The problem was, she didn't know how this jumping from place to place worked.

She bit down on her lower lips and squeezed her eyes shut. *Please, please take me down to Mom and Dad.*

A loud screech sent a shiver up Liv's spine and her eyes flew open. With a quick look around, she realized her plea had worked. She was back on the ground, but was across the camp from where Daher was standing.

Her mother was on the ground at Daher's feet next to a Dracuzian who was missing the top part of his head.

THIRTY-SEVEN

A beam of light streaked down from the hilltop. Daher screamed out as the beam ripped past his cheek and hit one of the Dracuzians in the center of the forehead. The enforcer crumpled to the ground without making a sound, taking Martina down with him.

"Mommm!" Liv's agonizing scream echoed off the mounds.

Sofia jumped.

"No, Livy! Stay back," Zach shouted and raced to intercept her before she got to Daher.

Sofia, too, took off in a run straight toward the mayhem, noticing the wind wasn't as strong as it had been.

Daher hauled Martina up by the wrist, tucked her against his right side, and swung around to face Will. Dark crimson blood flowed down his right cheek from a deep gash running from his ear to almost his nose. He made a guttural sound in his throat and lifted his free hand, curling his fingers in like an eagle's claw.

Will's head jerked toward the sky and his body lifted six inches off the ground.

"You've always thought you were so much smarter than me," Daher hissed through his teeth.

A dozen Pleiadians rushed toward the Anunnaki.

The two remaining Dracuzian enforcers abandoned their hostages and charged forward. The Nukiri ran toward the battle as well and screams and grunts rang through the air as the two opposing groups came together.

Daher didn't even flinch.

"You're a fool to think you and your rag-tag team could waltz in here and take the humans from me right under my nose." Daher lifted Will another inch. "Now, you get to watch as I annihilate these humans and your troops. Then I will kill you, too."

"I've got this," Nick said confidently through the comm. "Kemen, get me over there."

Sofia craned her neck around just as Kemen reared back and threw the small drone like it was a baseball toward Daher.

The dragonfly wobbled backward a few inches in the wind, then shot forward as if powered by a jet engine, or more likely, Pleiadian power. The two small UV lights on the top of the drone were a blur as it flew up to the side of Daher's head, then exploded.

Daher let out a blood curdling screech and his hands flew to his face.

Both Martina and Will dropped to the ground.

"Martina!" Scott yelled as he pulled himself along the ground with his one good arm.

Martina seemed stunned, but then shook her head, rolled onto her hands and knees, and crawled towards Scott's voice.

"Mom!" Zach and Liv yelled in unison.

Zach reached her first and helped her up, keeping his body positioned between her and Daher. "Get Dad," he yelled to Liv.

Daher dropped his hands. Patches of the morphing skin he wore to mask his alien features had been burnt off the left side of his face, leaving black, scorched edges around exposed flesh that looked like raw meat.

The intense hatred exuding from Daher's hooded, piercing eyes stopped Sofia in her tracks.

"Your arrogance holds no bounds, Gilamu," Daher sneered. "But your luck has run out. Thanks to you, I now have the Guardians, and Earth will soon be mine."

Zach released Martina and spun around.

At the same moment, Will shot to his feet.

Right then time seemed to slow as everything happened at once.

Zach thrust out his hands.

Daher hurled a thin bladed knife.

Will took a leaping dive toward Zach.

A white beam streaked through the air, hitting Zach and knocking him backward, sending the energy blast meant for Daher flying off into the sky.

Will raised his head and looked down at the hilt of Daher's knife protruding from the center of his chest. His gaze turned to Sofia and a look of sorrow and regret streaked across his face. Then his chest rose and fell for one last time.

Sofia heard a gut-wrenching scream echo off the hills and realized it was coming from her. The next thing she knew there was a blinding white light before her eyes and the fireball of energy inside her detonated like an atomic bomb.

Liv threw off her helmet and knelt down beside Zach. As she hugged him to her chest and begged him to wake up, the earth beneath her began to violently tremble.

Loud cracking noises came from the vicinity of both rock mounds. Within seconds, giant boulders began to tumble down, knocking additional rocks free as they went.

"Pull back," Kemen yelled through the comm. "Krogen, Razin, Nerea help me recover Zach and the hostages. Everyone else get to the Zurits."

The quake knocked Daher to his knees and the vibrating sand quickly sucked him in up to his pelvis.

The Nukiri and the Sons of Ea both scrambled to get out of the way of the falling rocks, but the quake was strong and staying on their feet was next to impossible.

Kemen made his way to Liv and knelt down beside her. “Olivia, we need to get him out of here.”

Liv looked up at him, tears from her nose dripping off her chin. “Fix him.”

“Not here. We need to get him to a safe place, away from the Nukiri first.”

A fiery rage swept through Liv like molten iron. “This is Daher’s doing.”

She jumped up, turned around, and saw Will lying still on the ground, the shaft of a knife embedded in his chest.

Shock hit her like a bucket of ice had been dumped over her head and a pain split her heart in two.

Will’s words came back to her in a flash: *“You’ll never be as strong or as effective apart as you are together.”*

Liv choked back the lump that had jumped into her throat. *Why didn’t we listen to him?*

Her gaze moved to Daher, who was struggling to get out of the sand, and her vision turned red with rage.

“You’re going to see the true wrath of the Guardians now, you son-of-a-bitch.”

She jumped to Sofia’s side in the blink of an eye. “Let’s finish this.” She took hold of Sofia’s hand. “For Zach and Will.”

THIRTY-EIGHT

Sofia was barely conscious of Liv's hand in hers. All she knew was that the fiery ball in her abdomen began to pulsate again as if it'd been recharged. And she couldn't hold back the blast wave that erupted.

The air rippled out in concentric circles around her, and the earth gave a violent shudder. Then, with an ear shattering crack, the ground split open.

Trapped in the sand, Daher could do nothing but flail his arms as the sand flowed into the gaping crevice, carrying him and a half dozen of his guards down with it.

Sofia didn't know when Liv let go of her hand. She also didn't know how long she'd been standing there when Elleci's soft voice came through the comm, "You did good, wudala, but now you must stop."

She flinched and blinked several times before she realized where she was. She gasped for air and clawed at the strap of her helmet to get it off so she could breathe.

The wind was no longer blowing, but a cloud of dust still lingered in the sky. A pile of rubble now stood where the two rock mounds used to be. At the edge of the debris, steam rose from a long, jagged crevice that stretched across the ground into the distance.

"What …" Sofia's words trailed off as the world suddenly tilted. She felt herself falling to meet it, but before she hit the ground, a strong arm wrapped around her back, and another slipped under her knees, lifting her up.

"It's okay, little one, I've got you," Krogen said, cradling her to his chest.

His strength and body heat were comforting, and Sofia clung to him for dear life. But as he started to walk away, the events of the last few minutes came rushing back. She sucked in a breath, reared up, and looked around.

"Zach! Where's Zach?"

"Kemen's taking him to the Zurits," Krogen answered.

"What about Liv and the hostages?"

"Everyone is being taken care of. You needn't worry."

Needn't worry? Those words repeated in her head as she surveyed the bodies strewn about the ground. Most of them were Nukiri, but a few were wearing the black jackets and helmets of their team. Her stomach pitched. Then her gaze landed on Will and her heart broke in half.

"Will! We can't leave him." She kicked her legs to get down.

Krogen tightened his grip, but she was wiggling too much for him to hold and he had to set her down.

"Our first priority is to get you and the other Guardians and hostages to safety," he said. "We'll send someone back for him and the others after you're out."

"But more of Daher's men are on their way. We can't let them get him."

"What we can't do is let them get *you*. You—"

"I will walk out on my own. You carry him," Sofia ordered, leaving no room for debate.

Krogen opened his mouth but must have seen the determination on her face. "If you can't keep up, I'll leave Will to carry you."

Sofia rushed to Will's side, knelt down, and gently placed a palm on his cheek, willing him to open his eyes.

He had said that plenty of people had already died for her, but she hadn't personally known any of them, nor had she witnessed their deaths. Her chest felt like it had been filled with cement.

"I'm so sorry," she whispered, choking back a sob.

Krogen touched her shoulder. "We have to go."

Sofia swiped her hand under her nose and got to her feet so Krogen could take Will. He lifted the Pleiadian leader as if he were a precious artifact and the pain on his face was like a knife stab to Sofia's heart.

"Are you sure you're okay?" Krogen asked once more before they started off.

"I'm sure," she replied, even though she wasn't sure she'd ever really be okay again.

By the time they reached the Zurits, Kemen had already left with Zach and two other Zurits were just pulling away, one with Liv and her mom, the other with Eneko and Scott.

"She won't get into the Zurit," Alazne said, tilting her head toward Meredith, who was sitting on the ground, her knees drawn into her chest and her forehead resting on them.

Sofia's strength was all but gone and she wasn't in the mood to deal with Meredith's dramatics, but she felt responsible for Meredith being there in the first place.

"I'll take care of it," she said with a weary sigh and tottered over to her old roommate.

"Meredith," she said softly, putting a hand on Meredith's shoulder.

Meredith reared back with a high-pitched cry, her eyes going as wide as golf balls. Then without warning, she lunged forward and wrapped her arms around Sofia as if Sofia was a lifeline.

"God, it was so awful." Meredith's voice was strangled, and her shoulders shook, making Sofia feel all the more guilty.

"It's okay," she cooed in Meredith's ear as she rubbed her back. "You're okay now."

"Those guys …" Meredith pulled back a little to look Sofia in the face, "were they with the show? Mr. Daher never said people might get hurt in the rescue. But …" Her bottom lip started to quiver. Then her face crumpled, and she pulled Sofia in close again.

"You know Hollywood can make anything look real. Right?" Sofia said, then pulled back. "But what did Daher tell you about the rescue? How did he know about it?"

Meredith sniffed. "What do you mean? How could he not know? He's the producer of the show."

"So, he told you this was part of the TV show?"

"Yeah … it was your last challenge."

Sofia exchanged a meaningful look with Krogen.

"But I don't think those men were acting. I think they might really be dead. Look," Meredith held up her hands, which were stained with blood. "This is real blood."

Sofia's heart skipped a beat. "Are you hurt?"

"No, it's Scott's blood."

"I'm sure—"

"And you …" Meredith's eyes widened again. "You just stood there in the middle of everything. Your hair was standing straight up and the air around you was kind of wavering like …" She sucked in a sharp breath and her brow furrowed with confusion. "Did you cause the earthquake?"

Sofia glanced up at Krogen for help.

"I'm sorry to interrupt, but we really need to get going," Krogen said. "The helicopter is waiting."

"Look, let's get you out of this desert," Sofia said. "You'll feel a lot better after you get cleaned up. Okay?"

"Meredith, you'll come with me," Alazne said, swinging her arm toward one of the Zurits.

Sofia kept her arm around Meredith's shoulders and guided her to the Zurit, then helped her climb in. "I'll be right behind you," she said and closed the hatch.

As Krogen walked away with Sofia, he said, "I have a feeling she might be a problem."

Sofia didn't respond. She couldn't. The shock of what had

happened had caught up to her and her mind and body had begun to shut down.

Krogen took one look at her, lifted her in his arms, and carried her to the last Zurit.

"It's going to be okay," he said as he buckled her in. "Just rest."

Sofia turned her head away so he couldn't see the tears running from her nose. Will and Elleci had both tried to warn the three of them of the dangers, but they hadn't really understood the scope of it all. And maybe they were a little too cocky after defeating Daher in the pyramid.

Whatever the reason … their naivety had cost Will his life and she was going to have to live with that the rest of her life.

An intense ache ripped through her chest. She gasped and curled in on herself as the heartache and sorrow swept in. And for once in her life, she let the emotions engulf her and didn't push them aside after sixty seconds.

THIRTY-NINE

Sofia?

Sofia's eyes shot open, and she sat up so fast, the room spun.

She was sure she heard Zach call her name, but she was alone in a high-ceilinged room. She swung her legs over the side of a bed, placing her feet on a cool brick tile floor.

The room had no windows and was bare except for the bed and a small end table that held a lamp that had flicked on the moment she'd sat up. She didn't know where she was, but it was definitely not the apartment in Cairo.

"Hello?" she called out.

The word echoed back to her.

"Hello," she said a little louder as she got to her feet.

The door creaked open an inch, then a foot pushed it open more and Elleci came in, carrying a tray with a steaming cup.

"Good, you are already awake," she said with a smile. "I brought you some ginseng tea. It will help restore your energy."

"Where's Zach?" Sofia asked anxiously. "Is he okay?"

"He's resting in a CDT unit."

Sofia's knees gave out and she plopped down on the bed. "I was afraid he …" she looked down at her hands, unable to finish the thought. Then she jerked her head up. "Will? Is he ..."

"Will is dead." Elleci set the tray on the table, then sat down beside Sofia and took her hand. "Do not feel bad. His whole life was dedicated to protecting you three. He always said he would gladly give up his life before he would let anything happen to you. I am sure he regrets nothing."

"Oh, God, we didn't mean for it to end this way."

"Shhh," Elleci said, stroking Sofia's hair. "It is not your fault. You did not throw the knife."

"Daher." Sofia spat out the name as if it was a curse. "I wish he'd died in the pyramid. Then he couldn't have ..."

She leaned over her knees and covered her face with her hands.

"Zach was asking about you earlier," Elleci said. "He is worried about you. I think it would help him rest if you went to see him. If you are feeling up to it, that is."

Sofia raised her head. "Yes! I want to see him. Can we go now?"

Elleci nodded and led the way out the door and down a hall lined with tall marble columns that supported the underground ceiling of an ancient cistern in the city of Istanbul — the Pleiadian base of *Anides*.

A short distance ahead, another door opened and Kemen stepped into the hallway. A sad smile lifted the corners of his mouth as Sofia ran up and hugged him.

"I'm so sorry about Will," she said into his chest.

He hugged her back. "I'm glad to see you up. How are you feeling?"

"I'm okay."

"That's good, because we need to discuss your friend, Meredith." He walked Sofia away from the door. "She's asking us to send her back to France and wants us to pay her to stay quiet."

Sofia snorted and rolled her eyes. "Ohmigod, she never quits." She looked back at Kemen. "You aren't going to do it, are you?"

"She's seen a lot and knows about your powers. Can she be trusted with that knowledge?"

This time, Sofia let out a short laugh. “Are you kidding? I wouldn’t trust her to walk my dog if I had one.”

Kemen squared his jaw. “That was the impression I got as well. In that case, I don’t see how we can release her and risk her exposing us.”

“So, what are we going to do? Lock her up somewhere?”

“We could send her up to Atlantis II,” Elleci piped in.

“And let her see we have a space station?” Sofia exclaimed. “Then she’d know for sure we’re aliens!”

“We should talk this over with the others,” Kemen said.

“I was taking Sofia to see Zach now,” Elleci said.

“Good, I’ll walk with you,” Kemen replied, and together, they started down the hall again.

Meredith, her ear to a crack in the door, listened for the footsteps to fade, then pushed the door open a little further and peeked out.

Sofia’s an alien! How did I not know? It explains so much. Her mind raced to process what she’d heard. *They want to lock me up so I don’t tell anyone. Well, fuck that.*

She fingered the necklace Daher had given her and thought about his instructions. He must have known all along that they were aliens and that’s why he wanted to know where their base was. That had to be why he had to kill that man, too.

He was defending the world from the aliens.

Meredith bit down on her bottom lip. *The government or the CIA needs to know there are aliens running around on Earth.*

She closed her eyes to think. *But would Mr. Daher be okay with me telling them? What if he gets mad and won’t give me the money to live in France?*

She pondered that thought.

He obviously hasn’t already told people about the aliens, so he must have a plan to take care of them himself. And he probably wouldn’t like it if I let the cat out of the bag. So, I’d be giving up my once in a lifetime chance to live like a princess, and for what?

She pursed her lips. *I'd have to be a fuckin' moron to do that. Who would believe me, anyway?*

I would be helping humanity by letting Daher take care of Sofia and her bunch. And I'll be free then to go off and marry a rich, exotic French man, and live happily ever after.

Meredith smiled as she pictured herself lying on a beach in the French Riviera next to a bronzed hunk.

And with a dreamy sigh, she pushed the ruby on the necklace.

A Note From the Author

Thank you so much for reading,
THE GUARDIANS' GIFTS
THE RISE OF THE THREE Book II
I hope you enjoyed it. It was great fun to write.

If you could take a minute to post a review, it would mean a lot to me. I always love to hear readers' thoughts.

To follow M.J. and stayed informed on new projects, please 'like' her Facebook page, MJ Bell Author, or go to her website: www.mj-bell.com

Happy reading!

ACKNOWLEGMENTS

I'd be remiss if I didn't take a moment to thank a few very special people.

First off, my daughter, Tiffany Lopo, and good friends, Janie Gianotsos, Charmayne Sobon, and Barb Buffington for spending countless hours with me brainstorming and perfecting the characters and plot. I don't know that I could have pulled this story together without them. I love you all 3,000.

Sometimes it really does take a village, and I am fortunate to have a wonderful critique group from Rocky Mountain Fiction Writers in mine! I could always count on them to give me wonderful feedback and suggestions that helped fine tune the story. You guys are the greatest.

I'd also like to thank my editor, DeAnna Knippling. I so respect your knowledge of writing and appreciate your patience with me, even when I question your suggestions. (And you are seldom wrong.) I not only consider you one of the best editors out there, but a very good friend.

And, of course, none of this would happen without the support of my husband, who puts up with me and doesn't complain when I forgo cleaning the house to write. I love you more than you know.

Lastly, I would like to thank all my readers who have followed me and supported me on this long road. You make it all worthwhile and the journey would be very lonely without you. Can't wait to reconnect with you in person at future Comic Cons!

About the Author

MJ Bell's love of reading and everything magical is what motived her to jump headfirst into a writing career. Little did she know that only a few years later she would be an award-winning author (Gold award from Mom's Choice Awards), and have six books published, with more on the way.

Though MJ grew up in Iowa, she now calls Colorado her home, where she lives with her husband and Keeshound, Tallie. Her family is a source of pride and joy to her, as well as a great source of inspiration, which she uses to bring a little more magic into the world.

She loves to hear from readers through her FB page: **MJ Bell Author**, or on her website: **www.mj-bell.com**

www.ingramcontent.com/pod-product-compliance
Lightning Source LLC
LaVergne TN
LVHW050623100826
845148LV00011B/1706

* 9 7 8 1 7 3 6 5 0 0 3 2 3 *